beachside kisses with my best friend

A SWEET ROMANTIC COMEDY

KRISTIN CANARY

To Lydia, Beth, Lindsey, and Kaci.
You guys got me through this one.
Thank you for all the encouragement, texts, memes, and prayers.
Jordan and Marilee's story is finished largely because of you.

And to the real-life Marilee.
Thank you for letting me steal your name, and for all the support
over the years. You really are the best!

author's note and content warnings

Hi, friend! I'm so glad you're here. This book is a long time coming, and while I may have taken some liberties with rules and timing of the legal system, I hope you'll dive in and fully enjoy with any suspension of beliefs necessary. 😆

While I do intend for my books to make you LOL and swoon, sometimes characters deal with things that might be triggering to you. Here are some things you'll find in this book:

- Death of parents (past event)
- Discussion of past miscarriages
- Discussion of an emotionally abusive past marriage
- A confrontation with an emotionally abusive ex (no harm comes to the female)
- An alcoholic (though non-violent) father

Also, this book contains no sex or swearing. Happy reading, and welcome back to Hallmark Beach!

Kristin

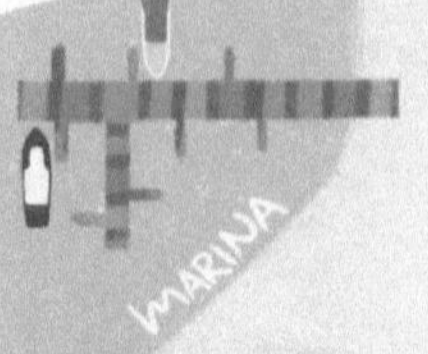

THE PURPLE SEASHELL
1

Olive Paradise
2

THE BLUESTOCKING BOOKSHOP
3

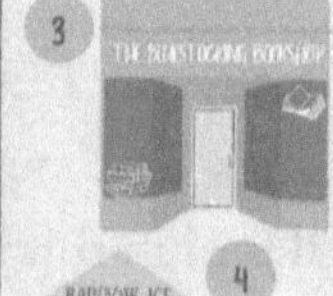

RAINBOW ICE
4

The Green Robin
5

Just Peachy Boutique
6

The Pink Rose
7

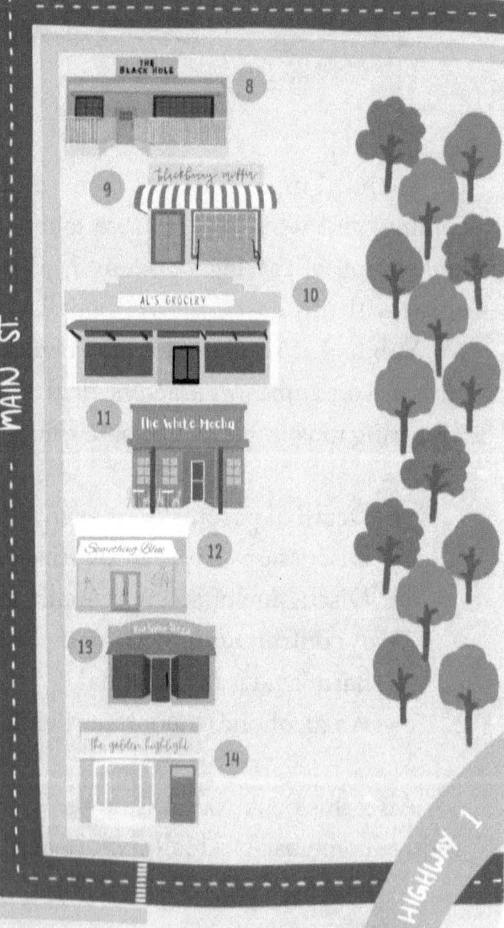

HALLMARK BEACH
hallmark beach

MARINA

LEGEND
1: The Purple Seashell
2: Olive Paradise
3: The Bluestocking Bookshop
4: Rainbow Ice
5: The Green Robin
6: Just Peachy Boutique
7: The Pink Rose
8: The Black Hole
9: The Blackberry Muffin
10: Al's Grocery
11: The White Mocha
12: Something Blue
13: Red Sauce Pizza
14: The Golden Highlight

MAIN ST.

THE BLACK HOLE
8

blackberry muffin
9

AL'S GROCERY
10

The White Mocha
11

Something Blue
12

Red Sauce Pizza
13

the golden highlight
14

HIGHWAY 1

one

JORDAN

15 years ago

You don't expect to meet the love of your life at age fourteen.

And you definitely don't expect to meet her in home economics—especially when you're a dude.

Not that I'm sexist. Far from it. But when you sign up for gym class at the new school you're transferring to just before the holidays and get put in cooking class instead...there's bound to be some confusion.

What school doesn't have any gym classes available? None of the ones I've been to—and that's a solid five in the last ten years alone. Thank you, military life.

But Dad's retired from the Air Force now—honorably discharged thanks to an injury that's left him reeling and reaching for the bottle more than he'd care to admit—and he wanted to move back to his home state of California. But he didn't want to return to Los Angeles. He wanted to be somewhere small. Quiet. Peaceful.

That's how the Carmichaels ended up in Hallmark Beach.

And that's how I ended up in this class.

With her.

I don't know her name—I don't know anyone's name—but as I shift my backpack from one shoulder to the other, I can't take my eyes off of her.

There's a red apron tied around her petite waist, her brown hair is piled on top of her head, flour dots her cheeks, and she's smiling while she frosts cookies, off in her own world while her classmates—well, *our* classmates, I guess—are chatting and joking around.

She's beautiful, but the kind where she doesn't seem to know she's beautiful. She seems oblivious to her charm.

But I'm not.

"Jordan."

I straighten, jerking my attention to the administrative assistant—a Mrs. Benson, I think?—smiling kindly at me from behind her cat-eye glasses. She's the lucky one who got to escort me around Hallmark Beach High's campus, which took all of five minutes. "Sorry. What?"

She pats her white curls and nods toward the middle-aged teacher, who is busy instructing a student standing behind a burner built into a table. "That's Ms. White. I think you'll like her. She gives a lot of creative freedom. And you'll only be in this class for a few weeks until second semester starts. Then there should be a spot open in gym class."

"Great." I say the word, but there's a lack of enthusiasm in it. My eyes have drifted once again to the girl standing at the last table in the back of the room.

Mrs. Benson chuckles. "Would you like me to introduce you?"

"What?" I turn, shaking my head with so much force that I might be mistaken for a bobblehead. "No. No, I'm good."

At that moment, Ms. White glances up and sees us, says

something to the student she's helping, and walks across the noisy room to join us. She's probably my parents' age—forty-ish—with small wisps of gray salting her dark hair. "Hi, there. You must be our new student. Jordan, right?"

"Yes, ma'am."

"Wonderful. Thank you for escorting him, Mrs. Benson."

"Of course." Mrs. Benson's mouth hooks into a wry grin. "I don't think Jordan has any experience baking, so perhaps you might consider pairing him with your best student." She flashes me a quick wink before heading out the door.

What the...?

Ms. White seems to consider me, then nods. "That's not a bad idea. Come on, Jordan. Follow me." She weaves through the tables, calling out encouragements to others, some of whom look up at me with curious expressions. A few turn to whisper and giggle—probably because I'm the only guy in here.

That's okay. I'm used to being the new kid. Their stares and laughs don't bother me. Like water off a duck's back...

Then I see where Ms. White is leading me—and my palms begin to sweat.

Now I understand why Mrs. Benson winked at me.

Before I can protest this partner pairing, Ms. White stops in front of the girl who caught my attention from the very second I stepped into the room. But the girl doesn't look up. She's humming a tune—"Jingle Bells," I think, though she's really off tune.

It's kind of adorable though.

"Marilee, dear."

She finally glances up and startles. "Oh! Hi! Sorry, were you saying something?"

Ms. White offers a sincere smile—I have a feeling this girl, this *Marilee*, is a favorite—and gestures toward me. "We have a new student. Jordan Carmichael. Would you mind showing him the ropes?"

"Of course not." Turning toward me, a huge grin splashes across Marilee's face, and if I thought she was beautiful before, well...I didn't know what beautiful was. Because the sight of her smiling at *me*, her green eyes sparkling, makes me lose my breath. "Hi. I'm Marilee Moffitt."

"Hi." My voice cracks, and dang, I wanna crawl under the table. Wouldn't be very manly of me though. I cough, lower my voice. "Hey." I've never been the smoothest with the ladies. With how much we've moved, there's never been a point. Mostly, I just keep to myself, do my schoolwork, and don't do anything to rock the boat. Eventually, I make a few friends.

But this time, if Dad can be believed, we're staying, and since I'm just a freshman, I've still got three and a half years left here. Can't afford to be branded the pathetic loser who can't even talk to a pretty girl.

Thankfully, Marilee just keeps smiling at me. "Nice to meet you. You're going to love it here in Hallmark Beach. I've lived here my whole life, and it's such a warm, friendly place." She reaches out and pats my upper arm while addressing our teacher. "I'll take good care of him, Ms. White."

"I know you will, Marilee. Thank you. And Jordan, welcome here."

"Th-thank you." My backpack falls to the ground beside me.

Marilee's hand is still warm on my shoulder for a moment while our teacher walks away. Then she drops it and picks up a white tube with green frosting protruding from the tip. She holds it out to me. "Wanna give it a whirl?"

I look at it like it's a snake. "Like, try frosting cookies?"

She laughs, a magical tinkling sound like wind chimes. "Of course, silly. It's easy." Marilee points down at the cookies on a parchment-lined tray in front of us. There's a whole array of sugar cookie shapes—candy canes, snowmen, bells, Christmas trees. And each one is expertly decorated with precision and bursts of creativity that make me smile.

I point to a little snowman family, each one with a different outfit in reds, greens, and whites that must have taken hours to complete. "That doesn't look all that easy."

"It is once you practice." She wiggles the tube at me again. "Come on."

"Baking isn't really my thing. How about you show me first? So I can observe and make sure to get it right."

"There is no *getting it right*. There's just...I don't know. Feeling your way through it."

I chuckle at her exuberance. "Not sure I've felt my way through anything in my life."

"Really?" She leans over the cookie with the tube, releasing the green in even, beautiful lines. "Why not?"

"I dunno. My dad's in—well, *was* in—the military."

"Oh. High expectations, then?"

"Yep. Of me and my sister."

"You have a sister? I have an older brother. Blake. He's a junior."

"Cool. Claire's already in college. She goes to Berkeley."

"Wow. You weren't kidding about high expectations." She huffs, the beginnings of a frown on her lips for the first time. "I understand that all too well."

I want to ask her what she means, but then she moves on, chatting about all the wonderful things about Hallmark Beach, all the while pumping out more frosting. I've never been one to pay attention to the details on decorated baked goods. A cookie is a cookie, and it tastes the same no matter what the decorations look like. But right now, I'm mesmerized by the way her experienced hands make artwork of something that's going to be consumed.

Even more mesmerized when she lifts the tube, nods in satisfaction at the little snowman dude wearing a top hat and pair of glasses, and flicks the remaining frosting off the tip with her pinky finger, sticking it into her pink mouth.

I swallow hard against a dry throat.

"Ten minutes until next period, people," Ms. White calls from the front. "Time to clean up."

Marilee looks up at me—I've got a good six inches on her at least—and blinks. Then laughs. "Sorry, I've been talking the whole time. Off in my own world. I do that a lot." Marilee gestures toward her apron smudged with flour and frosting. "I'm a mess, I know."

"I don't mind the talking." I really don't. It's nice, actually. "And you're not a mess."

"That's not what Don—" She freezes, then shakes off whatever she was going to say. "Anyway, tell me more about yourself." Marilee busies herself with cleanup, unscrewing the lid on the pastry tube.

I step forward to grab a paper towel and sweep some stray sprinkles from the counter into my waiting hand. "Not much to tell, honestly." I toss the sprinkles into the trash.

"Well, what do you do for fun?"

"Run."

"Like, away from your problems?" Her eyes sparkle as she kicks on the sink beside our station and washes out the frosting tube.

I snort. "Maybe sometimes. But I was talking more like track and field."

"Ah, makes sense. You look like a runner."

"Uh, thank you?" By that, I hope she doesn't mean I look scrawny. I'd like to add more bulk to my body, but I'm not really sure where to start. Maybe my gym teacher can give me some pointers next semester. I'd ask Dad, but he's not really in any condition right now to be giving advice on physical fitness. And even if he was, he wouldn't have time for me anyway. "What else can I do to help?" Most of the materials and tools are still out on the table. "Seems like there's still a lot to clean."

"We don't have to have everything put away since there's a class after us. Maybe take that tray of cookies to the room across the hall?" She's washing out a mixing bowl, yellow gloves on her hands, but she uses her chin to indicate the door. "We're storing them in Mrs. Lincoln's room. She's the student government teacher and will keep them safe in containers until the bake sale this weekend."

"Bake sale? So I don't get to sample one now?" I tease.

"Nope. You'll need to wait for Friday night's football game. We're in the championships. You should come."

I like sports, but attending sporting events has never been on my radar. Still... "Will you be there?"

She dries her hands on a towel, unhooks her apron, and tosses it onto our table. "Of course. You can sit with me and my friends."

Maybe this new high school won't be so bad. "That'd be great. Thanks." I take the tray of cookies in hand and make my way through the classroom, where other pairs are also straightening up and grabbing their things. Glancing at the clock, I pick up the pace. There's only a minute or so until the bell rings if the schedule I memorized yesterday is correct.

I plow my way through the door, out to the hallway, and start to cross.

That's when I hear, "Watch out, freak!" and see a football careen toward me. Protecting the cookies, I turn away from the flying object, and the football slams into my back.

I suck in air as I hear laughter ring through the hallway.

"Jordan?" Marilee's voice lifts behind me, and then she's squatting there, her hand on my back, rubbing where the ball hit. "Are you all right?"

I want to scream not really, because that's definitely gonna leave a mark. Instead, "Yeah, I think so."

"Good." Marilee looks down, where I safely set the cookie sheet after the football landed. "You saved the cookies!" There's pure delight in her tone, and suddenly, I care nothing for my bruised back.

In that moment, I'm Marilee Moffitt's hero. And I have a feeling there's nothing better than that.

Marilee stands and dusts off her hands before tugging on my sleeve.

I stand too, leaning down to grab the precious cookie tray.

"You sure you're okay?" she asks again.

"He's fine, babe." Another voice joins our conversation, one with a sneer and an uncanny resemblance to the person who yelled for me to "watch out, freak" just a few moments ago.

We turn to find a broad guy in a blue varsity football jacket strutting toward us from down the hall, his black spiked hair as pointed as the glare he's giving me.

"Donny?" Marilee squeals as he approaches us. "What are you doing here? Your next class is across campus."

The bell chooses that moment to ring, and students pour from their classes. And even though I feel like a complete third wheel—because of course, Marilee is taken, and of course this jerk is her boyfriend—and I know I should move on, my feet don't agree.

"Eh, it's just with Coach Jensen. He's cool if I'm a few minutes late to history. Jimmy and I snuck over so we could walk our girls to their next class." He nods toward another football player—the one who must have been meant to catch the ball Donny threw. The guy's leaning up against a row of lockers, making out with a girl with long blonde curls.

"That's so sweet."

"I'm a sweet guy."

"Oh, hey, I wanted you to meet a new friend. Donny, this is Jordan Carmichael. Jordan, this is my boyfriend, Donny Franklin. He's one of the football team's quarterbacks."

Donny pastes on the fakest smile I've ever seen. "Sup. Good to meet ya. I'll take care of my girl from here, though."

Marilee opens her mouth to protest, but Donny leans down, tipping her chin up, and gives her a kiss. A really passionate kiss.

Marilee lifts on her tiptoes and responds.

I know I literally just met her, but the sight is a knife in my gut. Bitter disappointment, maybe? It's really stupid is what it is, and I definitely should not be here watching like a freak show. Besides, I've got another classroom to find, and only five minutes to do so. Being late on the first day isn't a good look.

My shoe squeaks on the linoleum as I turn to deliver the cookies to the desk in Mrs. Lincoln's empty room. Then I duck back into the hallway and ignore the way Donny's holding Marilee. Like he owns her. I head into Ms. White's room and grab my backpack. After a second of contemplation, I grab Marilee's too.

When I'm back in the hallway, I do the most awkward thing ever and clear my throat. Finally, when it's obvious they're not coming up for air, I tap her on the shoulder mid-kiss.

"Jordan?" She steps away from Donny, whose eyes flash murder at me. "Hey, sorry." Her cheeks are flushed, her lips kind of swollen.

I hate it. Again, for no logical discernible reason.

"No worries. Just thought you might need this." I hold her backpack out.

"Thank you." She smiles and slips it on. "You have no idea how many times I've left this thing in a classroom."

"No problem."

Donny steps forward and wraps his big, beefy arm around Marilee's shoulders. "That was nice of you, Johnny." There's a predatory gleam in his eyes.

"It's Jordan." But of course, he probably knows that. I've met plenty of guys like him, and I'm not letting him intimidate me. I turn my attention back to Marilee. "Let me know the plans for Friday night."

"Plans?" Donny says, a challenge in his voice.

Marilee shrinks a bit, turning into Donny and patting his chest. "I invited him to hang with the gang to watch you kick butt at the game!"

"I *am* gonna kick butt, especially if Kev's arm isn't back to normal and I get off the bench. I know I can bring it home for us."

"Of course you can. You're the best."

Donny puffs out his chest. I can see what he sees in her, but what does she see in this dude?

"I kind of am, huh?" Then he studies her, maybe for the first time. Laughing, he swipes at a streak of flour on her forehead. "You're such a mess, babe."

I don't know why I'm still standing here, but those words leaving his mouth... They make me honestly want to deck him.

I don't have a right to deck him. And like I said, I just met this girl.

But the way her whole face crumples at the statement makes me want to protect her. To go to bat for her. To tell her, again, that she's *not* a mess. That she's perfect.

Geez. When did I turn into such a sap?

"Oh. I know." Marilee's cheeks go red as she scrubs her palms across her face, wiping away the excess flour. "Sorry."

Then she rubs at a patch of white on his chest. "Oh, shoot. I got your jacket."

"It's fine. You can clean it for me later."

Her mouth turns downward into a frown. He pulls her back in, kisses the side of her head. "Kidding, kidding."

Something like a relieved smile crosses her face, and she melts into his side. "Right. Of course. I knew that."

And as she flashes me a wave and shouts, "I'll let you know the deets about Friday soon," something settles in my spirit.

A deep knowing.

That somehow, that girl is going to be important to me— even if she's taken, and all I can ever be is her friend.

MARILEE

Present day

Every year, without fail, whenever it's time to take down the Christmas tree, I die a thousand tiny deaths inside. That's why I wait as long as is humanly possible.

Or until my roommates—i.e., my brother Blake and his recently eloped wife, Lucy—start to complain.

"It smells like death in here, Squirt."

My head lifts from my spot at the kitchen counter, where I'm currently halfway through decorating a cake, to find my brother just inside the front door of the home in Hallmark Beach where we both grew up. It's late afternoon on a Monday, which means he's just returning from a supply run into San Luis Obispo to stock his gourmet grilled cheese food truck for the week. "What?"

He hangs his keys on a rack and shrugs out of his brown Harrington jacket before pointing to the Christmas tree next to the mantel, which, fine, is maybe a few days past its prime, with wrinkled bark and several brown needles, many of which cover our living room floor. Some of my favorite ornaments—like a tiny spatula (the last one Mom gave me before she and Dad died almost seven years ago)—are drooping, right along with the branches they're hooked on.

"It's gotta go, Mare. Lucy nearly threw up this morning on her way to the restaurant."

Using my favorite small star tip, I pipe a row of red around the edge of the round cake, which will hopefully soon resemble Captain America's shield. He's Ryder's favorite superhero, and the birthday boy gets what the birthday boy wants. "Most things make Lucy nearly throw up these days." Tossing my brother a saucy wink, I ignore the internal pinch at the thought that one of my best friends is pregnant.

Because I'm seriously happy for her—for both of them—but it doesn't stop me from grieving my own secret losses.

I don't think about them all the time, but I never forget.

Still, I'm going to be an aunt, and that really *is* worth celebrating. Come early August, this kid's gonna be spoiled, that's for sure. He or she will have all the cupcakes, cookies, and baked goods I can sneak them. Plus all the snuggles and kisses too.

Blake plops onto the stool across the kitchen island from me, exhaling heavily at the same time he pushes a hand through his short brown hair. "I thought we'd have a bit more time married and alone before becoming parents."

That word—*alone*—captures my attention, and I blink at the cake in front of me. It's only half finished but I feel the urge to start from scratch. I open my mouth to say what I'm thinking —that they're hardly alone with me here, that I'd move out and give them the whole house if I could afford to—but Blake keeps on talking.

"Still, I'm happy, you know?"

"I know." I smile at him, pushing my large-framed glasses

up my nose. "As you should be." Blake and Lucy's path to a relationship was filled with ups and downs, supposed "hatred" and love. But they finally found their way to each other, and I've enjoyed watching them go from falling in love last summer to getting engaged and quickly eloping a few months ago to this —starting a family.

Blake and I have always been different—him so put together, me such a mess—so it's no surprise that he's succeeded in all the ways I've failed. Donny and I may have been married for six years (after dating for five), but our relationship was never like Blake and Lucy's.

And I didn't see it. All those years...

Then, when I did, I was too scared to change it.

Too broken.

I fill in the edges of the shield, frowning when I muss a spot. Normally I can decorate without thinking—it's my happy place. But Donny and the past aside, there are a lot of other things swirling around in my brain right now. It started with Lucy and Blake's Christmas morning announcement nearly two weeks ago and continued when my boss Marla Thompkins asked me last week if I was interested in buying The Blackberry Muffin bakery from her, as she's ready to retire.

Standing, Blake grabs an apple out of a bowl in the center of the island and tosses it into the air a few times before spearing me with a look. "So... Do you think Jordan would loan you his truck so we can haul that thing away? Or maybe he can use it as firewood for one of his camping trips this spring?"

"I'll ask him tonight." My chest tightens at the thought of losing another Christmas tree. Of another year passing without Mom and Dad.

"Tonight? You guys are doing dinner together *again*?" Blake may think he's being nonchalant with his question, but I want so badly to roll my eyes at the implication in his tone. "Weren't you just over there a bunch this weekend?"

"This weekend, I was helping to watch Ryder so Jordan could get in extra work after the holidays. And tonight, it's Ryder's birthday dinner. His grandparents on both sides are going to be there too."

I want to add a "so there!" to the end of my declaration and stick out my tongue for good measure, but it's no use. Jordan Carmichael has been my friend since freshman year of high school, and that's never changed, despite him leaving Hallmark Beach to attend college and graduate business school in Phoenix and then swooping back into my life not long after my parents died in a car accident.

But ever since my ex-husband left me nearly four years ago (and my divorce was finalized one year later), I've received countless amounts of teasing smiles and coy looks over how close Jordan and I have been since he moved back. I usually shrug it off, declaring us "just friends."

But after a while, it's exhausting.

I'm pretty sure Jordan doesn't care for me as anything more than a friend, anyway. He's never said so, even though sometimes, there's a look he gives me that makes me think I might be wrong. But I hope for his sake I'm *not* wrong, because I just can't afford to think of him in that way.

Can't afford to think of *anyone* like that again.

Because I won't inflict my mess on anyone else. Won't let my poor decision-making ruin anyone else's life the way it's ruined mine. I mean look at me. I'm twenty-nine, single, and used up, without a dime to my name because my ex-husband— the guy I chose to give my *forever* to—blew my inheritance on gambling and other women.

Why Marla would ask *me* of all people to buy the bakery from her is a wonder. Guess I've got her fooled.

"Earth to Squirt." Blake waves his hand in front of my face, and I startle.

"Sorry." Because there I go again, retreating into my thoughts. "What'd you say?"

He chuckles and shakes his head. "Never mind. Have fun at the party." Taking a bite of his apple, he turns and walks through the living room and down the hall, toward the master bedroom he and Lucy now share. I gave them my room when they came back from a national parks tour married in November.

"I *will* have fun at the party," I murmur to myself. I've got to focus and get this cake finished, though, because time is ticking away, and I've still got to shower.

A few hours later, I'm parked in front of Jordan's two-bedroom bungalow, leaning into my car to grab the cake box. Surprisingly, I'm the first one here, even though I'm a half hour late.

The front door squeaks open, and a little blur of red and blue careens toward me. "Lee-Lee! You're finally here!" Ryder stops just before crashing into me and throws his little arms around my waist.

Laughing, I set the cake on top of my car and wrap him up in a hug. Then I step back to study him and put on a confused face. "Wait, who is hugging me right now? I didn't know Captain America lived here!"

Ryder's blue eyes—the same light shade as his daddy's—stare at me from behind the mask with an A in the middle of his forehead. "Lee-Lee!" He giggles. "It's me. Ryder."

"Seriously? *You're* Captain America? What happened to Steve Rogers?"

"I'll bet you're pretty proud of yourself for knowing that reference," says a deeper voice from the front porch.

Glancing up, I see Jordan leaning against the doorway, his

strong forearms crossed over his chest, his signature backwards hat on his head, as he smirks at me.

"I am, actually." Because despite having a brother, I grew up on a steady diet of Audrey Hepburn movies and modern-day romcoms like *While You Were Sleeping*—my mom's favorite. I redirect my attention to Ryder, who is wearing a costume with a puffy "muscled" chest. "Wow, I'm super impressed with your muscles. You'll have to share your workout routine with me."

"It's easy. You just run and run and run. And a-fore you know it, you've got mus-ckles!" Ryder giggles again and runs a circle around my car. Goodness, even for a five-year-old, he's got energy to burn.

I reach for the cake on the top of my car, but then Jordan's there swooping it down. I catch a whiff of his familiar woodsy scent with hints of cedarwood, clove, and patchouli—like a warm blanket during a camping trip. Not that I'm a camping-type girl usually, but being Jordan's best friend has meant expanding my horizons. I've hiked and camped more in the last few years than in my whole life combined before that. And Jordan lives for it—it's why he started his adventure tours business when he moved back to town a little over six years ago.

"Thanks." I smile at him as I follow him up the few stairs into his house. It's small, with a kitchen that opens to a living room, two bedrooms, and one bathroom, but it's been his home since he found out Georgia was expecting Ryder. She never lived here, as the two of them didn't ever date, so it's got the mark of Jordan all over it. Masculine but comfortable, with the comfiest brown leather couch, a sleek fifty-inch TV, and a Padres-themed fleece blanket thrown over the back of a recliner.

Shoved into the only available corner is his artificial Christmas tree. He used to take it down as soon as the calendar hit January, but I suspect he's started leaving it up longer just for me—the girl who wears Christmas sweaters and Grinch pajamas year-round.

Christmas reminds me of my parents. It was my mom's favorite, and keeping the season alive all year is my small way of keeping them close always.

Ryder runs back inside and zooms down the hallway, yelling something about a new toy he wants to show me. And also about needing to poop.

I grin. Kids.

Jordan sets the cake on the granite kitchen island and taps the top of the container. "Thanks for bringing this. Ryder's gonna flip when he sees it." He flashes a dimpled grin at me. "You sure are talented, Lee."

"Oh, stop." I wave my hand in the air. "It was nothing."

"Don't do that. It's not nothing." Walking to the oven, he flips it open and pulls out a white box with the familiar Red Sauce Pizza logo. "We both know you're the most talented baker in all the land."

"All the land, huh?" Setting my small purse on the counter, I lean forward, elbows on the island, and inhale the delicious aroma of pepperoni and cheese.

"Yep, all the land. Have you given any more thought to Marla's offer?"

"I mean, a bit."

"But?"

Frowning, I tap my stubby fingernails against the gleaming, black countertop. "I still don't understand why she'd ask me. Sure, I can bake, but operate a business? That's a stretch. I'd probably run the thing Marla's built into the ground."

"What are you talking about? You're super smart." He washes his hands in the sink.

"No, *you're* super smart, Mr. MBA." I round the island to grab a handful of plates and napkins from his cupboards.

"Whatever." Jordan shuts off the faucet and flicks me with some water.

I squeal and push on his muscled arm. "Hey!" Leaning down, I use the sleeve of his Henley to wipe away the moisture. "It's true. I'm no business genius." I settle back against the counter and sigh. "Then again, Marla's already built the business. If I just keep things exactly as she has them, maybe it'd be okay. There's just the whole matter of getting a loan to be able to buy her out. And that would be next to impossible."

Because we both know that Donny shot a hole in my credit with all the ways he drained our accounts and racked up debt on our joint credit cards before he left me to shovel my way out. I've been working hard to get out from under it all, but even now, it feels heavy.

"You never know. Maybe Pete over at the bank would give you a shot. He's known you forever." He dries his hands on a towel and reaches out to rub my elbow.

"Maybe. But unlikely." His touch is the reassurance I need to shake off the gloom of the past. "I've been thinking that I could maybe sell my half of the house to Blake and Lucy."

"Wow. Are you really ready to do that? I know what that house means to you."

"I know, but with the baby coming...I just sort of feel in the way, you know?"

"I'm sure *they* don't feel like you are."

"Not yet, maybe." I shrug, heat stinging the back of my eyes. "But I want them to have time to truly be alone before the baby comes. I could sell to them, find an apartment, and use the extra money to buy out Marla."

"You could."

I sense the hesitation in Jordan's tone. Craning my neck

upward—because Jordan's got a good twelve or fourteen inches on me ever since his massive growth spurt junior year of high school—I study him. "What?"

"Nothing."

Going up on my tiptoes, I steal his hat and ruffle my hands quickly through his blond hair, which he's let grow a bit longer than usual. "Nope. Unacceptable answer." Moving away, I turn and hop up onto the island across from him, sticking his hat on my head instead.

He laughs. "Dork."

I open my arms and pretend to bow my head as if I'm curt-sying. "Why thank you. I resemble that remark. Now." I wag my finger at him. "Exactly what are you thinking, Jordan Thad-deus Carmichael?"

"I'm thinking that I regret telling you my middle name."

"Ha ha. I'm being serious here. I value your opinion, and you're one of the only ones I trust to always tell me the truth."

He blinks at me for a moment before sighing and crossing his arms. "I guess I just wonder if you really *want* to take over the bakery. What about your own cake decorating business? I thought you were considering doing that."

"I was, but..." My mouth scrunches. "There's a lot of risk in it, you know? I need the security of a job. I've enjoyed taking on some cake decorating on the side, as much as Marla will let me, but she seems to think there's not enough of a demand in town to be a sustainable part of her business. And she's been running The Blackberry Muffin for thirty years. She would know."

"Not necessarily. Things change. More people have moved to this area, and she's never really tried it, other than letting you take on a handful of commissions this last year."

"I guess." Either way, this is an opportunity to really think about what I want to do with my life. The only for sure is that I want to stay here, with my friends and family. And I want to bake in some way. But what I make right now at the bakery—even full time—isn't necessarily sustainable in the long-term.

I blow out a breath.

Jordan steps forward and places his hands on my shoulders. "It'll be okay, Lee. You don't have to make any decisions right now."

"You're right. Thank you." Smiling, I place my hands over his. Something swoops in my stomach. Must be hunger pangs. "What I need to do right now is eat. When is everyone else getting here?"

Jordan drops his hands and moves to the pizza box. "You're actually it. Sorry, I would have texted you, but I just found out right before you arrived."

"Found out what?"

"Mom's had a flare-up, so she can't make it. And I'm not sure Dad was going to come anyway."

"Oh no. I'm sorry." Jordan's mom has multiple sclerosis, and it's worsened over the last few years. That, combined with the fact his dad is a high-functioning (though thankfully non-abusive) alcoholic, means Jordan can't rely on them to watch Ryder as much as he could when Ryder was a baby.

And now that Georgia's gone, her parents and I are the only regular caretakers who can help Jordan with Ryder when he's in his busy work season during the spring and summer.

"What about Larry and Constance? I thought they were coming."

He gives me a look. "They never actually accepted my invitation."

"What do you mean? I thought things were better between you?"

Jordan just shrugs as he serves up pizza slices on the plates I slide his way.

Georgia's parents, who live one town over, have never been

Jordan's biggest fan, but since he and Georgia co-parented with respect for each other, they always held their tongues.

Until Georgia died from cancer. In recent months, Constance especially has not held back her opinions on Jordan's parenting. But to not come over for Ryder's birthday?

"That's just rude. I'm sorry."

"It's fine. I think they're just really struggling. It's been almost a year since Georgia died. But I don't want any tension for Ryder's sake." He runs a hand down his face, then seems to shake off his anxiety over the situation. "Anyway, you're enough of a guest to make this a celebration. And speaking of the birthday boy, I'm gonna go make sure he didn't fall into the toilet. Be right back."

"Okay." I say the word, but my whole body hums as Jordan leaves the kitchen. His words carry me—*you're enough.*

It's so strange to hear someone say that after years of enduring Donny's emotional abuse. So easy to settle into it, to want to make a home there. To make a home here.

But as much as Jordan and Ryder and I feel like some strange little family—with two platonic parents, of course—I know it'll never last. Jordan's too good of a guy to not marry someone someday. And I want that for him. I do. I won't stand in the way of it.

Which means I need to remember my place.

That this is *not* my home.

But neither is my actual home. Not anymore. It's Blake and Lucy's home, and I'm just living in it.

So maybe I need a New Year's resolution—to figure out where I *do* actually belong.

And then, maybe I can finally believe that I am enough. That the world I've built for myself is enough. And somehow, stop worrying that it's all going to fall apart if I make one more poor decision.

three

JORDAN

The best part about living in a small town like Hallmark Beach is all the people who care about you.

The worst part about living in a small town?

All the people who care about you.

Because this Tuesday morning, all I want is to grab a coffee from The White Mocha and be on my merry way. But as I'm waiting for my Americano near the pickup counter, Earl Flanders and Ned Chamberlain hop up from a round, black metal table in the corner—their usual spot—and make a beeline for me.

"Jordan, my boy." Earl sidles up beside me, stretching a bony arm around my shoulders. The Old Spice aroma he douses himself in every day wafts upward and tickles my nose. "We've got a question for the Town Guru on All Things Sports."

"Good morning, Earl." It's only eight-thirty, but the place is already hopping, with a line stretching out the door and onto Main Street. From the large picture window out front, I catch a glimpse of the rising January sun glinting off the windows of Rainbow Ice across the road. "And wow, that's quite the title."

Bespectacled Ned stomps up and lightly shoves Earl's arm away from me. "Now, don't go getting all warm and fuzzy with him in hopes he'll agree with you, Flanders."

"Pshaw. As if I would." Earl flashes me a mischievous grin, and I know without a doubt he *definitely* would.

Even though I'm in a hurry, I can't help but laugh and indulge them. I'll be here a few minutes waiting for my order anyway. "All right, guys. What's the question?"

"In your fine opinion"—Earl's bushy eyebrows dance and disappear underneath the brim of his cowboy hat as he emphasizes each word—"which is better: pig wrestling or underwater hockey?"

If I'd been drinking my as-yet-to-be-served coffee, I'd have sputtered it all over the burnished wood floor. "Um. Well. That's a very…interesting question, gentlemen." One for which I have no answer.

Because… What the what?

My hesitation is covered by the sound of the coffee grinder whirring behind the pickup counter, where Amy, the younger sister of coffee shop owner Thomas Montrose, works on filling orders.

She flicks me a smile. I glance away. Not because she isn't pretty. With her blonde braid and slim figure, she definitely is.

Just not as pretty as…

"Baseball," I say, moving my attention back to the two seventy-something chuckleheads that have come to be like crazy great-uncles to me. "Baseball is definitely the best sport."

"Aw, come on. It's okay. You can tell us the truth." Earl leans in close and whisper-yells, "We both know it's pig wrestling."

"Gentlemen, gentlemen." I hold up my hands in defense. "I choose to abstain from this…er, discussion." Not only because it's ridiculous, but because at my core, I'm a peacemaker.

Though in reality, nobody has been able to keep peace between Ned and Earl, who have been best friends since grade school. They're always arguing about something. Thankfully, they do it in love.

They're proof that people *can* say what they're thinking without losing someone's affection and respect.

If only I'd experienced that in my own life.

"That's because for the hundredth time, Earl, pig wrestling's not a sport!" Ned shakes his head in disgust. I catch a whiff of some sort of olive oil wafting off his flannel shirt. His family has owned Olive Paradise for as long as I can remember —and he's smelled this way for as long as I can remember too.

"Is too! My granddaddy wrestled pigs with the best of 'em." Tipping his hat upward with the thrust of his pointer finger, Earl struts back toward their table.

Grunting, Ned follows, muttering something about how Earl's old and that means his granddaddy probably wrestled pigs one hundred years ago.

I can't help but grin at their nonsense when Amy finally calls my name. Turning, I find her there, smiling at me again, my Americano clutched in her hands. "Morning, Jordan." Her eyes are bright and eager. She's a bit younger than me—maybe five years?—and she's really sweet. In any other life, I'd ask her out in a heartbeat.

But she's just not my person.

Not that my person knows how I feel. And even if I could summon the courage to tell her, I'm not sure she'll ever be ready to hear it.

"Hey, Amy." I don't want to encourage the poor woman's attention if she does have feelings for me, but I also can't be rude. "How are you?"

"Fine." Biting her lip, she runs her thumb along the lid of the cup. She opens her mouth to say something else, but before she can, her brother—who is taking orders in his signature, bright-orange Hawaiian shirt—asks if she can get some more coffee beans from the back.

"Sure, Tommy." With a sheepish glance my way, she slides the coffee across the counter. "Enjoy your drink and have a good day."

"Thanks. You too."

She heads through the kitchen door behind the glass display case featuring a variety of breakfast sandwiches, yogurt parfaits, and specialty sodas.

Shaking off the discomfort I feel over the interaction, I grab my coffee, its warmth seeping through my hand, and turn, nearly smacking into Bea Reynolds. "Oh geez, sorry, Mrs. Reynolds!" Just my luck. She's one of the chattiest town members around, and I'm short on time as it is.

I guess this is what I get for coming to the town's only coffee shop instead of making my own cuppa Joe at home. But I was nearly late dropping Ryder at preschool as it was.

"Jordan Carmichael! We haven't seen you in ages, sugar." The Texas charm oozes off of Bea, who just happens to be the aunt of Marilee's other best friend, Lucy, and the mother of their mutual friend, April. "And you know, it's Bea. We don't stand on formality here."

"She's right." Aaaaaand she's not alone. Her sister-in-law, Janine—owner of The Purple Seashell, the town's only inn— peeks from behind her. "You're keeping yourself far too busy these days."

Both women are looking at me with big, sympathetic eyes, like I'm a cartoon bunny they just want to wrap up in a motherly hug.

Like I said. Small towns.

I chuckle. "I believe we all saw each other Saturday night at the barbecue in your very own backyard, Bea." Lucy and Blake invited their closest family and friends over to announce their pregnancy, and Burt and Bea hosted.

Bea waves her hand in the air. "That hardly counts. I didn't get a chance to catch up. How's your mama doing? We've missed her at book club."

"She's feeling a bit better than last week. She had to miss Ryder's birthday dinner and felt really bad about it."

"Oh, how's the little man doing?" Janine asks.

"He's great. Loving being five now." I take a sip of my coffee while glancing surreptitiously at the white clock hanging on the black brick wall behind the counter. A stitch of impatience pulls at my chest. Because the clockface tells me all I need to know—I've got only a handful of hours left until preschool is over, and I'll either be able to finish the work that's piling up or calling in yet another favor to Marilee, who I've been relying on far too much lately.

Marilee, whose words from last week I can't get out of my brain: *"I value your opinion, and you're one of the only ones I trust to always tell me the truth."*

The truth?

Ha. She couldn't handle my truth.

"The poor dear."

Bea's words snap my attention back to the town matriarchs beside me. "What's that?" I say.

Janine tuts and pushes a strand of her gray bob behind her ear. "Is he still having nightmares about his mama being gone?"

I feel the band around my chest tighten. I know it's not my fault Ryder's going through this. But he already had to deal with parents who didn't live together, who didn't even love each other.

Who were only in each other's lives permanently after a one-night stand—something I've never done before and have never done since, the combined effect of rejection and alcohol.

He already had to live with the consequences of my poor decisions and broken heart, but then to lose his mom when he was just barely four years old?

I want so much more for my little man than the year he's had. Than the life I've been able to give him.

I clear my throat. "He's back to sleeping in his own room, thankfully. Of course there are still some nights when the bad dreams come..."

"Of course, dear, of course." Bea's strong arm pats my shoulder. "You're such a good daddy."

What do I even say to that? Because I want to be. But I can't help feeling like I've failed him. I try not to take work home, to be fully present for him when I'm there. But that doesn't help during my busy season, when I can't be home at all. Because when you run an adventure tours company and are one of the only guides...well, sometimes you literally *can't* bring it home.

Thankfully, I make enough to support us. But being a small business owner at a start-up company—and being a dad on top of that—is not for the faint of heart.

I don't want much in this life, just to take care of my people as best I can. To make things as smooth and easy for them as possible.

But Mom's sick, Dad's an alcoholic, and they're living paycheck to paycheck. Ryder's mom-less and has to be over at his other grandparents' house or with Marilee more than he's with me. And Marilee...

I shift my weight from one foot to the other. "You're kind to say so."

Janine leans in close like she's divulging a secret. "So—"

"I know that look." Bea yanks Janine upright. "Leave the poor man alone."

"What?" Janine presses a hand to her chest, her mouth

screwed into a smile that's about as innocent as a toddler with a dirty diaper. "I was merely going to ask—"

"I know what you were going to ask," Bea says. "And you don't need to."

I'm glad Bea is sure, because I've got no clue. But now that the flow of conversation is broken, it's the perfect place to finally assert myself and escape. "It was great running into you ladies, but I'm needed at work. Mandy's holding down the fort alone." Not that my assistant minds. She's used to my wonky schedule.

"Of course. Get on, now." Bea makes a shooing motion, and I take the chance to get out of Dodge.

A breeze greets me as I duck out of the building. I toss a wave to Adam Painter across the street, where he's sweeping sand off the deck of Rainbow Ice. In between the ice cream shop and The Green Robin restaurant sits Blake's black-and-white food truck, its serving window shuttered until about eleven, when he'll start grilling up some of the town's best fare. His wife alternates between working as a waitress inside the Robin and helping him out at the truck, which has turned into a thriving business.

The man's got it all. Plus a kid on the way.

He did things in the order I'd have preferred to. But I can't regret Ryder for a second, so I try not to think about my mistakes too much.

I hustle down the street—past the early morning joggers, headed for the boardwalk on the other side of the row of buildings to my right, past the Golden Highlight salon and the Pink Rose flower shop, all coming to life after a nighttime of sleep—and finally, after rounding the bend, I catch sight of the bright-green facade of Go Round Adventures. Colorfully painted surfboards are mounted on the front wall beside the yellow door, the sight of which always makes me smile, because

Marilee chose that particular shade. I would have made it all blue, but she insisted it needed to be bright and happy.

She didn't need to say anything else. All I needed to see was the light in her eyes—light that that jerk of a husband Donny had slowly chiseled at in the years since I'd been away at school—to say okay and ask when she was free to help me pick out the exact right color.

Of course, it had to be a night Donny was out. Because while it was completely fine for *him* to be gone until two a.m. with no explanation of his whereabouts, if he got wind that Marilee and I were hanging out at all, she'd hear about it.

Other than a few cars, the street is fairly deserted—not surprising, as winter isn't the most popular time to come to the beach, even though our weather stays fairly temperate with a high of mid-sixties.

Just as I'm approaching the front door, it swings open, and a guy who looks around my age steps out wearing a red polo and jeans, with a messenger bag strung across his chest.

His eyes fix on me. "Jordan Carmichael?"

"Yes?" I don't think I've ever seen him before, but he seems to know me. Maybe Mandy told him I was on the way and he wanted to talk with the owner.

The guy whips an envelope out of his bag and has it in my hands before I know what's happening. "You've been served. Have a nice day."

"Wait." I turn, blinking as I watch him cross the street to a parked, white car. "What is this?"

He looks over his shoulder, shrugs. "Not sure, but I suggest you read it ASAP."

Sitting on the bench, I rip open the crisp white envelope and pull out the paper inside. The letterhead reads *Superior Court of California.* My neck heats despite the cool breeze blowing up off the Pacific as I read the words.

Words that, honestly, make no sense.

Because if my eyes can be believed, Larry and Constance Comer—Georgia's parents—are petitioning the court for custody of Ryder.

But that can't be right. I mean, sure, they never loved me, but they also never said I was an unfit parent. And yet, there it is, in writing, questioning whether being with me is in Ryder's best interest.

Surely—*surely*—this is a mistake. Standing, I tug my phone from my pocket and dial Larry's number. A quiet accountant, he's always had a good head on his shoulders, even when Constance's loudly stating her opinions.

The phone rings once, twice, three times.

Voicemail.

Nope. I hit redial. Again. And again.

Finally, the ringing stops, and Larry clears his throat on the other side of the line. "Jordan."

"Larry, please tell me this is a joke."

The man sighs, and I can picture him running his thumb and middle finger along his thin brow. "Afraid not."

"But..." I mean, what do I say? As I pace back and forth along the store porch, the wood creaks beneath my weight. "Why?"

Another sigh. "Look, son. It's nothing personal—"

"It feels a little bit personal." I inhale deeply, trying to calm myself. Spouting off and getting angry won't solve this problem. I may hate confrontation, but I won't let anyone take my son from me. "Sorry, this was just a surprise. I thought we were doing okay—me letting you see Ryder as often as you'd like, you helping me out when I need to work. I thought it was a win-win."

A muffled voice in the background—which sounds an awful lot like Constance—fills the space for a moment. Then Larry finally answers me. "Well, see, Constance recently found Georgia's will when she was cleaning out her house. It says she wanted us to have custody of Ryder if anything ever happened to her."

"Okay." I mean, I guess I get that. But *I'm* his father. And I'm still here. "I can understand how that would be upsetting—"

"Upsetting?" Constance's shrill voice banks in my ear, and I have to pull the phone away for a moment. "Yes, it's quite upsetting when your only child dies, Jordan."

I close my eyes. "Constance—"

"No, don't *Constance* me. Our daughter's dying wish was for us to take care of her child—a child you rarely see because you're a workaholic. He'd be better off with us, and our attorney agrees. Don't contact us again. We won't answer."

I pinch the bridge of my nose. "But what about Ryder? Are you going to shut him out too?"

"Well, no, of course not." She seems to falter there. "Fine, you can text us about watching Ryder, because of course we want to see him. And I pray you're not cruel enough to keep him from us."

Me, cruel? The irony.

She continues. "But we will not talk to you about this court petition. The court date is in five weeks, and we can discuss it then. Good day."

The phone goes dead. I pull it away, stare at it in my hand. Run my hand down my face. My breathing hitches, and my palms go sweaty. What am I going to do?

My response is automatic. I pick the phone back up and text the one person I know will be here in a matter of minutes.

SOS.

The phone rings almost immediately. Marilee's picture—one I took of her baking something in my kitchen, adorable, with her hair up and glasses falling down her nose, unaware I was taking a photo—pops up on the screen. "Hey, Lee."

"Jordan?" I can hear the noise of the bakery, the steady stream of classical music Marla Thompkins keeps playing, eking into our conversation. "Hang on." The noise suddenly stops. "Sorry, I had to step into the kitchen. What's going on? Where are you? Are you okay? Who do I need to beat up?"

She says the last part jokingly, and it is rather laughable to think of sweet Marilee Moffitt beating anyone up with her petite frame and kindness that wouldn't harm a fly. But then again, she has no idea why I'm SOS-ing her.

"Um. Sorry. I didn't know you were working today."

"Don't apologize. Lexi had an appointment, so Marla asked me to fill in up front. But she actually just got back, so it's good timing." A pause. "Where are you?"

"At work."

"K. I'll be there in five."

"You don't have to—"

"I said I'll be there in five, Jay."

I smile at the nickname she gave me in high school after I first called her Lee. She said it was only fair that if I got to shorten her name, she got to shorten mine. "Let's actually meet on the beach."

"Okay."

I don't even have to tell her which spot—she just knows. It's the spot where we always go, down past the Pink Rose, south of most of the major Main Street buildings, where a path diverges down to the water and there's a grassy bluff always sporting a spray of flowers, even in the winter.

After I pop inside the store to let Mandy know I'll be gone a bit longer than usual, I head to the place where the boardwalk ends, and Marilee's already waiting there for me, two white pastry bags clutched in her fist—because of course she couldn't come empty-handed.

"Hi." She tilts her head, studying me from behind her black-rimmed glasses. Today she's got on jeans, red Converse sneakers, and a white cable knit sweater with a large, green Christmas tree on the front. Her long, brown hair is tied loosely back in a low ponytail pulled over one shoulder—a different look than her high bun, but it's still enough to give me a view of her graceful neck.

What can I say? I'm a glutton for punishment.

"Hi." I stop in front of her. "Thanks for coming."

"Duh. You sounded..."

"Panicked? Yeah. A bit."

"Why? What's going on?"

"Let's go sit."

"Please tell me now. I'm really worried, and don't think I can last an extra minute."

I glance away, toward the waves flicking up against the sand. Ebbing and flowing, no matter how much my own world is imploding. "Constance and Larry are trying to take Ryder away from me."

"I'm sorry, what?"

"It's true." Reaching into the back pocket of my jeans, I pull out the letter and hand it to her. She sets the pastry bags on the worn but sturdy wooden planks under our feet. Her fingertips skim mine as she reaches for the letter. Opening it, she reads. Huffs indignantly. Her mouth falls open, and her glasses scoot to the tip of her nose.

Finally, she looks back up at me. "I can't... What...?" The hand holding the paper flies to her hip, effectively crumpling the page in her fist. "Just who do they think they are? They must be crazy."

Marilee never speaks out against anyone, so under normal circumstances, I'd find her indignation cute.

But these are not normal circumstances.

I stuff my hands into my pockets. "I dunno. Maybe they're right. I've worked a lot lately—"

"Because you own a business. Would they rather you be a bum? I mean, you're setting a great example for Ryder, showing him that hard work pays off."

"Yeah, but is it too much? Am I gone too often? I've had to rely on the Comers, and on you, so much."

"You know I don't mind."

"I know, but you've got your own life."

"Jay, look at me."

I do. Marilee is usually soft spoken, but right now, her voice is firm. Reaching out, she touches my arm. "When I help with Ryder, I'm right where I want to be. I love you guys, okay? I don't mind helping you out one bit. Goodness knows you've helped me."

I'm guessing she means after Donny left—since then, we've grown even closer. There were days I literally (and lovingly) dragged her out of bed. Between me and Lucy, we kept her going. Kept her drinking water and eating, until she had shaken off the mantle of despair that creep left on her shoulders.

But that's just what best friends do.

I only wish when she said she *loved* us that she meant...

No. That's not what this is about. I shake my head. "I don't even know a lawyer, Lee. How am I going to fight this, however ridiculous it is?"

"Don't worry. I know someone."

"You do?" Surely she wouldn't recommend that terrible attorney who represented her during her divorce proceedings. The guy met with her a grand total of one time, charged a ton, and didn't even get Marilee retribution for what Donny stole from her. Meanwhile, Donny had a great attorney—one he was clearly sleeping with, if the way they couldn't keep their hands off each other outside of the mediation proceedings were any indication.

"Yep. One of my dad's college roommates works in San Luis Obispo." Marilee grins, and it's like all the clouds in the sky suddenly run scared and poof—disappear. That's what her smile does to me, to my world. "I'll call him up and see if he can meet with us tomorrow."

"With *us*? Lee, you don't have to—"

"Stop it right now. If it involves helping you, I'm there." For a moment, she frowns. "Unless you don't need me there. Which is totally fine, but I just want to support you however I can."

Her hand starts to drop, and I catch it before she can pull away completely.

"Honestly, I couldn't do it without you, Lee."

"Good. Because I won't let you." Without a moment's hesitation, she steps forward, arms outstretched, and I wrap mine around her. Tilting her head, she looks up at me. "We're gonna figure this out, Jay. I promise. I won't let anyone take Ryder from you. We'll do whatever we have to, okay?"

Words burn in my throat, so I just nod. She burrows into me, pulling me tight, and I place my chin on the top of her head, taking the first deep breath since I read the court's summons.

"It's gonna be all right," she says.

And somehow, I kind of, almost, believe her.

"Daddy, do you think if I eat too many carrots, my face will turn orange?"

I blink away the thoughts that have been looping in my brain since receiving the court summons just over forty-eight hours ago and glance down at Ryder. His little hand is tucked in mine, and he's wearing his favorite green dinosaur backpack since I just picked him up from preschool. "What's that, bud?"

"Carrots. Miss Angie says that we should eat a lot of 'em because they're crunchy and delicious. But Evan told me that if you eat too many, you'll turn orange." Ryder scrunches his freckled nose up at me. "And I think that would be really cool, because my hair is already kinda orange."

"You *would* look pretty cool with an orange face."

"I know."

This kid. His confidence, his swagger, his sweetness. He's everything cool, and I don't deserve him. But somehow, he's mine.

And I have to do whatever it takes to keep it that way.

A breeze blows dead tree leaves down Hillside Drive, a road that overlooks downtown. Most of Hallmark Beach's residents live in the neighborhood that spreads out to the east, including me and Ryder. My parents are only a few blocks away, as is Miss Angie's in-home preschool where Ryder's attended regularly since Georgia died.

I worked this morning at the office as best I could and then headed home to throw on some slacks and a button-up shirt since I'm guessing my normal joggers and Henley aren't appropriate fare for meeting with an attorney. But what do I know about that? Georgia and I never met with attorneys when we had Ryder. We were able to amicably split custody and responsibilities without a third-party mediator.

But now she's gone, and I suppose I can't take anything for granted anymore.

As I walk Ryder to my parents' house—where Marilee will meet me in a few minutes—my whole body feels like a twig blowing in the wind, risking a snap at any moment. I just don't know when the breaking will come.

"So, Daddy. Is it true?"

"What?"

He huffs, as if my ignorance is the silliest thing he's heard all day. "About the carrots! I mean, Evan lies a lot, so I don't think he's probably telling me the truth. But I kinda *want* it to be true. So maybe I just pretend?"

How do I answer him? I don't want to steal his innocence, that special spark of light he's got. Don't want to tell him that pretending doesn't make something true.

I've pretended in my own mind enough times that Marilee, Ryder, and I are a family. And look how that's turned out.

But I just squeeze his hand and smile at him. "I don't think there's ever anything wrong with dreaming."

His tiny-toothed grin—which I know will someday soon have gaps in it—is a balm to my soul. "Oh good. Because sometimes the impossible comes true."

What's the saying? From the mouth of babes?

Yeah.

I ruffle his hair. "Never stop dreaming, Ry."

"You too, Daddy."

Ah, geez. This kid.

We approach my parents' small white home with green trim, where they've lived since settling in Hallmark Beach fifteen years ago. The grass in front is dead, and not just from the winter. The paint is in desperate need of a fresh coat, and the weeds borne of the winter rain we've gotten have overtaken the rocky side yard. A huge mesquite has a cracked branch that should have been taken care of weeks ago, but I haven't had the time to come over and do anything about it.

And Dad... Well, Dad's not been in any shape to do much of anything for a long time.

Senior year, I tried telling him what I'd seen his alcohol consumption do to him. To us. Tried to ask him to get help, to deal with his PTSD in a healthier way.

That's when he told me he thought it'd be best for me to go away for college.

Ryder darts away from me and runs up the front porch steps, flinging open the door and shouting, "Grandma! Grandpa!"

Thank goodness that, despite my dad's lack of emotional engagement with me, he's at least decent to my son.

I follow after him, shutting the door behind me. The house smells like burnt toast and coffee. It's dark despite the afternoon sun, since the light can sometimes give Mom a headache. I duck into the living room to find Ryder up on Dad's lap in his trusty, battered recliner. He's got a can of Bud Light in one hand, the remote in the other, and some Western is on the television.

Ryder's chattering away, and I can't tell if Dad's listening to him or to the TV, which is set to low volume.

I pick up Ryder's backpack from the middle of the floor where he left it. "Hey, Dad."

"Son." He doesn't even glance at me. From here, I can see he's wearing his favorite Dodgers cap over his balding head, and a white T-shirt is pulled snug over his beer belly.

"Where's Mom?" When I called to ask if she was feeling up to watching Ryder today, she assured me she was fine. But if she's not, maybe Lucy or Chloe would be willing to take a few hours off to babysit.

"Bathroom. She'll be out in a sec."

"Okay." I glance down the small hallway. The carpet's been freshly vacuumed, a sign that maybe Mom is past her last flare-up. The bathroom door's closed, but the light's on underneath. I settle on the edge of the brown couch and wait. Look at the clock mounted above the TV. Marilee should be here soon.

I glance back at my dad and Ryder, who's fallen silent against his chest, asleep in minutes. Preschool must have worn him out today.

Gaze still steady on the television, Dad lifts his can of beer and shakes it. "Grab me another, will you?"

I want to say absolutely not, but I know he'll just ask Mom when she gets in here if I don't. So I trudge into the small galley kitchen, where I see the black toast in question sitting on a plate, strawberry jelly spread in a thin layer over top, one singular bite removed. Opening the fridge, I grab another beer from Dad's daily six-pack. There are only two left.

"Go ahead and grab yourself one too," Dad calls from the living room.

I shut the fridge, the single can of Bud gripped in my hand, and rejoin him, holding the beer out.

He finally looks at me, squints in the dim light. "You didn't want one?"

"Thanks, but you know I don't drink, Dad." After seeing what alcohol did to him, I never have.

Except that one night—the one when I met Georgia in a bar, just as lonely after a breakup as I'd been. Alcohol and my own heartache were the reasons I made a choice to be that guy I never wanted to be.

And I've never touched a drop of the stuff since, not even socially.

Dad shrugs, takes the can, and pops the crisp top. Takes a swig and turns up the volume on the TV.

"Jordan, you're here." Mom's sweet voice floats into the room, and I turn to find her coming down the hall in her slacks and sweater, her gray-blonde hair styled around her shoulders in soft curls. She looks like she's headed out to church instead of spending the afternoon watching her five-year-old grandson. Other than the bags under her eyes and the fact she's lost weight over the last few months, I wouldn't know Lydia Carmichael had anything wrong with her. She's a strong woman and a saint, my mother.

"Hey, Mom." I pull her into a quick hug. "Thanks again for watching Ryder today."

"It'll be fun." She gestures for me to follow her into the kitchen, which I do. There she pulls a pot from beneath a cabinet and fills it with water, setting it on the stovetop. A box of mac and cheese sits nearby. "I still just think this whole thing is ridiculous. Did you already fill the attorney in on everything?"

"I sent a copy of the court summons, and he asked for an extra day to dig into things so he could give advice when Marilee and I get there."

Mom looks slyly at me from the corner of her eye as she flicks on the burner. "It's nice of her to go with you."

"It *is* nice." I grab a water bottle from the fridge, twist off the lid. "She just wants to support me."

"Of course she does. She's a special woman, that one." Mom cocks her head as I take a swig of water. "So, when are you finally going to tell her you love her?"

I inhale the water down the wrong pipe and sputter, coughing.

Mom just stands there, looking unconcerned. "Well?"

Wiping my mouth with the back of my hand, I set the water on the counter and avert my eyes. "I don't—"

"Don't you dare deny it, because I'm not blind, Jordan Carmichael. And I'm not getting any younger, you know. I'd like to see my only son happily married. Maybe with more children while you're at it..."

"Geez, Mom." Not that I haven't dreamed of the same things. "Are my feelings that obvious?"

"They are to me. You've loved that girl as long as you've known her."

"Maybe. But she's never been interested in me."

"Only because she was with her ex when the two of you met. That man kept a hold on her for a while."

"Exactly. And even though she's divorced now, he still has a grip on her, in a way. She's not really healed from it all."

"Who better to help her heal than you?" Mom pats my arm. "A good man, who loves her for who she is."

"It's complicated."

"I know. You're best friends. You don't want to mess that up. You don't want to lose her."

"It's not just that. I mean, yeah, sure, I'd worry things would change between us, but that's the point. Marilee's lost so much already—first her parents, then her marriage, then her inheritance." I shrug. "She's told me how much our relationship is a comfort for her, and I don't want her to lose that too. And if I tell her I love her, and she doesn't feel the same way..."

Mom's face softens. "I think that's unlikely. Are you sure you're not staying quiet for *your* sake just as much as for hers?"

My lips press together. Hard. "Are you saying I'm being a coward, Mom?" I don't know. Maybe I am.

"No. I just think sometimes you don't say what you need to say because you're worried about rocking the boat. But change can be the catalyst for some of the best things in life." Mom gives me her look—the one that tells me she means business. "Jordan, perhaps it's time to tell her how you feel, before someone else sweeps her up."

The thought snaps something inside of me.

The water on the stove starts to bubble. Soon it's a rolling boil.

"I wouldn't even know where to start. If I say something and scare her off, I'll never be able to forgive myself. I'd have ruined one of the best things in my life." I almost ruined it nearly six years ago, when I finally told Marilee what I thought about Donny.

And she rejected my advice—rejected *me*—for saying my piece.

"I know it might seem scary, but this living in limbo isn't healthy for either one of you." Mom tears open the box of pasta and pours it into the pot. "Because if she doesn't love you back, maybe it's time to let her go, so you can move on and find someone who does."

"Yeah. Maybe." I push a hand through my hair just as the doorbell rings. It's a stark reminder of why I'm here in the first place. Of where I'm headed. "But right now, I've got to focus on Ryder. He's what matters most."

But as I answer the door, give Marilee a hug, and say good-bye to my parents, taking off for the attorney's office, I can't help but think about what my mom said. About how impossible it all feels.

But also, about what Ryder said earlier too—"*Sometimes the impossible comes true.*"

First things first, though.

I've got a fight to win.

MARILEE

I am not an angry person.

I do, of course, get angry just like everyone. I am quite an emotional person. But often, my emotions are delayed. I need time to process them.

For the last two days, since I heard about Constance and Larry's petition though?

Hi, I'm Marilee Moffitt, the woman with a raging pool of protective-best-friend lava oozing from her pores.

Nice to meet you.

"Every time I think about it, my heart races and I wanna hit something." I snatch my plastic cup from the center console of Jordan's truck and sip up the last of my iced coffee from The White Mocha. Not even that can calm my nerves as he turns the vehicle east, away from the ocean and onward, toward San Luis Obispo, which is about forty-five minutes from Hallmark Beach. "And unfortunately, I've been holding an icing bag the last few times it's happened. Icing went everywhere. I've ruined like three cakes."

Jordan chuckles. "Oops." His hands sit calmly on the steering wheel as he navigates Highway 1, and his shoulders are relaxed. Even though we're heading to talk to an attorney about something potentially life changing, I'm not surprised, because Jordan isn't one to express his emotions. It's not like he's a robot, but he's just calmer all around. I'm not sure I've ever seen him cry, to be honest. He's just super steady, super chill.

Well, that's not totally true. I've seen him angry a few times.

Usually, it involved Donny and his treatment of me.

Even with this situation, after that initial shock of finding out about the petition, he's gone into problem-solving mode. I can sense an underlying tension, but he's come down a lot from that moment when I met him on the boardwalk and he wrapped me up in his arms and held on for dear life.

That moment is seared into my brain forever. The fact he was looking to me for comfort instead of the other way around. The way we stood there for so long, I lost track of time. The way his warmth blended with mine, and despite the chilly breeze blowing up off the ocean, I wasn't cold in the slightest.

"Seriously," I say. The plastic cup bends and crackles underneath my fingertips because, oops, I'm doing it again. Wanting to hit something. But my energy would be better spent trying to cheer Jordan up. To distract him. "Three cakes. One was supposed to be a brown puppy dog, and it ended up looking like a pile of poop."

"I'm sure it wasn't that bad." Jordan tugs at the collar of his purple shirt. It's strange seeing him dressed up. He's even ditched his hat and must have gone to see Glinda over at The Golden Highlight for a trim, as his hair is cut and gelled to perfection. I kind of prefer it a bit longer, though, where the ends curl over the edge of his shirt...

"Oh, it was bad." I stick the cup back in the cup holder and smooth my hands over the green skirt I'm wearing. "Marla came in right afterward and gave me a face that looked just like the gritted teeth emoji."

Still smiling, Jordan keeps his eyes on the road. "Speaking of Marla, what's going on there? I meant to ask Tuesday, but then..." His smile disappears.

I'd do anything to get it back. Unfortunately, I don't think this particular conversation will do that.

I clear my throat and fiddle with the air vent, directing some of the heat my way. "I visited Pete. Just to see if getting a loan would even be an option."

"And?"

"And he confirmed what I figured. My credit... Well, as much as he likes me as a person and respected my parents, I'm just not a good risk."

Tell me something I don't know, Pete.

"That's harsh." His glance flashes over at me, then back to the road, where I can see buildings and stoplights ahead. We're almost there. "So where does that leave you? Are you going to see if Blake and Lucy want to buy your portion of the house from you?"

"I haven't decided. It's a big decision, you know?" And I don't have the best track record with decisions.

"For sure. You should absolutely take your time." Jordan follows his phone's GPS a few more blocks to a brick building in a nice part of town. He parks, turns off the ignition, and sits back. Breathes in. Out. Then turns to me. "You ready?"

"I am." I tilt my head. "It's gonna be okay, all right, Jay?"

"Yep. Right." He smiles but it doesn't reach his eyes. And I don't blame him one bit. This meeting will tell us a lot about what next steps need to be taken.

About how likely the Comers are to succeed in this petition.

Together, we exit the truck and walk up the steps into a

multi-office building, then follow the signs for Samuel Granger's office on the second floor. I've actually only met Sam a few times when I was much younger, but his information was in my dad's old contact book. When I reached out on Tuesday, he was very kind and accommodating. Doesn't mean he won't charge Jordan an arm and a leg, but hopefully his experience with family court will mean this is an open-and-shut case.

Jordan holds open the door for me, then follows me into the small lobby. There are only a handful of chairs in the waiting room and a pleasant-looking woman with glasses and a gray ponytail who smiles at us from behind the receptionist's desk. The run-of-the-mill carpet is a bit worn on the way from the door to the desk, but everything is very clean, and a small fountain on the edge of the woman's desk trickles a calming waterfall. "How can I help you today?"

"Afternoon, ma'am," Jordan says. "We're here to see Mr. Granger. I'm Jordan Carmichael."

"Ah, yes. One moment while I let him know you're here." She picks up her phone.

Jordan taps his finger on the edge of the desk. Then runs his hand through his hair. Then across his jaw.

I grab his hand and pull it down, keeping it firmly tucked in mine.

His gaze shifts to me, and he blows out a breath, nods.

"Okay, Mr. Granger will see you now," the receptionist says. "It's the second door on the left, down that hallway there."

"Thank you." Jordan starts walking and, since he's still got ahold of my hand, I do too.

When we reach the door, we knock and enter after a gruff "Come in" greets us. Mr. Granger sits behind a large desk flanked with oak bookcases, a window on the wall to our right boasting a gorgeous view of downtown. He's a nice-looking man, fairly fit and in his fifties, and his full head of salt and pepper hair adds to his distinguished air. He glances up from a stack of papers and sits upright in his chair, running one hand down the length of his silk, black tie before indicating the two chairs across the desk from him. "Please, sit."

Jordan leads me to the chair on the right and pulls it out just a bit for me, then reaches out and shakes Mr. Granger's hand. "Thank you so much for meeting with us last minute like this, Mr. Granger."

"Of course, of course. But please, call me Sam." He turns to me, and his eyes crinkle at the corners as he takes me in. "Marilee, so good to see you again. Goodness, you look just like Holly."

My eyes burn at the sudden and unexpected praise, because my mother was the most beautiful woman I've ever known, inside and out. "Thank you for the compliment, sir." I place my hands in my lap and start fidgeting with the bottom of my blouse. A lump lodges in my throat.

Now it's Jordan's turn to reach over and grab my hand, to steady me like he always does.

Sam taps the paper stack on his desk. "I've been reviewing your file and all of the information you gave me over the phone, then chatted with the Comers' attorney to gather some details. The good news is they're only asking for partial custody, same as their daughter had. But I understand you never had a formal agreement drawn up between the two of you?"

"Correct. We didn't see the need."

"While I'm glad you had the kind of relationship with your son's mother to allow for that, it does make it a bit tricky, as I'm told the mother's will didn't say anything about you. She only mentioned wanting her parents to have custody. But of course, as Ryder's father, you have rights too."

I squeeze Jordan's hand.

But he doesn't look my way. He's frowning. "While I can

appreciate their position, the truth is that he's my son. If I can provide for him, and especially if I'm willing to allow them to have a relationship with him, I don't understand why they think they have any sort of legal right to even partial custody."

"Honestly, I'm surprised their attorney was willing to entertain the petition, but some people will do anything for a buck." Sam shakes his head. "There have been a few cases—and they had extenuating circumstances—in which a deceased parent was able to appoint a guardian other than the secondary parent, but neglect of some sort had to be proven first."

"And Jordan is the best dad in the world, so that's going to be impossible." I smile at Jordan and flash him a satisfied look that I hope says, *See? It's going to be okay.*

He sends a look back my way that's all soft around the edges. I could sink into that look.

My stomach twists.

"While I appreciate your ringing endorsement, Marilee, with the allegations the Comers have raised—"

"What allegations, exactly?" Jordan's eyebrows bunch together.

"Accusations of poor parenting decisions." Sam flips through the papers until settling on one. "It says here that you frequently keep your child out late when he should be in bed. A Fourth of July festival was cited?"

I sit up straighter. "Everyone was out late that night. That's a terrible example."

"And the Comers say they are frequently asked last minute to watch Ryder for you, and he's left there overnight most of the time?" Sam studies Jordan. "Is that true?"

"I'm a single dad, and I own a business. So yeah, sometimes I have to ask them to help out. But they've told me they don't mind. They know my parents aren't capable all of the time of watching him for me, and I often lead adventure tours all day and sometimes overnight, especially in the spring and summer."

"That's good information to know. Your business is relatively new, correct?"

"It's about six years old."

"Which means it's probably just starting to turn a real profit only in the last year or two?"

"Yes." Jordan draws the word out, slow, like a string of molasses suspended in the air.

"Have you ever had trouble paying your bills?"

Jordan scratches his neck. "I had to push a rent payment or two at the very beginning, but other than that, no."

He did? I didn't know that. I frown. "Sam, believe me when I say that you're not going to find a more trustworthy or honest person than Jordan Carmichael. He's as steady and stable as they come."

Sam sighs. "I believe you, Marilee, but I happen to know this attorney, and I have to warn you that she's a shark. She will take anything and spin it out of proportion. We've got a judge who is new to the area assigned to this case, so I'm not quite sure how he's going to react when there are examples of what could be perceived as neglect."

Squeaking with indignation, I start to protest. He holds up his hand before I can get any words out. "So while I don't think it's very likely the Comers' request will be granted, I just need to let you know that there's a tiny chance."

"So." Jordan's got a death grip on my hand. "That's it, then? There's nothing we can do?"

"I didn't say that. If you agree to engage my services—"

"I do. Done." Jordan leans forward slightly, nodding. "I don't care what it costs. I'm not letting them take my son, even for part of the time. They might poison him against me for all I know. Or have different ways of doing things. This whole petition thing is proof of that."

"I understand completely." Sam sits back in his chair and steeples his fingers over his stomach. "What we need to do is use the next four and half weeks to make you look like the most stable guy on the planet. Job, friendships, community involvement—it's all important. And relationship status too." He glances between us. "The two of you aren't by chance engaged, are you?"

I blink at Sam's question. It's not like he's the first to assume Jordan and I are a couple, and I could see how the way we're holding hands would throw him off. "Oh. Um."

Jordan coughs. "Uh—"

"Because if so, being engaged is good, but being married is even better. A marriage would go a long way in showing just how stable things are in your home. Shows you're not afraid of commitment. Especially since, as I understand it—and I'm not judging here, but the Comers' attorney just might—you never were in an actual relationship with Ryder's mom."

The words pinch something inside of me. I can see it now, Jordan's reputation being publicly torn to shreds over one decision. I know how that feels. At least his decision led him to Ryder. I wasn't so lucky. But then again, people warned me. Over and over again, I turned a blind eye to Donny and what he was.

Jordan, for whatever reason—he's never told me—had one lapse in judgement one time. But the Comers don't get to crucify him over it. It's just not right.

"Jordan's not afraid of commitment." My nostrils flare. "The fact he didn't walk away when Georgia told him she was pregnant is proof of that."

"And that is definitely going to be in our favor. But we need to find a way to address the other concerns. If you were married, all of the Comers' objections about you not being available to juggle everything alone would disappear. And it would showcase you as the family man you are, with a stable home life."

Turning wide eyes to me, Jordan swallows hard. "The thing is, we're not—"

"Just think about it, okay?" The full weight of Sam's stare bores into me. "I know you've probably got some big fancy wedding planned, and you don't have to change those plans necessarily. You can still keep your big ceremony and reception. Hey, keep the honeymoon the same for all I care—"

Jordan coughs again.

"—but if you're planning to get married anyway, there would be a benefit to doing it sooner than later. It might just save you a lot of time, money, and heartache."

Meaning, marriage might just make this whole petition a non-issue.

My brain starts whirring. It's like when I get a new idea for a cake. A corner of my mind grabs onto the idea, tosses it around like a pizza, high in the air, until it's got something ready to bake and decorate.

"I don't think that's going to work, sir." Jordan lets go of my hand, leans forward so his elbows are on his knees, and rubs his hands down his face. "We need to figure out another plan."

Sam flashes me a grim look. "All right, well, it's just a thought. Stick it in your pocket. Ponder it. Marriage could be the answer to all of this. It's the best way for you to look respectable and stable in a short amount of time."

Jordan shakes his head and opens his mouth to say something—probably to inform Sam that we are not even dating, much less engaged—but I jump in with a question of my own. "But won't the judge think it's awfully convenient if we get married right before this? You don't think the quickness of it would raise any red flags?"

"If you were already together, already planning to get married, I don't think anyone could say anything against it. We could say you realized that getting married sooner would provide more stability for Ryder, and that his well-being is the most important priority for you."

"Hmm. Okay."

Sam smiles. "So you'll consider it, then?"

"Yes. We'll consider all options." I say it with confidence, but I can feel the heat of Jordan's stare. Turning to him, I find him blinking at me, confusion in his gaze.

Trust me, I mouth.

Then I turn back to Sam. "What else do we need to know?"

JORDAN

I'm pretty sure I've entered a twilight zone—one in which my attorney suggested I marry my best friend.

One in which my best friend didn't run for the hills at the suggestion. She didn't even laugh off his assumptions like she always does whenever someone else implies we're together.

In fact, she sat there and responded with questions of her own, as if what he was suggesting might actually be a possibility.

Yeah. Definitely the Twilight Zone. One that looks and sounds and *feels* very real.

As soon as Marilee and I step out of Sam Granger's office thirty minutes later, I snag her elbow gently and turn to her. "Hey."

She flips her gaze upward, eyes big and soft green. "I know what you're thinking."

Oh, I don't think you do. She couldn't possibly have any idea what I'm thinking. "And what's that?"

She glances back toward the door, then around the hallway, where a few people in business suits talk as they walk toward us. "Let's get a bite to eat and go talk somewhere. There was

57

some sort of sandwich shop on the other side of the street and a park right next to it."

I study her for a moment before nodding, my jaw tight. "All right."

After grabbing a few subs in relative silence, we're situated across from each other at a concrete picnic table under the spread of a California sycamore. This is a decent-sized park, with walking trails, a few basketball hoops, sports fields, and a playground. It's nearly time for most elementary schools to let out, but for now, the place is rather deserted. The sun is shining, and the paper around our sandwiches rustles as we unwrap them.

Marilee snuggles down in her jacket, which she snatched from my truck on the way to the sandwich shop. "So, how do you feel that went? I liked him. He seems really competent, right?"

"Yeah." I eye her. "But Lee—"

"And"—she rushes on—"that means he knows the best plan for ensuring you get to keep full custody of Ryder."

I squint at her from behind my sunglasses. "Sure. He seems to understand what the risks are and gave some solid advice for how to make sure we show up at court prepared to defend against the Comers' baseless accusations."

"Right." Staring at her food, Marilee fiddles with the edge of her paper. She hasn't yet touched her sandwich.

Then again, I haven't touched mine.

Because there's an elephant in this park, and he's sitting on this table. Makes it a little difficult to think about eating.

And we can't ignore it. "Sorry if any of his suggestions made you uncomfortable." I pop open my bag of plain kettle chips.

Her eyes finally meet mine. "They didn't."

Oh.

I clear my throat. "I tried to jump in and explain that we aren't together like that, but then—"

"I got an idea, Jay."

"What kind of idea?"

"What if..." She frowns, nibbles on her bottom lip in that way she does when deep in thought. "What if he's right? That you being married is the best way to save you grief, time, and money?"

I stare at this woman I've known half of my life. I've always known what she's thinking. She's not the kind to hide her emotions. To hide much of anything from me.

But right now? I feel completely in the dark.

"You feeling okay, Lee?" I force a chuckle as birds chatter and call in the tree above us. "You do know I'm not engaged to anyone, right? And haven't exactly been on a date in years, either."

"I know that." She huffs. "Look, this might be a really weird suggestion, and you can absolutely say no, but...what if *we* got married? In name only, of course. But it makes sense, right?"

There's a buzzing in my ears, like bees have suddenly descended on our picnic. I glance right, left, but nope, nothing.

"Jordan?"

Inhaling sharply, my gaze reconnects with hers. She's shrunk in on herself, huddled there, not just from cold, but a hit to her self-confidence. It's the same posture she used to take when Donny was in the picture.

I hate that something I've said or done would cause her to sit that way.

Scratching my eyebrow, I weigh my words carefully. "Lee, that's an incredibly generous offer, but I could never let you do that for me."

"Well...maybe it would solve my problems too."

I sit forward. "What problems?"

She shrugs. "If we got married for, say, a year, I could give Blake and Lucy the house without having to sell my portion to them. Give them their own space, try it out, without having to make a hasty decision. And, if you were okay with it, I could move into your house and not pay rent, so I could keep paying off my debt and maybe save up some extra money to either buy Marla out or—"

"Or finally start your own cake decorating business?"

"Maybe." Another shrug. "It just gives me a little time and space to figure out what I want to do next, you know? And I'd be happy to pick Ryder up from school every day and kind of take on a nanny role for him so that you could focus more on work in your busy season."

But she wouldn't be a nanny. She'd be my...

I swallow.

Geez. Nope. I can't even entertain the thought.

Because the thing I've wanted more than anything is being offered to me here, on a shiny silver platter. But it comes with an expiration date.

And it would be an imitation of the real thing—like drinking diet soda instead of the good stuff.

But how do I tell Marilee that, when she has no idea how living with her—being *married* to her—would make it so much harder for me to not give in to my daily impulse to kiss her?

Not to mention, if we were married as friends, I definitely couldn't tell her my feelings without risking our arrangement. Not without making it extremely awkward for both of us.

And yet. What she's saying also makes sense.

Marriage *would* solve my problem with the Comers breathing down my neck. And being married a year would allow me to establish my business even more, to get Ryder through preschool and into full-day kindergarten, to help him adjust even more to his mother's death.

And Marilee would get something she's never been allowed before—the chance to take a risk on herself.

I drum my fingers on the concrete table. "I'm not saying yes yet."

Something sparks in her eyes, and she sits upright. "I'll take *yet.*"

"But if you did this for me, you'd absolutely be able to live with me free of charge. No rent, no contributions to groceries, none of it. I'm guessing Blake and Lucy would pay you a monthly rent, or you could rent your room out to someone else if they weren't able to do that. Either way, you'd be getting some money paid to you for your portion of homeownership." I take a quick breath, knowing this last part might be a deal-breaker for her. "And you'd have to let me cosign a loan for you, or pay you back in some way."

"Jay, no. That's not why I'm doing this. You wouldn't have to pay me back. You're my best friend." Her eyes get misty. "I'd do anything for you and Ryder. And if this would help..."

"I know you would—but there's still a really good chance that we don't need to get married in order for me to keep Ryder."

"You heard what Sam said. The Comers' attorney is a shark. Sharks go for the jugular. And Jay, you're too good a person to..." She pushes a tear away. *Aw, Lee.* "I don't want you and Ryder to have to go through that. Not if we can fix it."

I take a chip from my bag, break it in half. Hold the pieces in my hands. "But Lee, this isn't just some small thing. It's marriage. And I thought you told me you never wanted to get married again."

The words are out before I can stop them. It's something I don't like to think about—that night when she cried in my arms after Donny had served her with divorce papers. When I told her that she was going to survive this, and that someday, she'd marry someone who saw the amazing person she was.

She'd responded with a declaration of her own.

"Yeah, well." She juts her chin—a move I always find adorable. "It's not a real marriage. Just on paper. If it makes you feel any better, we can establish some ground rules."

I lift my eyebrows at this. "Like what?" My stomach growls, and I finally pop my broken chip into my mouth. The crunch sounds loud in my ears.

"I don't know. Like, I'll sleep on the couch."

"Nice try. *I'll* sleep on the couch."

She rolls her eyes. "It's your house." Then she takes a bite of her turkey sandwich.

"I won't even entertain this idea if you're going to insist on sleeping on the couch." Thank goodness she didn't suggest we share a bed. I respect the heck out of her, but a year of sleeping next to the woman I love without snuggling up next to her, embracing her, kissing her neck in the early morning?

Yeah. I'd prefer torture, thanks.

She chews, her eyes narrow, but finally swallows and smiles. "Fine. You win."

Do I, though? I shake away my inner voice. "What else should go on this supposed list of rules?" Whoa, are we really thinking about doing this? I can't truly consider what it would mean. Have to keep focused on the facts. The list. A contract. That should keep us safe, right? It would provide us a baseline, so there's no confusion.

Otherwise, I know my brain—and my heart—might start thinking things are real and cross a line from which there's no return.

I pull out my phone. "I can type the list out and then print it. We can even sign it. Make things official."

"That would be good." She averts her eyes, and is it the

breeze or some other reason her cheeks look red? "Um, so I guess the biggest question would be about who we tell what. Because I don't know about you, but I really don't want to lie to our friends about our reasons for marriage."

Pressure I didn't realize was clamping my lungs releases, and I blow out a solid breath. "Me either. And my parents too."

"Agreed. But we'd have to swear them to secrecy. I don't think that would be a problem though, do you?"

"Definitely not. My dad doesn't really go out or talk to anyone. And Mom..." Well, Mom might have a few words to say about it, but she would also do anything for Ryder. "It won't be a problem."

"But the rest of the town..." Marilee pulls a piece off her ciabatta roll, squishes it between her thumb and forefinger. Then she looks up at me, a question there. "We act like a couple in front of them?"

And reality crashes back in. My thumb freezes over the phone screen, and the cursor in my Notes app blinks back at me. Accusing. "I mean, we'd probably have to in order to make it believable. But if you're not comfortable with that—"

"No, it's fine."

She's so quick to agree. It makes me wonder...

But no. She's just an affectionate person. We don't hold hands often, but she's always patting or squeezing my arm, resting her head on my shoulder when we watch a movie on the couch, giving hugs.

Still, there's one glaring difference between friendly touching...and more than friendly. My throat burns with the question, but it has to be asked. "What about kissing?"

The bread tumbles from Marilee's fingers onto the table. In the distance, the excited shouts of kids brim to the surface. But Marilee and I are still here, in this strange bubble, with this strange question hanging between us.

"Oh. Um." Shaking herself, she picks up the bread again and tosses it onto the ground. A pigeon dive-bombs it. "I don't think we have to make a big deal out of it, right? We're both adults. If the need arises for us to kiss, we kiss."

Like it's so simple.

Like it wouldn't be life changing. Earth shattering. A defining moment where time would only exist in the before and the after...

Then again, to her, it probably wouldn't be any of those things. Just to me.

And, if it means more stability for Ryder, a chance to give Marilee the freedom to choose her path, to allow her space to discover herself, what she really wants for her future—I'm willing to face the torment of kissing Marilee and knowing it doesn't mean the same thing to her.

I'm willing to marry my best friend for a year.

I set the phone down and study her. "Are you sure about this, Lee? Because we can eat our lunch, talk about the weather, go home, and never discuss this again if you have any doubts in your mind."

She blinks back at me, taking a while before she answers. "That's the weird thing, Jay. I know I'm not the best at making good decisions. But one that means helping out the people I love best in the world?" Marilee tilts her head, and her cascade of hair falls to the side, shimmering in the sun. "That's a no-brainer. Let's do it. Let's get married."

Today is my wedding day.

Again.

But this feels nothing like that did. Back then, at the tender age of nineteen—ten whole years ago—I pretended to be sure. Convinced myself I was. Ignored any concern that any friends or my mom expressed. I just figured they didn't understand the love Donny and I shared.

Turns out, what we had wasn't love. It was control.

But this? Helping Jordan, my best friend in the world, who would never do anything to hurt me?

Today *is* about love.

Maybe it's platonic love, but love all the same. And it's my decision to make.

Which is why, if Lucy asks me if I'm *sure* one more time, I might scream.

"Don't." As I exit my closet wearing a strappy lavender dress that's probably more appropriate for summertime, I hold my finger up to my sister-in-law's mouth, which is opening— I'm *positive*—to repeat the question that's been part of every conversation we've had for the last four days since I told her about my decision to marry Jordan for a year.

She's sitting against the headboard of my bed, her blonde hair down for once, a hand on her stomach, which is still flat despite growing my niece or nephew. Her color is a bit better today, though I think she's only consumed a few crackers and some ginger ale. "But—"

"But nothing. Yes, I'm sure about marrying him. What I'm not sure about is this dress." As I turn a one-eighty, the skirt flares out a bit. "Thoughts?" I study my reflection in the full-length mirror hanging on the back of my door.

"You look gorgeous as always."

I glance over my shoulder. "But?"

"But it looks like something you'd wear to church or out to dinner, not to get married in." Lucy takes the end of her hair and plays with it—a sure sign she's got more to say but is nervous about doing so. "And look, obviously I'm not weirded out that you're sort of eloping. I mean, Blake and I did. But that was different." She sighs. "Mare..."

"Lucy, we've been over this." I sit on the edge of the bed, careful not to wrinkle the skirt. "I know you're worried about me, but marrying Jordan will be a win-win for all of us. You and Blake will get some alone time—"

"Which is never something we wanted, you know." She tugs on her hair, and ouch, how does that not hurt? "I hope you're not doing this for us."

"Of course not. But I was already thinking about moving out to give you guys some space."

"That kills me. You know you're my best friend."

"I know. And I love you. I love my brother too. But you guys deserve to have your own place. You're married now. And soon, I will be too." I glance at the clock on my bedside table.

Shoot. "In less than an hour, to be precise. I really need to decide what to wear."

Of course, that's me—Ms. Procrastination. Hopping back up, I head into my closet again, searching for something, anything, that will make me feel pretty.

My hand hovers over a green silk dress I usually reserve for Christmas parties. Wait. Why do I care about being pretty?

I don't. I mean, not for Jordan's sake. He's seen me without a stitch of makeup and also with all of my makeup smudged from hours of crying. In flannel pants and a baggy shirt. He doesn't care what I look like.

But I still find that I want to look nice.

It *is* a wedding, after all—however fake and small and underwhelming it might be.

Lucy appears at the closet door, her presence startling me out of my thoughts. She leans against the door and pulls a white, zippered bag down from the rack. "What about your mom's dress?" Her voice is soft, full of questions.

"No." I shake my head vehemently, taking the dress from her hands and re-hanging it. "This isn't that kind of wedding." I didn't wear my mom's dress to my wedding with Donny either. Even though I've always loved it—a timeless A-line with delicate straps and a dropped waist—Donny chose my dress for our ceremony: a strapless gown that showed off more cleavage than I was really comfortable with.

And honestly? I'm grateful I didn't waste Mom's dress on him.

But wearing it to a fake wedding would be even worse.

I snatch the green dress off the rack and maneuver past Lucy into the bedroom, unhooking the back of the purple dress and shoving it to the ground before stepping into the silky hug of the green option. It's got flowing sleeves that button at the wrists and an empire waist that makes me look taller than my five-two. I reach for the back zipper.

"Here." Lucy zips me up. Then she puts her arms around me from behind—she's got about eight or nine inches on me—and sets her nose against my hair. "I love you, you know. As a friend and a sister. I just don't want to see anyone get hurt here."

I hug her hands and then turn out of her embrace, pulling her hands into mine and looking deep into her blue eyes. "I know you love me. But I'm going to be fine. This is Jordan. He won't hurt me."

She chews her lip. "But will *you* hurt him?"

"Of course not." I bat away the words as I head for my dresser and stick in my favorite jingle bell earrings. "We made a solid agreement. Signed and everything. And I'm doing this to help him, remember?"

"I know, but Mare...I'm pretty sure the guy's crazy about you."

"You're wrong." I *hope* she's wrong. Because if Jordan really does care about me like that, then this whole thing *would* be crazy. But I gave him time to back out—all weekend, in fact. He hasn't.

"And you're sure there's no part of you that loves him?"

I whirl. "What? No! Not like that, anyway."

She puts her hands up in defense. "Okay, okay. Like I said. I don't want you to get hurt." Lucy moves to the door. "I just hope you know what you're doing." Turning, she does a once-over on me. "That dress is killer, by the way. If Jordan *did* love you, you'd make him keel over." Then she flashes me her famous Lucy smile, and my sassy sister is back. "Sweet macaroni, you probably will either way."

"Get out of here." Laughing, I open the door and push her

into the hallway. "You're going to make us late if you aren't dressed soon."

She salutes me and hurries toward the master bedroom.

I slip on my black heels—which I never wear—and turn back to the mirror, exhaling as I smooth out the skirt and my hair, which Lucy helped me curl earlier. It falls in soft waves down my back, all the way nearly to my rear. Usually it just gets in my way, but today it feels like a safety blanket of sorts.

Okay, then. I'm ready to marry my best friend.

As ready as I'm going to be, anyway.

Twenty minutes later, I'm in the back of Blake's car, with him and Lucy sitting up front. My brother's eyes keep finding me in the rearview mirror, his gaze alternating between concern and a scowl. I know he, like Lucy, is hesitant about this, but when I asked them to be our witnesses, he still agreed after making sure it was what I really wanted.

It made me realize that I haven't really focused on what *I* want in a long time. I've been too busy healing, trying to ferret my way out of the hole Donny dug for me. That I dug for myself.

And honestly, I don't know if I really want to *marry* Jordan. But I *do* want to help him, and this seems to be the best way to do that.

I also don't hate the idea of having a little bit of flexibility to make a decision about my future. I talked with Pete from the bank on Saturday, and he confirmed that he'd happily give me a loan if Jordan cosigned. Of course, I didn't mention that Jordan would be doing so as my spouse. You drop a bomb like that in Hallmark Beach, and everyone will know by lunchtime. For now, Blake and Lucy are the only ones who know. I don't need any more voices in my head. It's hard enough to make decisions without listening to everyone else.

No, I'm set on this, if only because my best friend needs me

—and goodness knows he's always been there for me when *I've* needed *him*.

After driving for about fifteen minutes, Blake pulls into the parking lot of a tiny chapel. It's north of Hallmark Beach, set along the coast between it and the next town over. Cutting the ignition, he turns in his seat. "Ready, Squirt?"

"Yep," I say with all the brightness I can. Then I climb from the sports car and glance up at the decades-old building, which is on a bluff overlooking the ocean, flanked by coast live oak trees on all sides and encased in glass and wood. I haven't been here in ages. There's another church around the corner from Main Street where some of my friends and family attend services, but this one... This one's special.

It's where my parents got married. And, when I was ten, they renewed their vows in this very spot.

Ironically, I didn't choose the location. Jordan did, and he made all the arrangements too. He thought it would be nicer than seeing a justice of the peace, and getting married on a Monday afternoon meant it happened to be available—and that Blake could be here, since Monday is the only day he closes the food truck.

Lucy and Blake follow me to the front steps, where Jordan is sitting, chin in his hands. He doesn't look up at first, which gives me a chance to study him. It's the rare occasion he dresses up, but he's got on a dark suit that's cut to perfection, hugging his muscles and accentuating his smooth, tan skin. His hair is tousled with gel, and something about the way it's lying so perfectly makes me want to run my fingers through it. To loosen it.

My breath catches when he glances up, and I see the deep green tie he's wearing.

It matches my dress exactly.

It's a coincidence, I know, but something about it comforts

me. Reminds me that Jordan knows me better than I know myself. That we'll be okay, even when we're doing something as crazy as entering into a temporary marriage of convenience.

His jaw twitches. He stands, sticking his hands in his pockets. "Lee, you look... Wow."

I feel heat rise in my cheeks, which is ridiculous, because Jordan has definitely seen me in this dress before at some event or another. "This old thing?" I swish the skirt dramatically, just to lessen whatever new tension this is between us. Guess it makes sense. Maybe he's nervous.

But he doesn't need to be. It's just me. And it's just him. We are *us*—the same people we've always been.

I step forward to give him a quick hug, but before I can, he reaches around me toward Blake. "Thanks for coming, guys."

My brother takes his hand but doesn't release it right away. "I will always be here when my sister asks." Then he pulls him in close and whispers something—probably threatening him as any good brother should. It makes me smile that he thinks he needs to warn Jordan about anything.

Jordan, who has always been careful with my heart.

Staring at the two men I love most in this world, that very heart twists and thumps, and I feel tears prick my eyes.

Lucy slips her arm through mine. "Come on." She tugs me away from the men, who follow closely behind.

When we reach the doors, Jordan bounds up the stairs and opens the glass door with the wooden handle. Lucy and Blake head on in before us. Even from here, I can see inside the church. It's small, with maybe ten red-backed velvet pews on either side of a short aisle, but every wall is made almost entirely of glass. When we step inside, Jordan's hand brushes the small of my back as he leads me toward the front. And is it just me, or do his fingers rustle through the ends of my hair?

I shiver at the contact.

What's wrong with me? This isn't the first time Jordan's touched me like that. But I suppose it's the first time he's touched me like that *as my fiancé.*

Holy cupcakes, my fiancé. I'm about to get married again.

I stop walking toward the front, where Lucy and Blake have taken a seat in the front pew, and a skinny man with a clipboard, who looks to be in his thirties, is waiting under an arch of wood that gives a gorgeous view of the vista in front of us. The clouds from this morning have dissipated, leaving brilliant sunshine glinting off the surface of the ocean. At once, we are in the middle of a forest of trees *and* on the edge of the world. And it's beautiful.

"Lee."

"Hmm?" I turn to find Jordan close, looking down at me with eyebrows notched together. His cologne surrounds me, and I feel like I'm tucked into the hollow of a tree, safe and warm.

"Last chance to back out." Jordan is not a goofball, but he's not overly serious either. Neither of us are the life of the party or the party poopers. We are solidly in the middle—and in the middle together.

But right now, he's giving off seriously solemn vibes.

"Do *you* want to back out?" I ask.

He hesitates, frowns. "I don't want either of us to regret this. Maybe we should think—"

"Maybe we should. But I think I'd arrive at the same conclusion. Ryder's what matters, yes?"

"Well, yeah, of course."

"And no matter what happens, we will continue to be best friends. Remember our agreement?"

When composing our list of rules to sign, I suggested that if either of us wanted out sooner than a year, we'd do it, so long as it wouldn't negatively affect Jordan's custody battle or my financial situation.

We both signed it, and thinking of that reminds me that this will all be okay. We have an out in our back pocket.

Slowly, Jordan nods and blows out another breath. "All right, then. Let's do this."

"Let's. Except..."

"Except?"

My eyes search the chapel, almost frantic. Despite the glass, something about being inside suddenly makes my chest tighten. "I need air."

"Okay. We can take a few extra min—"

"No, not like that." I purse my lips, my gaze finally landing on a patch of grass near the bluff outside. "Can we do the ceremony out there?"

His brow furrows. "Sure..."

"It's just." How do I explain? "I love that you chose a place that means a lot to me. That we aren't doing this at some sterile justice of the peace, because that's not who we are. But something about being married in a church, knowing..." *Knowing that we are saying vows that are just for now. Just to save Ryder.* "Well, I don't really want to get struck by lightning on my wedding day."

He laughs, a sound that eases the tightness in my chest. "You're the last person in the world that would happen to. But I understand. Hang tight while I go talk with the site coordinator and see if we can move things outdoors."

"K."

He heads up front, pulling the man aside and talking with him. Lucy looks back at me, eyebrows raised. I turn toward the window again, meditating on the peace I will surely feel when all of this is over.

A touch on my elbow startles me.

"Sorry." Jordan's there, his voice low as he turns me round-about to face him and Clipboard Man. "Marilee, this is the site's event coordinator and officiant, Terry Maxson."

"Hi, Marilee. Call me Terry." Terry reaches out with his smooth, pale hand, and his mustache twitches as he smiles. "Jordan tells me you'd like to move things outside, and that's perfectly acceptable. If you'll just follow me, we'll get things going."

And before I have a chance to respond, he's headed out a side door, Lucy and Blake close on his trail.

"You good?" Jordan reaches for my hand.

I swallow, take it. "All good."

My heels click on the polished wood floor as we approach the door, hand in hand. My breathing ratchets up as my dress swishes against my legs, but Jordan is my anchor as he's so often been. His hands aren't soft, and I wouldn't expect them to be with the way he's outdoors and rock climbing and constantly doing sporty things. All of my attention zeroes in on a callus on his thumb, which wends its way back and forth over the top of my hand.

Why is that tiny motion so...intoxicating? All-consuming?

We step out onto stone steps that lead down into a small clearing. Here, my nose catches the sea-salted air, and my ears catch the whistling breeze. Then, we stand facing each other as my eyes catch a wink of something diving in the distance. A whale, maybe?

I haven't gone whale watching in forever, but it's something Mom and I liked to do together. So this... It feels almost like a gift, an assurance that everything is going to be okay.

Blake and Lucy stand off to one side as Terry dives right into the ceremony. But I couldn't tell you one word of what was said. It's like when I was a kid, and my mom would put eardrops in to prevent ear infections after I went swimming.

There's cotton in there now, and all I can do is force a smile and nod. My stomach feels like it's going to bottom out but keeps dropping. And it's oddly not due to nerves.

It's because of Jordan's darn thumb.

The tiny point of connection between us—two people who have touched more times than I can count. It doesn't make sense that this would be so utterly distracting to me, especially in a moment like this.

But oh. My. Sheet cake.

I think...I think I'm attracted to my best friend.

My eyes jerk upward and find his, which are on me. They're sharp around the edges, not missing anything, but gooey in the middle like brownies, fresh out of the oven, and oh wow, I wanna just sink into his gaze.

What? No, no, noooooooo.

Why have I never known—like, *really* known—how attractive this man is? I mean, I've always noticed he was good looking, but just kind of...I don't know, ignored it? First, because I was with Donny, and then... Well, maybe I've always known.

But now, I can't unknow it.

This is bad. Very, very bad.

"Lee." Jordan's voice slices through all the noise in my head to bring me back to reality—where I think I'm cutting off his circulation with how hard I'm gripping his hand.

I loosen my grip. "What? Sorry." I turn to Terry, who watches me with a question in his gaze.

"I asked if you take this man to be your husband?" He says it like a question, like he's unsure of my reply.

I don't blame him. He probably doesn't get a lot of space cadet brides in front of him.

"Sure do!" I say with all the brightness I can muster.

"Do you have rings?"

Jordan reaches into his pocket and pulls out two simple

silver bands. He shifts, clearing his throat. "I figured we could get you something fancier...later."

Code for: probably *never*, but we can't say that in front of Terry. Got it.

I nod, and we exchange rings.

Then Terry speaks again. "By the power vested in me by the state of California, I now pronounce you husband and wife. Jordan..." He pauses dramatically. "You may kiss your bride."

Oh, cookie crumbs.

Um, look, don't judge me, but I don't always think things through. I applaud myself for thinking of how I'd have to live with Jordan and how I'd get to hang out more with him and Ryder, and how we'd unfortunately have to lie to a few people and how I'd be able to finally stop worrying about finances for just a little while.

But somehow, I didn't think about this moment—when the officiant would tell Jordan to kiss me.

Maybe it wouldn't have bothered me *before*. But now that I think Jordan is not just handsome but attractive?

I...I'm without a thought in my brain. What do I do?

Jordan takes a step toward me, studying me for a moment— and then leans in.

I squeeze my eyes forcefully shut and wait for the peck on the lips I'm sure is coming. Because we *did* agree to kiss if absolutely necessary, and I kind of think our wedding ceremony would fit that particular bill.

But then, there's a tiny bit of pressure on my hand, and I feel the warmth of Jordan's breath hug my ear as he whispers, "Just breathe, Lee," and presses his lips to my cheek.

My eyes pop open as his face retreats and he straightens.

And my chest unexpectedly deflates.

Terry clears his throat. "Hmm, well. All right, then. This

would be the part where I announce you to your audience, but—"

"But it's just us," Lucy teases from the side. She flashes me wide eyes filled with questions. My friend knows me well, and I'm guessing she can't wait to get me alone and ask why I'm acting so strange. But how am I supposed to tell her, when I don't understand it myself?

Terry gestures for us to walk back toward the church, but before we do, Jordan pulls me into a hug. "Did we just really do that?" His voice is muffled against my hair.

The familiarity of it calms me. Whatever insane attraction I just felt was just a result of the heightened emotions. It had to be. Because this is Jordan—my *friend*. He didn't sign up for a wife who's attracted to him or for things to be awkward or complicated between us.

So I will take those emotions and stuff them far, far away, praying they are a one-time thing.

He pulls away from our embrace and smooths down my hair where his hug ruffled it. "All right, then. Let's go home."

Home.

How strange that my definition of that just shifted in a matter of seconds. Though as I stand here in the shelter of his arms, I can't help but wonder if it's been the same all along. That I just didn't realize it until now.

Nope. Friends.

As it's always been.

As it's gotta stay.

It's just as unbelievable as it is official—I have a wife.

Even more unbelievable, *Marilee* is my wife.

Fake wife. I know that. But a wife all the same.

It's several hours after our wedding ceremony, and all kinds of thoughts and memories swirl around me where I sit on the couch, my right knee bouncing as I attempt to watch a football game. The TV is on low, so I can hear Marilee banging around down the hall, presumably getting things arranged and situated in my bedroom.

Well, now it's *her* bedroom for the next year.

I'll keep my clothes and toiletries in there but made plenty of space in the dresser and closet for Lee's things. But the bed... It's all hers. Good thing I sprung for the extra comfy couch when I bought the leather number underneath me, because we are going to become fast friends each and every night. I don't mind, though. Not if it means Marilee is comfortable.

The air feels sticky even though I peeled off my suit jacket the first chance I got, so I stand and crack open the back door, which leads to a small grassy yard littered with a scooter, a kid-sized basketball hoop, a tee and whiffle ball. The matching bat's nowhere to be found. Probably buried somewhere in my son's room. A breeze cools my face as I run my hands through my hair and take in the chaos of toys. My heart pinches at the sight —at the thought that I could have lost this. But now, thanks to Marilee, my attorney is confident that I won't.

Sam was overjoyed when we called him this afternoon to relay the news of our marriage. He still thinks this is the ace in the pocket we need to convince the judge there are no legs to Constance and Larry's petition. I sure hope he's right.

There's a noise behind me, and I turn to find Lee at the kitchen counter, grabbing a handful of popcorn. She's dressed in a pair of red-checkered flannel pants, an oversized T-shirt that hangs slightly off one shoulder, and Rudolph slippers on her feet. Her hair is piled on top of her head, but for a moment, I'm returned to the memory of this afternoon, when it flowed freely down her back. When, so help me, I couldn't resist allowing my fingers to graze the silken strands as I led her to the proverbial altar.

She just looked so beautiful. I mean, she always does—she does right now, in her pajamas—but there was just something about knowing she was there, all dressed up...for me.

Though actually, it was for Ryder. And that's an important distinction. Something I need to remember.

Even if my son wasn't there today—we didn't want to create a core memory that would be confusing later when Marilee and I decide to go our separate ways, so my mom watched him all day, and he's there overnight too—he's the reason for all of this.

Though I swear, today, the way Marilee looked at me during the ceremony...

It was almost as if she saw *me* the way I've always seen her.

Shoot. That's some wishful thinking there. Wishful...and dangerous.

"Hey." I leave the door open behind me as I join her in the kitchen. "You all settled in?"

Squeaking, she drops a few kernels of popcorn. "You scared me!"

I chuckle. "Sorry." Walking back around to the couch, which I've already arranged with a few pillows and quilts, I sink back into the cushions. "So? Need anything else?"

She plops down beside me, bowl of popcorn in hand. "I don't think so." Her fingers travel along the patches of the quilt my grandma made before she passed. "I still feel bad you're staying out here."

"Nah, it's fine."

She throws a kernel at my head. "Your back is going to be killing you after a week or two."

"You know I tent camp on the hard ground several nights a week when I'm taking groups out on tours, right?" Picking up the discarded kernel, I toss it in the air and catch it in my mouth.

"I know, but..." She huffs, and her glasses steam momentarily. Removing them, she cleans them with the edge of her shirt, giving me the tiniest glimpse of the pale white skin above the rim of her pants.

I glance away. "There aren't any good alternatives. I don't want Ryder to lose his room—that's sure to get back to Constance and Larry. And I'm not making you share either. I want your new home to be as comfortable as possible."

"I know. I still feel bad, though."

"Don't. You're helping me out of a jam. It's worth it."

"You're helping me too." Sighing, she grows quiet, and I don't have much else to say, so I turn up the volume on the TV and watch the Rams get crushed by the 49ers, over and over again.

Marilee lays her head back against the couch cushion and,

grabbing her phone, flips to an e-book app—probably to read the latest novel by Abigail Fox, her favorite romance author. I love that she'll sit here with me even if she doesn't care at all about sports.

At halftime, I stand to refill the popcorn bowl, which I've demolished, when there's a knock on my door. "Did you invite anyone over?"

Her head pops up over the back of the couch. "No."

I set the bowl on the counter, stride toward the front door, and look through the peephole, but it's dark. Covered. Are the neighbor kids being obnoxious again? I fling open the door. "Gotcha!"

But instead of surprised teens, I find an entire group of friends spread out on my front lawn. A chorus of voices cries out, "Congratulations!"

Broad-shouldered Landon Bennett and Blake have got a banner stretched between them, brunette twins Kelsey and Elisse Loveland—along with Lucy and her cousin April Reynolds—are carrying platters of food. And former bodyguard Frederick Shaw and his newly affianced Princess Chloe Huntington flank them all, carrying bottles of wine.

"Uh." It's all I can say, because what in the world? "Lee?"

She appears at my elbow, wrapped in one of my quilts. Her eyes are wide. "What are you guys doing?"

"We are here to celebrate your nuptials," Chloe says in her British-like accent as she looks at Lucy beside her. "A little bird told us the two of you finally got married."

Finally, huh? Geez. *Subtle, Chloe.*

Lucy flashes us an apologetic smile. "Sorry. I know they weren't our beans to spill, but Chloe can be very scary when she's sniffing out a secret."

"What can I say? It's a gift." The princess, who is all dignity and grace, holds up the wine and flutes in her hand. "Now, can we come inside, please? Since you insisted on leaving us out of the actual ceremony, we insist on throwing you a bit of a last-minute wedding shower."

"Um, sure. Come in, come in." Marilee waves to our friends, who rush forward and give us hugs.

Within seconds, everyone is inside. Food and drinks have been set on the counter, and Elisse has gone through my cabinets to find plates and napkins. Now all of our friends surround us, their eyes wide, expectant.

"Well?" April, who at five feet nothing is even shorter than Marilee, pushes her red bangs out of her eyes before brandishing a hand on her hip. "What gives, guys? How did this happen? When? Was it a secret romance?" She sighs happily. "Friends to lovers is my absolute favorite trope."

From what Marilee has told me, April—an aspiring author and avid reader—is always seeing things in story form, not reality.

"So. Um." I clear my throat. "The little bird who informed you of our marriage should have *also* told you that our marriage is...not exactly conventional."

"Exactly." Marilee twists her hands in front of her body. A nervous laugh titters out of her. "Jordan's custody of Ryder was questioned and—"

"Oh, the little bird *did* tell us all of that, including the fact that the reason for it is a secret." Elisse moves behind the kitchen island and begins to remove the foil from the dishes, shooing Landon out of the way as she goes. "But we all thought maybe it was just an excuse to finally be together without having to admit your true feelings."

I groan inwardly. Leave it to Elisse...

"Geez, woman." Landon reaches around her and pulls a chip from the bag she's just opened, dipping it into what looks like Elisse's famous homemade guacamole. "Have a little tact." He shoves the chip into his mouth and groans.

"Look who's talking. You wouldn't know tact if it hit you in the face."

They start bickering, the rest of the group dives into the food, and it looks like I owe Landon big time for distracting everyone from Elisse's question. Our friends stay for a few hours—the guys watching the rest of the game with me, the ladies gathered in the kitchen talking about Chloe and Frederick's upcoming engagement party on Friday night and a variety of other topics I'm not privy to.

We work as a group to devour the plates of brownies, seven-layer dip, and taco bar they brought over, but eventually, they start shuffling out the door, shouting once again their "congratulations" and winking that they're excited to keep our secret.

After Blake practically carries an exhausted Lucy to their car, I shut the door and lean back against it. Marilee's over in the corner of the room, looking up at the Christmas tree I haven't had the heart to take down, because I know how much she loves it.

The room rings with the sudden quiet.

Shoving my hands into my pockets, I approach. "Hey."

"Hey."

"You okay?"

"Mmm hmm." She spins the new ring on her left hand.

My heart stutters at the sight. "Liar."

That causes a tiny smile to appear. "I'm just processing everything that happened today." Her forehead wrinkles. "Do you think we made a mistake?"

"Lee, I hope you don't feel pushed into this. I never wanted that."

"It was my idea, remember?"

"Maybe I shouldn't have agreed."

She bites her thumbnail before blowing out a tremulous breath. "Until now, we've been in our bubble about this, only telling Blake and Lucy. But now, people are going to have their opinions, and we're going to have to let all the townspeople think that we're..."

I hate that she seems bothered by that, but Marilee's the most honest person I know. "I wondered if you would have a problem lying to people."

"I'm hoping that most people will just make assumptions, and we won't have to lie. I can tell them I love you, because I do. They don't have to know I mean as a friend, right?"

And I'll admit—her words are a dagger to my heart. Because if I had any hope that Marilee saw me differently, her declaration crushes it into dust. "Yeah. Right." My gaze latches onto an ornament made of popsicle sticks in the shape of a picture frame. The dried glue is clumpy and the sticks are crooked, but it's perfect, because nestled inside the frame, a photo of Ryder grins back at me. "We just have to stay focused on our reasons for doing this and not let other people's opinions get in the way. It's not their business, Lee."

"You're right." She leans her head against my upper arm. Her vanilla scent wafts upward, and the back of my hand brushes hers. It takes everything I have not to take hold of it, to weave our fingers together. But I'm going to have to ignore a thousand such impulses over the next year.

I thought I'd built up an immunity to the effect Marilee has on me, but living with her, being around her constantly, is going to test that resolve in a major way.

I reach out to straighten an ornament she gave me on my first Christmas with Ryder. It's one of those wooden figurine ornaments of a dad holding a new baby. "That being said, if you regret this—"

"No." The word is solid, punctuating the air with certainty and force.

"You sure?"

"I'm really tired of people asking me that." Her voice holds a tease, and I'm glad for the levity, however small.

"Sorry. It's just you asked me if we made a mistake. I mean, maybe we did. Either way, it doesn't really matter what *I* think." I pull away slightly and turn her shoulders so she's facing me. "If *you* feel like we did, that's enough for us to march ourselves right to the courthouse and get an annulment. I would never trap you in this, Lee. But if you're in it, so am I."

Her face softens, and she launches herself into my arms. "Thank you for having my back, and for giving me a choice."

"Always." I hug her tight to my chest. I want to say more, to scream that I'm not Donny and never will be. But some part of me wonders if by marrying Marilee, I'm taking advantage of her, if I'm being selfish like he was. "And we're going to make sure this marriage is a good thing for both of us, okay? So if you decide you're ready to secure that loan, I'll go with you to the bank and cosign on the dotted line. *Have* you decided yet?"

"Well." Her arms squeeze my torso before releasing me, retreating a bit into herself as she hugs her own chest. "Marla asked me if I had any updates in my thinking yesterday during my shift."

"And?" I start collecting dishes from around my living room, tossing the used paper products in the garbage and placing others next to the sink to deal with in the morning.

She follows me to the kitchen, filling the sink with hot, soapy water. "I told her I was still figuring out the loan stuff, and she said she didn't want to wait forever."

"So you've decided to go for it, then?" I set more dirty dishes on the counter beside her.

She plunges a bowl into the suds and scrubs. "I think so."

With the back of her hand, she tries to push away a few strands of hair that are stuck behind her glasses.

"Here. Let me." Without a second thought, I reach out. Her skin is oh so soft where my fingertips lightly graze her forehead as I tuck the hair behind her ear.

And I am a weak man, because my hand lingers there, cupping her ear as I get lost in her eyes. As if it's got a mind of its own, my thumb takes its dear sweet time skimming its way from the top of her ear, down the edge, all the way to the perfectly shaped lobe, where my thumb and forefinger rest on opposite sides.

My breathing stutters.

I've touched Marilee a thousand times before. But something about standing here in the stillness of my kitchen—now *our* kitchen—at midnight in the half-dim room, with moonlight streaming in through the windows, makes the air between us vibrate on a different current.

"Jay?" she whispers, her voice thick. "Are you okay?"

Shoot. I force my hand down and take a step backward.

She stares at me, her mouth slightly gaping. So much for self-control and resistance. *Get it together, Jordan.* I need to refocus, to remember that just because a few things have changed—like Marilee's address and the fact our names are linked on paper—doesn't mean that *everything*'s changed.

I clear my throat. "Yeah, of course. Everything's fine."

Everything except the fact I might be falling even more in love with my best friend than ever before.

And that is *not* the bargain we've struck.

MARILEE

I've been Jordan's wife for four days.

And other than Monday, when we had the actual ceremony and evening alone together before our friends dogpiled in to "celebrate" with us, I've hardly had a moment alone with him. With his busy season coming up at work, he's spent long days planning at the office. We've worked it out so he takes Ryder to school in the mornings and I pick him up after my extra-early shifts at the bakery. Then, I spend the rest of the afternoon and evening taking him to the playground, feeding him cheese crisps and homemade pizza bites, curling up on the couch and reading with him...

Ryder's adjusted to it all really well, and that's probably because, other than my change of address, the amount of time we spend together is honestly not that different than before Jordan and I were married.

Not much is different, really...except for this pesky feeling inside of me, the one that says I've finally found where I belong. And the warning that goes along with it—that it's temporary.

When that feeling comes, I snuff out any tendrils of attraction for Jordan and focus on my relationship with Ryder. I've always wanted to be a mom. Tried several times over to have babies with Donny.

Tried...and failed.

But now, I have a chance, for one year at least, to be a stepmom to the most precious little boy I can imagine. And I'm going to enjoy every second of that.

"Ryder!" I call down the hall from my place at the stovetop, where I'm making him a grilled cheese sandwich. "Time to eat, bud." After checking the underside of the bread, I flip it. Blake may be the grilled cheese connoisseur of the family, but Mom also taught me how to cook, so what can I say? The golden-brown crust speaks volumes.

At least in this—the realm of the kitchen—I am not a mess.

"Woohoo!" My charge gallops out of his bedroom on a stick horse, a cowboy hat atop his head. As per a prearranged date, he spent several hours yesterday afternoon with Constance and Larry, the latter of which picked him up directly from school and then brought him home to me with the new toys.

I'll admit, it's hard not to see them as bribes. To not see *them* as the enemies.

No doubt someone has told them about our new relationship status, though Larry didn't even get out of the car when Ryder got home, so I can't be sure. Despite not living in our town directly, they come here all the time, and gossip spreads like a fire in Hallmark Beach. When I went into work on Tuesday, I got more pats on the back, hugs, and well wishes for "lots and lots of adorable babies"—and the winks to go along with that statement—than I can count.

The funny thing? Not one person asked me for the story of how Jordan and I got together. Like I hoped, they just assumed they knew it.

Which, I guess, says a lot.

I'm just not sure what exactly it's says...

"Grilled cheese? Yes!" Ryder drops the horse with a clatter onto the tiled floor and scrambles up the stool on the other side of the kitchen island. "That's my favorite."

"I know." Removing the sandwich from the skillet, I set it on a plate with a sliced apple, carrot chips, and some rolled lunch meat. Then I slide it in front of him. "Eat up, kid. Lexi will be here to babysit in about fifteen minutes."

He squints up at me from underneath the brim of his hat. "She's fun, but I wish you and Daddy didn't have to go somewhere tonight. I thought we were gonna watch *Garfield.*"

"We'll do that tomorrow night, okay?" I tip the hat up enough to lean in and give him a kiss on the forehead. "Tonight Daddy and I have to celebrate Miss Chloe and Mr. Freddy's engagement."

"That means they're getting married, right?"

"Sure does." I swipe a carrot from his plate and shove it in my mouth.

He chomps on an apple. "How's come nobody celebrated your engagement to Daddy then?"

A piece of carrot lodges in my throat. I cough, grabbing my drink tumbler to suck down some water. "Well." How to navigate this? So far, Ryder's just accepted the facts: that I decided to become Daddy's roommate, and the best way to do that was to get married. Curious as he normally is, he hasn't asked more questions—until now. Where's Jordan when I need him? "Our marriage happened kind of quickly, and it's different than Chloe and Frederick's because we were such good friends beforehand."

He studies me with his big eyes while he chews. The smell of butter and cheese turns my stomach as I wait for his next question. Lying to this little boy is not an option. I may go back and forth about whether it was a good idea to get married in the first place, but this is something that takes no decision-making, because I will *not* damage him or make him distrust me and Jordan later when we end up with an annulled marriage. Answering his questions just might requires some...creativity.

But instead of asking anything more, he just shrugs. "Okay." Then he takes a big bite of the sandwich, pulling a string of melted cheese away from his teeth and giggling. "Look, Lee-Lee. It's like lava."

Man, I love this kid. The joy he finds in the simple things. "Tasty lava, I hope."

He flashes me a thumbs up. "Oh, yeah. So good!"

The doorbell rings, and I leave him to keep eating. Pulling the door open, I find Marla's blonde-headed, nineteen-year-old granddaughter standing there, a few board games in her arms. "Hey, Lexi. Thanks for coming."

"Of course!" Her tall lanky figure steps past me. "I love hanging with Ryder."

"Ryder, look who's here." I shut the door.

He leaps from the stool and practically tackles Lexi, who laughs as she sets the board games on the counter and stoops to give him a full hug. "What's up, dude? I brought a few new games for us to play tonight."

"Sweet!" He pumps a fist. "First, I gotta finish my dinner, though."

"You do that." She turns to me, and I give her a few instructions for the evening, though clearly she's got this handled.

"I need to go finish getting ready, and then I'll take off. Probably be home around ten or eleven if that's okay?"

"Totally fine." She pats a messenger bag that looks extra full, probably with textbooks, since Lexi is attending online community college. "I've got to study for a test, so I'll be up late regardless." She tilts her head. "Is Mr. Carmichael meeting you there? Congrats on your marriage, by the way."

"Thank you." And there it is again, that flutter of something in my stomach. Maybe just worry, that I'll have to lie, have to figure out the right thing to say in front of a whole town full of people I care about. "And yes, he's been working all day and is meeting me there."

"Great." Without asking anything else, she sits on the stool next to Ryder and starts talking to him about his day.

I breathe a sigh of relief and head to the bedroom—the one I still feel a bit strange taking over. Even though the sweet smell of my aloe vera lotion now lingers in the air, my jewelry is spread on top of the dresser, my shoes kicked in the corner, my bra hanging haphazardly over a chair, the room is still thoroughly masculine, with its dark wood furniture, hunter green duvet, and large canvas prints of some of Jordan's favorite spots in nature, including Firestone Beach and Hallmark Lighthouse.

After tossing on a pair of jeans, a yellow blouse, and a pair of Christmas tree earrings, I brush out my hair and quickly decide the kinks are not worth dealing with tonight, so up into a messy bun it all goes. Then I slip on my favorite brown flats and, with a hug and a kiss to Ryder and a goodbye to Lexi, I'm off to Chloe and Freddy's engagement party.

Off to make the first real appearance in public as Jordan Carmichael's wife.

Here's hoping I don't blow it—because everything depends on people believing our story.

Finding parking along Main Street is next to impossible on a Friday night, so I decide to take the short walk down Hillside Drive. By the time I'm at The Green Robin, the sun is setting along the horizon, and I'm a bit chilled. Instead of entering through the front door, I head beachside to the steps leading to the raised patio off the back of the restaurant, which Chloe reserved for the party. Laughter and music greet me as I push through the small gate at the top of the stairs.

And wow, the place has been transformed from a casual dining space to a party wonderland—something I'm not surprised at, with event planner Chloe at the helm. Fairy lights are strung from poles mounted at the corners of the deck, and the lime green tables and chairs have been covered with fancy, white tablecloths and moved to make room for a small dance floor in the center. Stretched along the southern deck is a six-foot table piled with some of the Robin's signature dishes, along with a circular table with artfully arranged baked goodies, most of which I helped Marla make earlier this week at The Blackberry Muffin.

There are people everywhere, some sitting, some standing, and only a few dancing. My first instinct is to stick to the edges as I scan the crowd for my people. Not that everyone in town isn't "my people" to some degree—even seventy-something Alberta Jenkins, the owner of Al's Grocery and possessor of one of the sharpest tongues in Hallmark Beach, who is currently circled up near the baked goods table with her twin sister (and town librarian) Anita Draper and gossip queen Collette Flanagan. Alberta's eyes catch mine over Anita's head, and she looks like she might push through the crowd to talk with me. Probably because I haven't been by the grocery to tell her the news about me and Jordan myself.

"Mare!" A familiar voice rises over the crowd, and my head swivels to locate its owner.

Lucy's weaving her way toward me, her cousin April in tow, and I've never been happier to see them, because suddenly it feels like I'm in a wind tunnel and the blast of everyone's attention is focused solely on me. The music seems to fade into oblivion, and I can even hear April's dad Burt guffaw and say,

"Still can't believe them two finally got hitched after all these years!" Murmurs overrun the deck like ants on a dropped piece of cake.

Thankfully, when Lucy and April reach me and smother me with hugs, a whoosh sends people's conversations rolling again. "We wondered if you were coming," Lucy says, looking behind me. "Where's your hubby?" Her eyebrows dance playfully. She looks less pale than she has for a while. Maybe the morning sickness has subsided. I've been so caught up with life this week that we have hardly talked since the completely unnecessary celebration she and the others threw us on Monday.

"Working. He'll be here soon."

"Oh good. Chloe has someone she wants him to meet." She hooks her thumb over her shoulder, where Chloe, Freddy, and a good-looking guy in his thirties or forties stands in a blazer and jeans chatting with them, a dark-bottled drink in hand. "He's a new business associate who owns a glamping site with these really amazing stargazing tents. Chloe's planning a wedding up there this summer, but she thought maybe he and Jordan could hook up to offer some overnight experiences together."

A member of the Robin's staff comes by with a tray of waters, and I snag one with a smile. "That sounds right up his alley." I take a sip, and the cool liquid washes away my earlier dread at being the center of attention. "When he gets here, I'll be sure to let him know." I turn to April. "Who's watching Scarlett tonight?"

A single mom to the most precocious seven-year-old (who is sassy just like her mama), April just moved back to Hallmark Beach from San Francisco last summer. She lives with her parents and works at the Bluestocking Bookshop, and she doesn't talk a lot about herself, but I know things have been tough for her. Still, I don't think she regrets her decision to move back here, at the very least for Scar's sake. It gives her more time to work on her novel writing too. I just know someday she's going to be a best-selling author. Not that she's let anyone read her stuff yet. But I can just tell, because she's the determined sort.

"Mom's arthritis was bugging her, and she claimed she'd rather stay home and have a movie night with her granddaughter than come out, but we all know she never passes up an opportunity to be among her friends." April frowns as Michael Bublé's version of "Quando, Quando, Quando" lilts through the night air. "I feel bad asking her for so much help."

"Don't be so hard on yourself. Your parents want to help." I reach out and squeeze her hand.

"I know. It's why I moved home. But I have to run up to San Francisco for a thing tomorrow and won't be home until Monday evening. I'm worried Scar's energy is going to be too much for them all."

"Blake and I can take her tomorrow if you want," Lucy says. "But I'm driving down to meet Mom and Kevin in L.A. on Sunday and won't be home till Tuesday."

"Really? Even just one day would give Mom a break. Thanks, cuz." April's eyes get a little misty.

"If you want to give them the whole weekend off, I'm not working Sunday." I tilt my head. "I'm sure Ryder would love to have a playmate for the day. We can go do something fun. She can stay overnight, and I can grab her from school Monday until you're back."

"Seriously? You guys are the best. Thank you."

"Being a single parent is hard work." I shrug. "I know Jordan's struggled a lot too."

"Except he's not a single dad anymore, now is he?" A wry

grin overtakes the shadows on April's face. "Maybe I need to find someone to conveniently marry *me*."

"Shh." Lucy hip bumps her cousin. "Someone is going to hear you."

"Please." Rolling her eyes, April gestures toward the crowd, where nobody seems to be paying us any mind. "Even if they did, they wouldn't think anything about it. We all know Jordan's been making eyes at Mare for years."

"Ha ha." I down the rest of my water and place the empty cup on a nearby table. Overhead, stars have popped through the gauzy fabric of the night. "Not you too, April." That funny feeling wends its way through me again, chasing the question of "what if?"

The *what if* doesn't matter, though. Not when I know that Jordan deserves a lot better than someone like me. Donny used up everything good I had to give. That's why I'm never getting married again.

Well, never getting married *for real* again.

It just wouldn't be fair to the other person. I come with too much baggage, and I'd never want to pile that on someone else.

"Just gotta speak as I find." April laughs. "You know my favorite Abigail Fox story is the one about a marriage of convenience between a hockey player and a single mom. And remember how *that one* turned out?"

My cheeks heat at the thought. That book had some excellent kisses...

"Troublemaker." Lucy grins as she says the word, her eyes scanning the crowd. "Oh, hey, there's Jordan." She points toward the restaurant. "Uh oh."

"What? What's wrong?" I stand on my tiptoes, but the deck's only gotten more crowded, and my view is filled with shoulders and necks and arms. I see Freddy tipping Chloe back on the dance floor and one of Elisse and Kelsey's brothers flirting with Gemma Stone near the dessert table. I see both of Chloe's female bodyguards dressed in black suits, scanning the crowd for threats.

But I don't see Jordan.

I sure could use a few of Lucy's extra inches right about now. "What's wrong?" I repeat.

"Constance just pulled him away from talking to Landon and Blake. And she looks upset."

"What?" Everything in me prickles. I feel like a cat with an arched back, my claws at the ready. "Where exactly?"

She takes my shoulders and points me southeast. "Straight that way."

Before she can say anything else, I'm off, bobbing and weaving through the crowd like it's an Olympic sport and I'm a gold medalist.

I hear Constance before I see her. Her voice is tense, low. Nasty mean, like a cobra spitting poison. "I just find the whole thing very convenient, especially after claiming for years to be just friends."

"The good thing is, Constance, that you don't have to find it any particular way." Jordan's being very diplomatic, his voice calm and soothing, but tension rides the currents underneath. "You just need to accept it."

I pop through the crowd and find them standing along the deck railing near the door that leads between the patio and the inside of the restaurant. Constance is short and thin in a wraithlike way, but nothing about this woman is meek—from her large hands to her loud voice, hissing at my best friend. Even the graying hair pulled away from her tan, weathered face adds to the severity of her features.

Constance's husband is sitting at a table just inside, his face red as he strokes his bushy white mustache, watching the exchange. Once again, he's standing (or rather, sitting) by while his wife runs roughshod over the dad of their grandchild. Unbelievable. They must have been dining when she saw Jordan out here. Ironic. Constance said she didn't want Jordan to contact her about the court petition, but *she's* allowed to approach him in public?

Not cool. Not fair.

"I don't accept it either," she continues. "All I'm saying is, the judge might find it interesting to know the timeline."

"And all I'm saying is, *my* attorney doesn't agree with you. The timeline doesn't matter—not with the love we have for each other."

His words... They sound so *convincing*.

But this is what we said, that we'd refer to our mutual love. Which we have. It just so happens to be platonic love.

At least...I think so.

"And you expect me to believe you just recently discovered this love?" Snorting scornfully, Constance wags a meaty finger at Jordan, who is dressed in a green T-shirt, black Adidas track jacket, and jeans. He faces Constance, arms crossed over his chest, casual and effortless—except for the way his hands are white-knuckling his biceps. It's the only indication that this interaction bothers him. That and the way his Adam's apple bobs at her question.

Part of me wants to hang back, wants to hear what he has to say. The other part doesn't, because...it's irrelevant.

Either way, right now, he needs me.

"There you are." I smile like nothing's wrong as I walk straight toward him and slip my arm around his torso so we can face Constance together.

Our gazes connect as I blink up at him, hoping he feels my support—literally and figuratively.

He squeezes my waist, his hand momentarily splaying across my hip.

I suck in a sharp taste of salty air before moving my attention back to Constance, forcing a smile. "Good evening, Constance." I'd say *nice to see you*, but did I mention I really hate lying?

The woman—who I'd never have described as snake-like before now—stares at me with dark eyes that look like they want to devour me. Despite my long sleeves, a shiver courses up my spine, and Jordan moves his hand to my arm, rubbing it up and down, keeping me warm.

If only he knew *that* was making the shivering worse.

"Tell me." She seems to be studying me the way a scientist picks apart an experiment. "If the two of you love each other so much, why does Ryder tell me that you're sleeping on the couch, Jordan?"

He stiffens. "That's really not your business, Constance. And I don't appreciate you using my son to learn details about my life."

"The welfare of my grandchild is most definitely my business, and if the two of you are lying to a child—"

"Who says we're lying?" Jordan asks.

"I do," the woman says through clenched teeth. She steps forward, her voice hissing. I swear I see a forked tongue dart out as she speaks. "Either way, it's a bad look. You're sleeping separately, and it doesn't matter to me if the reason is because you're fighting—which, let's face it, less than a week in does not bode well—or because you're faking the whole thing to make Jordan appear to be a better dad by creating the appearance of a stable environment for Ryder."

Fudgesicles.

I want nothing more than to smack the obnoxious, gleeful look off her face. I mean, Constance Comer is not a bad person —I know this logically. She just misses her daughter and wants to feel closer to her by gaining some sort of custody over her daughter's son.

But to do all of that at the expense of Jordan?

I want to scream at her that this is not the way.

Instead, it looks like I'll need to show her. And there's no other option in my brain at the moment than to prove to her that her assumptions—while actually true—are false.

"Constance," I say sweetly, taking a step forward and out of Jordan's hold.

She tilts her chin upward. "What?"

Appropriately, Katy Perry's *Roar* plays in the background, each beat pumping me up to do something I never in a million years thought I would do.

"Does *this* look fake to you?"

Then I spin toward Jordan and snatch the front of his shirt. I see his wide eyes flicker down at me for a split second before lifting on my tiptoes, wrapping one arm around his neck, tugging him toward me—and aiming my mouth for his.

It's a moment of suspension in air, of my brain wondering what in the ding-dong donuts I'm doing, hoping that Jordan sees this as necessary, just like I do—praying that I'm not over-stepping.

Then, that moment's over, and it's clear Jordan agrees when his hands find my waist and he yanks me against him. Our mouths fuse together like they've done it a million times, and I can't help but melt against him like butter on a hot, delicious blueberry muffin.

His fingers flex against my hipbones, and suddenly I'm hyperaware of every point where our bodies connect. His lips are impossibly soft, moving against mine with a tenderness I never expected. This is Jordan—my best friend, my fake husband —but there's nothing pretend about the way he's holding me, like

I'm something precious, or how my knees have gone weak as I drown in the taste of him, in the warmth of his embrace, in the way his fingers trail up my spine to cradle the back of my head.

I've never been kissed like this, never felt so completely consumed by a single moment.

Then a loud whistle pierces the air, followed by whoops and a chorus of "Get a room!" Reality crashes in, and I stumble backward, my lips tingling, to find our entire group of friends and the rest of the town staring at us with knowing grins.

At least it seems like Constance believes us, given that she looks as if she just touched a burning hot stove.

I can relate to that feeling. My show for Constance has led to this—a heart thundering against my ribs, my entire body feeling like it's been lit from within.

And then, there's the realization that I didn't want it to stop.

What have I done?

nine

JORDAN

My converted garage-slash-man cave might be filled with dudes at the moment, but my head is even fuller. And not even our monthly Saturday guys' night can get me out of this funk.

"Oh, come on, mate!" Frederick tosses popcorn at the big-screen television from his seat on the black couch. "That's a definite penalty."

"Yikes." I lean on a cue stick near the pool table behind the couch, where I'm playing a solo game. "That looked like it hurt."

"It's downright criminal is what *that* was." Freddy cups his hand around his mouth and boos loudly.

Landon snickers, clapping Frederick on the shoulder. "Still cracks me up we've converted you into such a hockey fanatic, Freddy, old boy."

"I didn't know what I was missing, chaps. How can you not enjoy watching Ethan Fox killing it on the ice like that?" Freddy lifts a water bottle toward the sky, as if in toast to the Big Apple Blizzards' forward. "I really think it's likely he will lead them to the Stanley Cup this year, yeah?" His accent—which matches Chloe's, given they're both from the European country of Kentonia—sounds all sorts of dignified, and in direct contrast to the way he was screaming at the TV not moments ago.

"It looks promising, that's for sure." I line up my shot and take it.

Miss.

Shoot. I've even lost my ability to play a decent game of pool. Marilee's that much of a distraction, even out here.

"Agreed, but only if he can keep from being injured. Everyone's clearly gunning for him." Blake grabs a few cans of soda and two waters from my garage fridge, which is next to the door leading into the house—the house where Ryder's asleep and Marilee's spent all day baking up a storm. The smell of cinnamon and sugar and frosting have seeped through the doorway cracks. She's got a few cakes to finish up this weekend, and I didn't want to disturb her, so I took Ryder out for a long hike today so she could be alone.

Maybe, like me, she needs time to process last night's kiss.

It...well, I'm not gonna lie. It shattered my world in every kind of way. Shattered what I thought I knew. What I thought I wanted.

What I thought I could be content never having.

When Marilee Moffitt came for me, I don't think she intended anything more than putting Constance in her place. I didn't either—until I had her there, and the entire rest of the world disappeared, and Marilee turned to liquid in my arms.

Then, I honestly just forgot about anything but showing that woman how much I love her. I poured it all out, right there on that patio, and it *felt* like she responded in kind.

But then, the spell broke...and she looked horrified.

Horrified.

Yeah, that really makes a man feel good.

And now, I don't know what to think. We haven't spoken

about it. Haven't spoken much at all. She's been in her baking zone, where she retreats when the world is big and scary and she's trying to figure out her emotions.

But maybe her emotions are less about how she feels about me, and more about how to let me down easy.

Because I'm not sure there's any way she doesn't have a thousand percent clarity on how I feel about her—just like every other person on that deck who saw us kissing.

Silver lining—I think Constance was one of those people. She slunk back to her table with Larry and didn't bother us again. As for Marilee, well, she forced a smile that didn't reach her eyes, and we headed back to hang with our friends and toast Chloe and Freddy's wedding, which is planned for this fall in Kentonia.

"Yo, earth to Jordan."

I snap my attention back to Blake, who is now standing in front of me with a Dr. Pepper in his outstretched hand. "Oh. Thanks, man."

Taking the can, I set it on a nearby cocktail table and position myself to take another shot at the purple ball in front of me.

Instead of going back to join Freddy and Landon on the couch, Blake cracks open his Coke and studies me over the top of his can. "Want to go a round with me?"

I think he's talking about pool. I hope he's talking about pool.

Because I can't forget that Blake is Marilee's brother. And given the words of warning before our wedding ceremony, and the way he was also witness to that kiss yesterday, I'm guessing he has a few things to say. "Sure." I snatch another cue stick off the wall and hand it to him.

"So." He sets his soda down and grabs the chalk, rubbing it on the end of his stick while I collect the few balls I managed to send into the table pockets. "Any word from your attorney? Court date still a few weeks out?"

"Yeah, three weeks from Tuesday." I arrange the balls in the rack on the table, then remove it, leaving them in a triangular shape. "You can break."

Blake circles the table, his eyes on me just as much as the balls. Like a lion about to pounce on its prey.

I sigh. "Go ahead. Let me have it."

And he seems to understand exactly what I'm saying—that I'm not talking about pool. "Does the attorney know your marriage is a sham?" His jaw clenches and loosens. He finally comes to stand at one end of the table, lines up his cue stick, and lets it fly.

The snap of the white ball hitting the rest is like a whip cracking the air.

Four balls sail into various pockets.

Ouch.

I rub the back of my neck. "No."

"Don't you think that's risky?"

Freddy and Landon whoop from their spots on the couch, and from the corner of my eye I catch sight of a triumphant Ethan Fox holding his hands over his chest in the shape of a heart. Maybe he's got a girl in the stands, cheering him on.

Can't imagine *he's* been in love with the same woman for half of his life without any sort of reciprocation, hanging onto the barest of hopes that someday she might return his affection.

He's probably not as pathetic as some of us.

Blake banks another shot and sinks it. "Well?"

"I don't know, man. Probably. But my back was up against the wall." I open the soda he brought me and drain it, the cut of the carbonation burning my throat. "What was I supposed to do? Ryder's my kid. I'd do anything for him."

"I get it. I already feel that way about my kid, and he or she isn't even born yet." Blake frowns. "But I know my sister. She loves with her whole heart, and she'd do anything for anyone."

"You're right." And it's a precious thing. Too many people in this world are the exact opposite. Ungiving, undeserving. Selfish.

I fear I might be one of those people. I think Blake knows it too.

Blake chalks up again before taking another shot, but this time he scratches. Leaning down, he pulls the solid blue ball from a pocket and sets it on the table. "All I'm saying is, I don't like to see her taken advantage of. But I gave her my perspective on this whole thing, and she didn't want to hear it. So now, I'm telling you."

I retrieve the cue ball and set it down, line up to take a shot. "Telling me what?"

"I know what she means to you."

I miss. By a lot. "Do you?" My voice shakes and I look away, clearing my throat before I glance back.

"Yeah, it's kind of obvious, especially after that display last night."

"Oh." I figured, but hearing it confirmed...

Great.

"Okay, so... What?"

Blake runs his thumb down the top of the stick. "Donny really messed with her, and I didn't step in to stop it. That's one of my biggest regrets in life. I won't stand by again and watch her get hurt."

Shoot. Blake's a good guy, my friend, and more than that, Marilee's only close relative. I don't want him thinking badly of me. "Look, I need you to hear this. The last thing I want to do is hurt Marilee."

"I know, man, but this whole thing reeks of hurt. Lucy tells me I just need to be patient, to trust that what's supposed to happen will happen, but I can see a world in which Marilee feels obligated to love you back just because she's too afraid to hurt you. Or lose you."

I feel like he's jabbed his cue stick directly into my stomach. "I don't want that either." And maybe that kiss showed her all my cards. Maybe, without meaning to, I put too much pressure on her.

"Good." Blake sinks two balls in a row. "I'm glad we're on the same page." With one ball left, he's about to win.

Not that I care. This whole game is a sham—just like, apparently, my marriage.

But I knew that. I *know* that.

And I need to remember that, over and over again, until it's drilled into my brain and there's no room left for pesky things like hope.

Marilee did me a huge favor *only* because she cares about me as a friend.

And no matter how much I loved kissing her—or how much she seemed to enjoy kissing me back—I will not be another Donny in her life. I will not demand more of her than she's willing or able to give.

Even if I wish things could be different.

MARILEE

Parenting is an excellent distraction from the rest of life. It can be all consuming if you let it. And in this moment, I'm riding that train all the way to the sunset, baby.

First, because Ryder and Scarlett are absolute dolls, and I adore them with all that I am. And second, because I baked my fingers to the bone yesterday, and so today, baking can no longer serve to divert my attention from Friday night's Kiss-Gate—as my friends have taken to calling it in our group text thread.

So, kicking around a soccer ball and building sandcastles and picnicking on the beach?

Yep. Today, parenting is winning.

We've been here for hours—me and Ryder and Scarlett and Jordan—and the kids still have energy to burn. After stuffing them full of turkey sandwiches, chips, fruit, and peanut butter bars, they're ready to ramp up and go again, so Jordan's out there near the water, chasing them around in a rousing game of tag while I clean up.

My whole body sinks into the blanket as I finally close the

lid on the wicker picnic basket. The sand and grass are soft where I sit on the bluff overlooking the ocean, which gently undulates against the shore. I think that's one reason I like this spot so well—instead of rocking waves that crash and toss, the rounded shoreline allows for a slower pace. The water still laps, the tide still comes, but it's calmer. It allows the perfect opportunity for thinking.

For talking too.

Jordan and I still haven't discussed Kiss-Gate ourselves, but despite doing my best to put it off, I know it has to happen. We need to be adults and face this head on. I can sense he gave me space yesterday, and I did appreciate it. But now that I've got my emotions sorted—now that I've reminded myself of my priorities, of what I really want—it's time to talk.

So I suggested we come here, where other than the kitchen, I feel most like myself.

Because the rest of the world—and their voices, beloved as they might be—doesn't exist here.

Pulling my knees into my chest, I watch Jordan toss Ryder over his shoulder, growling like a bear as he chases Scarlett too. The little blondie screeches out a delighted scream and dashes away, her pigtails blowing in the wind behind her as she runs right through the sandcastle we built earlier.

Finally, Jordan sets Ryder down and pretends to get a cramp, collapsing on the ground. Both kids pile on top to tickle him. He giggles with a high-pitched laugh that is completely exaggerated, and my heart expands at what a good dad he is.

At how much he loves his son.

He's sacrificed more than most guys would, that's for sure. With his brilliant mind, he could have worked at a Fortune 500 company, but instead, he chose to come back to Hallmark Beach. Of course, that was before he had Ryder, so something else drew him back here—probably his parents, given his mom's diagnosis and his dad's inability to care for her. But still. He stayed.

He's the kind of guy who stays.

And maybe it shouldn't, but that's what terrifies me.

I sit that way, watching them for a bit, until Jordan glances up. Our gazes connect, and he says something to the kids, who clamber off of him and run back toward the soccer ball.

He brushes his gym shorts and walks up the small hill, plopping down beside me. "Couldn't have given me a little assist, there?"

"It looked like you had it handled."

"I could have used my wingwoman." A flash of sunlight peeks through the afternoon clouds, and he pulls the brim of his ball cap down a bit. "But who am I kidding? You would have been on their side."

"I'm glad you recognize the reality of the situation."

We both laugh, then settle into the silence that's been dogging us far too often the last forty-eight hours. Really, the last six days since we said "I do." If we are ever going to survive the next fifty-one weeks, this just can't continue.

I exhale. "Jay."

"Yeah, Lee?" He spreads his legs out in front of him, his muscular calves resting in the fine sand. I remember the first time I saw him in high school, how tall and spindly he was. The exact opposite of Donny, built like a juiced-up truck. Of course, for a while after Donny was injured at the end of his senior year, he stopped lifting. He grew weaker, while Jordan started lifting weights and grew stronger.

Donny never did forgive Jordan for that, I think.

Funny how their outward appearances finally came to match their insides.

I shake myself from the thought. Jordan may be Donny's

exact opposite, but I am still me—and my faults are plenty. "I wanted to apologize."

"For what?"

"Kiss-Gate."

He snorts. "Kiss what?"

I dig my toes into the sand at the edge of the blanket. "That's what Elisse took to calling it." Waving my hand in the air, I laugh with a dismissiveness I don't really feel. "Not important. The point is, I'm sorry."

He's quiet for a moment. "What exactly are you sorry about?"

Oh, he's not going to make this easy for me, is he?

A breeze wends its way up, carrying with it the sounds of Ryder and Scarlett's laughter as they retrieve the soccer ball from a hole in the sand.

I zip up my red hoodie, which is covered in flour that just didn't want to come off after yesterday's baking sesh. "That I made things awkward between us."

"You never have to feel awkward around me." He waits a beat. "Anything else?"

"I guess I'm sorry that I didn't ask you if it was okay before I sort of attacked you with that kiss."

His mouth tilts into a small smile. "Attacked me, huh?"

"Like a tiger." I wince. That particular analogy probably isn't the best, given how often people refer to being tigers in, um, well, certain places in their homes. Moving on... "I just got so riled at the smug look on Constance's face and wanted to do something to shut her up."

"Marilee Moffitt," Jordan says in a teasing tone. "Are you actually speaking ill of someone?" He clicks his tongue. "Never thought I'd see the day."

"She messed with someone I care about."

His eyes flick toward me briefly before finding the horizon

again. "Aw, come on, Lee. You don't have anything to apologize for. If anyone should say they're sorry, it's me. I, um..." His toes flex in front of him. "I shouldn't have gotten so into that kiss. You probably just meant to give me a peck and I...I took things too far."

The acknowledgement of the passion behind his kiss brings heat to my face. The memory of it turns my insides to boiling water.

Whew.

Nope. Can't think about that anymore.

I force a laugh. "Guess it's been too long since either of us has been good and kissed, right?" I honestly can't remember the last girl Jordan even dated. Someone in college, maybe. And then obviously there was Georgia, but they were never a couple.

Jordan doesn't laugh back. He's quiet, and I don't know exactly what his silence means.

But I have a suspicion. I hope I'm wrong, but I can no longer ignore that it's extremely likely my best friend has very real feelings for me.

Feelings I can't reciprocate.

I don't want to hurt him. But I also can't let him think of me like that. Because the worst thing in the world would be for him to fall for me—for me to fall for him. For him to eventually realize that I'm not *actually* what he wants. That I'm too broken to be the kind of partner I'd want to be to him.

And...he *will* realize it. It might take a while, but it's inevitable.

If Donny taught me anything, it was that.

But because Jordan is the opposite of Donny—who left when he finally tired of me—he would feel obligated to stay with me, stuck with my mess. He might even grow to resent me.

And I can't even fathom a world in which Jordan Carmichael resents me.

As his friend, I can give him his space—space to find someone else to fill that role he may or may not imagine me in right now. Someone who is whole and beautiful and untarnished by the scars brought on by her baggage—some of her own making, some tossed upon her.

He deserves that. I want that for him, because Jordan Carmichael is the best man I know.

And I fear, in this moment, given his continued silence, that maybe I've confused him. That kiss... It *was* confusing. But we can't lose sight of the goal, of the reason for all of this.

His custody battle.

And unfortunately, the other thing I need to discuss will probably also be confusing. But just like kissing him in public to prove our supposed "love," I think it's probably necessary. "So, there's something else we need to address."

He lifts his head. "Yeah? You ready to go sign papers at the bank?"

Oh. How do I admit to him that I haven't given the loan or the bakery purchase a second thought since our conversation about it nearly a week ago when we last discussed it? That I've instead been leaning into step-motherhood and baking in our joint kitchen, where I know I belong for now—*even though* it's just for now?

"Yes. Well, no, I mean. I'm still not sure." I wave my hand, flustered. "I'll let you know when I've made plans with Pete. If I do."

He studies me. "Okay. And if you decide you don't want to buy the bakery, that's totally all right too. But please, take advantage of me."

I spurt out a laugh, because my, did that sound...um, probably not how he meant it. "I'm sorry, what?"

He nudges me with his elbow. "I just mean, don't forget that I'm not the only one who's supposed to be benefiting from this situation. If you decide you don't want me to cosign a loan for you, then tell me what exactly you need from me to support you in your future career endeavors."

"Endeavors, huh? Well, that sounds official," I tease.

"I mean it, Lee."

"I know." I soften my tone. "And I appreciate it. Really, I do. I feel close to making a decision, though." I think. Maybe. Argh. "At the very least, Marla deserves some sort of answer soon."

"Don't rush your decision simply for her sake."

"Sure." I clear my throat. "Anyway, back on topic..."

"Right. Okay, so what else do we need to discuss?"

Whew. I shake out my suddenly sweaty hands. "What I was going to say is...we need to address the fact that Constance and Larry have a little spy living under our roof."

"Oh. That."

"Yeah. That." The whole reason for Constance's line of questioning the other night came because Ryder had reported our sleeping arrangements to his grandparents—of course not realizing that he was making our position more precarious. "I've been thinking... Dangerous, I know."

"Whatever, Brainiac."

I smile at the very misplaced compliment. Then sober at what I'm about to suggest. "Um, but yeah. I think-maybe-we-need-to-share-a-room."

He turns his entire upper body toward me. "What? We've talked about this. No."

"I knew you'd say that, but the whole reason you're saying no is because you don't want me to be uncomfortable, right?"

"Well..."

Seagulls caw in the distance.

"And I can assure you, sharing a room wouldn't be uncomfortable for me. In fact, I'd feel better knowing you weren't sleeping on that couch every night. I've seen you rub your lower back when you think I'm not looking."

"Nothing I can't handle. Really, Lee, it's fine."

"But it's not." I throw my hands in the air. "Ryder will continue to tell his grandparents we aren't sharing a room, and then this whole marriage is pointless!"

He winces, and I instantly regret my wording choice. It sounds brutal, but it's kind of true, right?

Before I can say more, he shakes his head. "I get it, but I can't in good faith..." Jordan presses his lips together. "I mean, that room isn't big enough for me to sleep on the ground, Lee." He hooks my gaze into his, and I feel the weight of his unspoken words.

We wouldn't just be sharing a room.

We'd be sharing a bed.

And if he really does care about me as more than a friend, then that might make things harder for him. Honestly, for me too. I haven't shared a bed with any man but Donny. Ever. And toward the end, he wasn't even in it half the time. I'd lie awake, just waiting...

So yeah. Sharing a bed with a guy holds some traumatic memories for me. But this would be different. Totally different. It wouldn't be a marriage bed... Not in the traditional sense.

I'm not sure what you'd call it—a best-friends-who-are-pretending-to-be-together-and-are-married-but-not-really bed?—but we're just going to have to figure it out for Ryder's sake.

"We can both be adults about this. I've known you half of our lives. I trust you, Jordan."

And I mean every word.

I feel like the sun sinks a whole mile before Jordan speaks again. "Fine."

"What's that?" I lean in, afraid I've misheard him. My glasses slide down my nose at the movement.

He pushes them back up for me, gives me a soft smile. "We can share a room." A pause. "But only if you're sure."

"I am."

And *that* may be the first lie I've ever told Jordan Carmichael.

JORDAN

Three weeks and one day until I find out if Sam Granger is right and my marriage to Marilee is indeed "pointless," as she so aptly put it yesterday.

But who's counting?

Standing at my desk, tucked away in the back corner of Go Round Adventures, I check the clock on my laptop again for the thousandth time. Just a few more minutes until I head out to pick up Marilee for a pre-lunch meeting with my attorney to go over the case and any prep work we need to do ahead of time. I just want the whole thing over with. I just want peace.

Not that I can get much peace with Marilee as my wife.

Thankfully, work has kept me busy this morning. I run a small operation here, only hiring a few other employees to lead day trips and run summer camps for kids but saving most of the overnight tours for myself. This puts extra burden on me, but when Georgia was alive, I simply scheduled around the weekends when she had Ryder. Now that Georgia's gone, it's putting a burden on my loved ones for me to work these long hours, but I'm not sure I have the funds to hire someone else. Maybe I should try to figure it out though.

The problem is the overnight tours are my most lucrative—and I do love them. Getting lost in nature, tuning out the rest of the world, immersing myself in the adventure of it all... Those are my favorite things. Even better when I can convince a few friends to come along.

And now, thanks to Chloe and her connection with Mitchell McGraff, I may have a new opportunity to woo customers who are willing to pay more for a high-end experience. More money per tour would be a boon that might help me be home more with my family.

Breathing out, I shoot off the email to Mitchell that I've been working on all morning and shut my laptop, stretching out my lower back, which still aches from the odd angle I slept at last night. Because despite my agreement to share a room with Marilee, when I finally got around to going to bed last night—she had hit the hay two hours before, thanks to having the early shift at work today—it just didn't feel right to climb in beside her without her being awake to acknowledge she was still one thousand percent okay with it.

So I slept in an old wooden kitchen chair shoved in the corner of my room instead.

Ouch.

Grabbing my keys, wallet, and phone, I leave my cozy den, which consists of a standing desk and portable treadmill, a huge window overlooking the forested hill behind my shop, and framed sports memorabilia on the walls, including a baseball signed by famed Padres pitcher Randy Jones. I shut my door behind me and step into the small yellow lobby, where there's a couple of sofas for people waiting for tours, a wall of rental equipment for the beach, and lots of eclectic pictures of past tour groups.

People clinging to zip lines as they fly over Pinot Noir vineyards and companion oaks, throwing their hands in the air through the open-air top of a dune buggy flying down the beach, popping their heads out of tiny tents they hauled through the forest themselves in the rain.

All smiling. All having the time of their lives.

Seeking the thrill, the adventure in the mundane.

And I get to foster that.

Man, I love my job. I just wish that the busy life it results in wasn't the main reason I'm going to court over the custody of my son.

"Everything okay, boss?"

I turn to find Mandy sitting atop the green stool behind the counter-height desk in the center of the room. The brunette—who is a former basketball player, sturdy and easily almost six feet tall—loves the outdoors as much as I do. About five years my junior, she's been with my company for the last two years, first working with her sister Sarah as camp counselors one summer. Now, she doubles as a tour guide and my office assistant.

"Yep. Just gotta head out for that appointment I told you about."

"Sounds good. I'll hold down the fort here." She tilts her head, and her ponytail falls over one shoulder. "So this email you copied me on just a minute ago... Who is this Mitchell guy?"

I shove my phone and wallet into the right pocket of my joggers and join Mandy at the desk. "Essentially, he owns a gussied-up camping site with incredible views near the foothills of the Santa Lucia Mountains. He's interested in partnering with us to get some tours up there at a discounted rate."

"Ooo, that might bring in a different clientele than we're used to. Expand the business." She shoots finger guns at me and winks. "Great idea, boss."

"Ha. That's the idea. Chloe vouches for him, so I've got a lot of confidence things could work out."

"But your email says you want to see the site before agreeing to anything."

"You know I don't do business with anyplace I haven't visited myself. That's disaster waiting to happen. I want to be sure it's perfect for our needs."

"Good point." She pulls up our Google calendar on her computer. "After he responds, do you want me to reach out to him with dates that work for you? How about Valentine's weekend? Doesn't look like any tours on the calendar then."

That's the weekend before our court date, but maybe it would be nice to get away from the pressure and stress. "I might not be able to make it, but why don't you see if that weekend or the following would work for him?"

"Will do." She clicks around before shooting me a sly look. "Will Marilee be going with you? You two didn't take a honeymoon, right? This would be the perfect opportunity to get away for a romantic weekend."

I groan internally. Like I need a romantic setting between us right now—because yeah, despite our talk yesterday, I can't get the kiss out of my brain. "I'm not sure she'll be available."

"All right." Mandy's eyebrows lift but she doesn't say anything more about it. "Just leave this with me. I'll get it all arranged with Mr. McGraff."

"Thanks. I'm off for my meeting with the attorney but will be back in once it's done."

"Good luck." She gives me a wave, and I'm out the door, driving the short distance to The Blackberry Muffin, where Marilee has been working since four a.m. She's got to be exhausted after taking care of Ryder and Scarlett all day yesterday, but at least she was completely out cold last night when I slunk into the bedroom, so I know she got some good sleep.

I pull up beside the building with the blue-and-white-striped awning, a brown bench in front of the large picture window through which I can see yellow tables sprinkled with customers. Marilee is behind the pastry counter chatting with Marla, a grandmotherly-type with round cheeks and a graying bun. She looks like Mrs. Claus minus the red dress.

They appear to be deep in discussion, so I lean back against the passenger side of my truck as I wait for Lee to join me. As if sensing me, she glances up and waves, holding up a pointer finger. I flash her a thumbs up before crossing my arms over my chest.

Hallmark Beach at the end of January isn't overly crowded with tourists, but the locals are out and about like usual—strolling along Main Street with Styrofoam containers from The Green Robin, walking their dogs and letting them stop to sniff the base of the wrought-iron black lampposts, and sitting on benches enjoying the sun that's burned away the clouds from this morning.

Just another day in this paradise we call home.

The front door of Al's Grocery pops open, and a young woman steps through holding two large paper bags. I can't see her face, but she's about to trip over a flower display, so I hop over to help. "Watch out." I steady the bags from my side and ease one out of the woman's arms.

Big, brown eyes greet from the other side. I smile at Amy Montrose. "Need some help?"

"Oh. Hi, Jordan." Her cheeks grow red. "Um, thank you. Tommy ran out of almond milk and a few other supplies and asked me to refresh our stock before the lunch rush." She nudges her chin toward The White Mocha. "Would you mind helping me get these into the kitchen?"

I glance back at the front door of the bakery, but Marilee's still not out here. "Sure." I follow Amy around the back and stop abruptly in front of the door while she fetches her key from the pocket of her jeans. I catch a whiff of lavender off her hair, which is just under my nose.

She glances up at me as she swings the door open, the brown paper bag on one hip. "Sorry to inconvenience you. Waiting for Marilee?" Something in her tone sounds wistful.

"Yeah."

"Hmm." Amy leads me through a hallway and into a bright kitchen with white cabinets and a gleaming marble-topped island spread with a few dirty mugs and baking supplies. She clears a spot and sets her bag down. "Thank you for your help."

I plop mine beside hers. "No problem. Glad to help." Turning to leave, I blink at Amy when she follows me.

"Sorry, I left one more bag at the register with Alberta."

"I could have carried it."

She bites her lip. "Yeah, I was flustered, I guess. At the heavy load, I mean. Didn't think about it."

We both exit and take the walkway in between the bakery and coffee shop. As she walks beside me, Amy tugs on the end of her braid. "I haven't seen you to offer my congratulations, but um, well...congrats. On your marriage."

"Oh. Thanks."

We stop near the front of Al's. She turns to me, squinting upward. "I always kind of wondered if the two of you were more than friends." And is it just me, or does she emit a tiny sigh? "But I'm so glad for you, that you found each other."

"Thanks, Amy." I reach out and squeeze her elbow.

Her face brightens, then reddens again as she takes a step backward. "I'd better go get that other bag, or Alberta's going to give it away to charity. I'll see you around, Jordan." Then she ducks back into the store and disappears.

When I swivel back to my truck, Marilee's standing there,

watching me. No smile, no real reaction. The woman just looks exhausted, like I knew she probably would be.

I approach and can't help but reach out my thumb, swiping underneath her glasses, where tinges of dark rim her eyes. "You look tired."

She seems to snap back from whatever world she'd retreated to in her mind. "Thanks, Jay. Just what every girl wants to hear." Again, no smile.

Oops. "I didn't mean—"

"I know." She waves it off as she pulls open the door and climbs inside.

I round the truck and get in beside her, turning on the ignition and pointing my vehicle toward San Luis Obispo. We're running a few minutes late, but I can make it up on the highway.

Marilee fiddles with her wedding band, spinning it round and round her finger.

"You know"—I say, tapping my thumbs to the beat of some country song that's popped on the radio, set at such a low volume I can't discern more than that—"if you decide to start your own cake decorating business, you could set your own hours. Aren't you sick of the early mornings? You used to be such a night owl."

"I was." She straightens. "But things change. We adapt as we need to."

There's something serious in her voice. I give her a sharp look before redirecting my attention to the road. "What's going on, Lee?"

After a few long moments, she finally answers me. "I've thought a lot about it, weighed all the options in my head. And yes, I do love decorating cakes—"

"Love seems rather a weak word to describe the joy that seeps from your very pores when you're doing it, but go on."

"Okay, Mr. Dramatic." She huffs a laugh, but I can tell there's something staid in it. Marilee is definitely in her head about something. "Yes, I love it, but I'm afraid it won't always pay the bills."

"Won't know unless you try. Go part time at the bakery. Heck, quit the bakery altogether. I make enough for us to live on for the next year. Spend time focusing on you, Lee. On *your* dreams."

"It's just not practical. Marla's got a solid business plan that's been working for her for thirty years. It's so seamless, even *I* can't mess it up."

"I hate it when you talk about my best friend that way." I try for a tease, but apparently, it falls flat, because it doesn't so much as lift the corners of her beautiful mouth.

"The fact is, we won't be married forever."

Geez, Lee, shoot me in the heart. "No, but—"

"And so if I quit the bakery and try to start my own thing, there's no guarantee whoever does buy the bakery will hire me back. And then where does that leave me? There isn't anything else I'm good at, nothing else I'd want to do for a job. Even selling the house to Blake and Lucy wouldn't make me enough money to live on indefinitely. I'd either have to do something I hated or move. And I'm not moving."

"Hey." I reach for her hand, and after a few moments, she gives it to me. I loop our fingers together and give her what I hope is a friendly squeeze. "You're basing your entire decision on what might happen. On the predication that you're going to fail. But what if you don't fail? What if instead, you fly?"

Marilee's hand trembles in mine before she pulls it away and tucks it into her lap. "It's hard to fly with a broken wing." Her words are soft, but they break me all the same. I want to pull this truck over to the side of the road. Want to grab her gently by the shoulders and wrap her into the tightest hug, to shelter her from all the doubts and worries and lies that life has thrown at her, from all the arrows being flung her way.

But they're coming from inside of her, and I don't know how to stop them. I don't know how to heal her. Probably, I can't. All I can do is reassure her that her brokenness doesn't scare me. That we're all a little broken, but that healing is possible.

Before I can find the words, she continues. "A few minutes ago, I told Marla I wanted to buy the bakery. All I need from you is to cosign the loan, but I will make sure I don't ever miss a payment." She blows out a breath. "I'm going to establish a life for myself, one that doesn't require anyone else to rescue me."

One that doesn't require any risk on her part, she means. That doesn't require her to ask anyone else to step into that risk with her. If only she knew that, if I could, I'd grab her hand and leap in with her head first, no questions asked.

Because that's what love does.

But love also has to let go. And maybe that's what I'm supposed to do. Maybe that's how I can love Marilee best.

I just wish I knew one way or the other.

MARILEE

I can barely keep my eyes open.

But since I'm still currently in charge of two small children, sleep is not an option.

Scarlett and Ryder pump their legs as they swing higher and higher over Jordan's grassy backyard. Scarlett yells out encouragements for Ryder to keep up with her. They've been going at it for a full thirty minutes after finishing their dinner at a breakneck speed because, as Scarlett said, "We only have a little more time to play before Mommy comes to get me. Hurry, hurry!"

And sweet little Ryder didn't mind being bossed one bit. He tossed back that lasagna like it was gourmet and followed April's daughter out the back door. I cleaned up their plates and set the pasta back in the oven on warm, ready for whenever Jordan gets home from his late-night working. He had to make up time after our meeting with Sam Granger ate into his work time earlier today. Thankfully, the meeting went smoothly, and we all feel pretty prepared for the court date that's three short weeks from tomorrow.

After cleanup, I join the kids outside, watching them play

while plying myself with coffee to try to stay awake. Although honestly, I'm not sure I could sleep with everything going on inside my head.

Like the sight of Amy Montrose and Jordan together earlier today. The woman clearly adores him. She's cute and sweet, and they made a striking pair standing beside each other. And I didn't like the way my stomach twisted watching them together.

Or the fact that being married to me is keeping Jordan from being with someone with real potential.

Ugh. *Go away, you obnoxious thoughts.* Shifting into the cushions of the resin wicker chair on Jordan's back patio, I soak in the warmth of the mug in my hands and the blanket covering my lower half.

"Knock, knock," comes a voice from behind.

I glance over my shoulder to find April, dressed not in her standard fare of yoga pants and an oversized shirt but slacks and a smart blue blouse that matches her bright eyes. "Hey—" I start, but am interrupted by a high-pitched squeal of "Mommy!" as a blur races past me and flings herself in April's arms.

April kisses Scarlett's head and gives her a hug. "Hi, Scar. Were you good for Ms. Marilee?"

Scarlett tilts her head up and nods emphatically. "Of course I was. She makes the best cookies and I wanted some."

"Oh yeah?" April's eyes laugh. Behind her, the porch light flickers on as dusk settles in. "And did she give you some?"

I hold up my mug. "Guilty as charged. Though I probably would have even if she was naughty."

Scarlett's face brightens. "Really?"

"Don't give her ideas, Mare." April taps Scarlett's freckled nose. "You ready to go?"

"Oh, can I please please pleeeeeeease have thirty more

minutes?" April's daughter folds her hands in front of her face like she's pleading for mercy in front of the queen.

April tucks a stray blonde curl behind Scarlett's ear. "I'm sure Ms. Marilee has lots to do—"

"Ms. Marilee does not." I pat the chair next to me. "Feel free to stay. I've got some lasagna and garlic bread left if you want to eat dinner and let the kiddos play a little longer."

"Twist my arm. Anytime I get the chance to eat your food is a no-brainer."

"And here I thought you enjoyed my company too." I make a face, sticking out my tongue slightly.

"So we can stay?" Scarlett bounces on her tiptoes.

"For a bit."

Pumping her hands in the air, Scarlett runs back to tell Ryder the good news.

I pop up from my seat, place my coffee on the small side table between the pair of wicker chairs, and pat the other one. "Sit. I'll grab you food."

"I shouldn't let you, but I'm exhausted from that drive. I forgot how nuts the city is."

"No problem." I shuffle inside and serve up some lasagna for April before returning to my seat.

"Thank you," she says as I hand her the steaming plate. She takes an inhale and closes her eyes. "This smells like heaven. I've been going all day on a protein bar."

"Poor thing." I settle back into my seat as she digs into her food. "Remind me—why did you go to San Francisco?"

April stops with a forkful of food hanging midair. She shoves it in and says around it, "Nuffin' important."

Hmmm. April's not the sort to hold back. She's more than willing to tell you all sorts of intimate details about her life—from Scarlett's birth story to the shocking reality of postpartum laughing and her bladder's inability to maintain decorum.

Other than not letting anyone read the books burning a hole in her computer—something I don't entirely blame her for, given she's still honing her craft—there's only one subject not fit for public consumption, or even her friends' consumption.

Scarlett's dad.

I'm not sure even Kelsey, her best friend, knows who he is. We only know that April came home from her freshman year of college pregnant and that she and the dad weren't together.

End of story.

I've never pried, but maybe here, in this small setting, she might open up if she knows I care. I pick up my coffee mug again and drum my fingers along the ceramic red surface. "Did your trip have anything to do with Scarlett's dad?"

Her head swivels toward me quick. "What?" April blinks like she's surprised. Then, "No."

The kids' laughter and an airplane flying overhead fill in the cracks of silence between us.

There I go, overstepping again. Seems to be my lot in life lately. "I'm sorry, April. I shouldn't have asked."

She sighs and puts her plate on the table, turning to face me. "It's okay. I just...I don't really talk about him."

"I shouldn't have been nosy." I press my lips together. "But I know how hard it is to suffer in silence, and I want you to know...I'm here if you ever want to talk."

"Thanks, Mare." Her slacks expose her ankles as she pulls her legs up and hugs them to her chest. "I haven't spoken to him since before Scarlett was born. So no, my trip had nothing to do with him."

"Was he a jerk when he found out about Scarlett?" My blood runs hot at the idea that someone wouldn't want to know the precious, spunky girl playing in the yard in front of me.

"No," she says, biting her lower lip. "He just...wasn't in a place to be a dad." There's something in the way she says it that tells me I'm not getting the whole story. That she's holding back some very crucial information. But that's okay. I feel honored she's sharing even this much.

"I'm sorry." I wait a beat before asking, "Do you still love him?" Maybe that's why I've never seen her so much as look at a guy with more than appreciation for his outward appearance.

"I didn't say that." April straightens, sets her legs back on the ground. "Let's just say that fiction is better than reality sometimes."

I reach out, waiting until she grabs my hand. I squeeze before releasing her hold. "Sometimes, I'd say you're right."

She eyes me. "But sometimes...maybe it's the same. Or even better than fiction."

"What do you mean?"

"Your case might be the exception."

My nose scrunches. "I'd hardly call my life a fairy tale."

"Maybe not your life with Donny. But you and Jordan..."

"Are just friends." I say it with finality—determined to believe every word.

"Girl, I'm not blind. I saw that kiss."

"You and the whole town," I mutter under my breath, taking a sip of the coffee. I blanch at its bitterness. Did I forget to add sugar? "We did it for Constance's sake. You should have heard what she was saying to him."

"Mmm hmm. I know that's what you're telling yourself. I'm on that text thread with the girls, remember? I've heard your protests loud and clear." April waggles her eyebrows, which lift up under her wispy bangs. "But sometimes I wonder if you are lying to yourself. Let me ask you this—what did you feel when you kissed him?"

"Nothing."

"I say this with all the love in my heart, dear, sweet, Marilee. That's a bald-faced lie."

"No, it's not." My breath leaves my lungs. I squeeze my eyes shut and shake my head. "It can't be. Because that would mean..."

"That you might have feelings for your best friend? Yep."

My eyes pop open as my heart pounds out an erratic rhythm. "I can't, though."

"And just why not?" April studies me. "You *deserve* happiness."

"I...I know." But do I? "But so does he." And with me, he wouldn't have it. Not long-term.

"I don't understand, Mare. You are one of the best people I know. He would be *so* lucky to end up with you."

My lips tremble, and my eyes burn. "It wouldn't last."

Stars make their appearance, dancing diamonds clustered like heavenly necklaces strung in the sky. Sometimes I wonder if Mom and Dad can look down from heaven. If Mom's cheering me on. If Dad's still disappointed in me. If they see the mess I've made and wonder—or know—if things will ever change in my life.

"Mare, I'm going to tell you something I wish I'd thought more about eight years ago."

I can only assume she means when she was pregnant with Scarlett. "Okay."

"Back then, I made a decision based on what-ifs. I can't go back and change that decision now. But sometimes...I wonder if I should have done more to be sure." She glances out at the yard, at her daughter, who is crowing at the top of the play structure, arms raised in the air, triumphant and full of joy. "To be honest, it haunts me sometimes. And I'd hate for the same thing to happen to you."

"I...I don't know how to be sure." Because I thought I was sure with Donny, and look how that turned out.

"Okay, maybe not *sure*. But open yourself to the possibility that you could be wrong. And ask yourself how that might change things between you and Jordan...and whether you want it to."

April's words haven't left me all week.

Through a meeting at the bank. Amid flour sifting and decorating a cake to look like a Minion. When playing with Ryder in the evenings.

And in the middle of the night, when I wake suddenly from a nightmare and glance over at the world's most uncomfortable wooden chair, where Jordan has taken to sleeping.

It's got to be even worse than the couch. But I haven't said a word about it, and neither has he. I'm not sure of his reasons for the silence, but as for me?

I'm scared of what will happen if I invite him in.

Not just into the bed—but into my life as more than a friend.

And yet, April's words swirl... *"I wonder if I should have done more to be sure."*

Now it's Friday night and I've just finished tucking sweet Ryder into bed, reading to him from his Avengers storybook for what feels like the hundredth time—and I'm sick of hearing myself think. More than that, I miss my best friend. Because I can feel it. We're both in our heads about all of this. The last week, since that kiss, has felt like walking a tightrope, neither of us willing to advance or meet in the middle. We've just stood on either end, staring at each other, constantly trying to stay balanced and not fall splat to the ground.

Snicking Ryder's door closed behind me, I inhale deeply, willing myself the courage to walk back into the living room to face Jordan instead of retreating to the bedroom and tucking in for another night of loneliness. Finally, I wipe my sweaty palms on my black lounge pants and pad in my slouchy socks toward the kitchen.

Jordan's back is to me as he cleans up from dinner, a black dish towel slung over one shoulder, hat sitting backwards on his head. He's got some Taylor Swift playing from his phone and is singing along softly, shaking it off lyrically and with his hips.

My chest loosens. Because this is my best friend as I'm used to seeing him.

I giggle, and he turns, eyebrows lifted as he continues to sing. He grabs the towel from his shoulder and dries off his soapy hands, flinging it dramatically back to the counter as he busts out moves Justin Timberlake would be proud of. Then, at a pause in the music, he tilts his head. "Dance battle?"

"Dance battle," I confirm.

Grinning, he flicks up the volume on his phone—Ryder's white noise machine will ensure our shenanigans don't wake him—and he flourishes his hands at me.

Guess I'm going first.

And look, I'm no Taylor or Shakira or Beyoncé. And I can't sing worth a flip. But I do at least have the gift of rhythm. I'm fairly certain I look ridiculous as I shake my hips and shimmy around Jordan, whose eyes laugh at me while he cups his mouth and whoops.

I take a break, arms folded back as I lean against the counter. "Top that."

He taps the tip of my nose. "Easy." Then he walks it back like he's Michael Jackson and adds a little robot action in there.

I pretend to be chill, but on the inside, I'm lighting up like the Christmas tree that's *still* in the living room. There's nothing like this feeling, laughing and being ridiculous with someone who just gets you.

When he's done, swiping off his shoulders like his moves were "no big deal," I jump back in, and so does he, until we're three songs deep and both belly laughing at how we've devolved into utterly ridiculous moves like the shopping cart, the sprinkler, and my personal fave, the chicken dance.

Finally, Jordan flips off the music and removes his hat, fanning himself. "Okay, I needed that."

"Me too." I pull my hair from my bun. It's sweaty at the base of my neck, and I comb it out with my fingers before tossing it back up.

I feel his eyes on me the whole time, burning in their intensity.

And suddenly, the levity's gone.

I swallow hard. "Rough week?" I shouldn't have to ask. Normally, I'd know, because we'd have eaten every lunch together, hung out more than once. But other than our drive to San Luis Obispo on Monday, we haven't spent more than ten minutes alone together. Not unless you count sleeping the same room.

But since we're not both awake for most of that, I don't.

He runs a hand through his hair before setting his hat on the kitchen counter. "Just busy."

"Did you ever hear back from Mitchell McGraff?"

"Yeah, I think I'm going to go check out the tents and stay overnight the weekend after next if that's okay." He pauses, his brow furrowed like he wants to say more. But then he shakes his head. "How about you? Seemed like you and Ryder had a good afternoon? Something about a scooter race?"

I laugh. "Yeah, he thought he could beat me around the block." I make a face. "He was right. How'd you know about that?"

"He told me while you were making dinner."

"Right." I nearly burnt the chicken earlier, too distracted by watching him push Ryder on the swings out back through the window over the kitchen table. The sight had my heart doing all sorts of naughty things like squeezing and thumping and tap dancing. "Well, Ryder is a doll, as always. But fair warning—he said he's over the scooter and wants you to teach him how to ride a bike now. So watch out. The request is coming."

"Oh, it already came. He'll be a tyrant on wheels, that one." Jordan chuckles, then tilts his head, studying me. "And the bakery? How's that going?"

"Fine. Marla hasn't really had time to walk me through the business plan or anything."

"Gotcha. Oh hey, I've got some free time Monday if you want to go sign the loan documents at the bank."

"That might work. Pete was still drawing them up, I think." But I'm not in a rush. Because ever since I said yes to Marla, I've had an unexplainable pit in my stomach. Probably just nerves. Change is hard. Nerves would make sense.

"Just say the word when you need me." Jordan rounds the couch and plops down, reaching for the remote. Maybe he wants his privacy. I should go... But no. That will only make things more awkward.

And how am I supposed to follow April's advice—to explore the possibility of *more*—if I'm constantly retreating from what's uncomfortable?

So, I sit down beside Jordan.

He wiggles the remote. "You wanna pick?"

"Sure." Our fingers brush—I shiver—as he hands it over. I navigate to a movie I didn't get a chance to watch over Christmas this year. Sandra Bullock and Bill Pullman's faces smile at each other on the screen. "This okay?"

"You kidding?" He stands, grabs a few blankets, and offers me one. "I'm always in a *While You Were Sleeping* mood."

"Ha ha. And thanks," I say as I take a fuzzy red blanket.

Tucking it around my legs, I shift and lean back against the pillow on the opposite side of the couch from him, stretching out my legs so my feet sit against his thigh. "Me too."

"Hey, I'm serious. It's a good movie. Your mom's favorite, right?"

"Mmm hmm." He's so good at remembering those kinds of details. Pressing my lips together, I tap the side of the remote and lower it to my lap without starting the movie. "Other than baking, watching movies with her was my favorite thing to do. She knew every line by heart, and soon, I did too. We'd take turns saying things in silly voices. Sigh at the swoony parts. It was the best."

"She was really great."

"She was." I sigh, the ache of missing her coming swift and strong.

Jordan sets his hand absently on the top of my right foot, which is buried under the blanket and my sock.

And yet, I feel the electric pulse of his touch through all of the material.

How did this happen? He's touched me so many times, just like this, right here on this very couch. So how did I never feel this before?

"You're so much like her, Lee." His soothing palm moves back and forth over my foot. "So sweet, so caring. So maternal, taking care of everyone around you. Ryder has been so lucky to have you as a mom, even if it's only temporary."

A tear slips unbidden down my cheek. Then another.

His hand stills. "Oh no, what did I say to make you cry?"

I backhand away the moisture. "Nothing. No, it's not you."

"What then?"

And this is the moment—the one where I make a decision of my own. Not necessarily to know anything for sure, but to open up. To tell Jordan just how broken I am. To see what he does with that information.

My insides quake.

"It's just that..." I blow out a breath.

"Hey," he says, looking at me with a concerned ripple in his brow. "Come here."

Jordan opens his arms and, weak woman that I am, I go. I sit right beside this man, my legs tucked to one side while I snuggle into him on the other. He's solid and warm, and he holds me while tucking his blanket over us both. Then oh so gently, he tilts my chin up and watches me with his tender blue gaze. "What's wrong, Lee? Talk to me."

I am so touched by the absolute love radiating from this man that I can't speak for several long moments. But finally, the words come as I set my head into the crook of his arm. "I've wanted nothing more my whole life than to be a mom. To be to someone else what my mom was to me—a safe space to nurture and grow them, to help them reach their potential. To pour out my love into a love that will never die, even when I do." Tears fall onto Jordan's T-shirt. I press my fingertips into them, feel the beating heart beneath his chest. "And Ryder... Well, he's the most special little boy. I'm so grateful you've let me be in his life."

"We're both grateful you're willing to be here. More grateful than you know."

I nod. "But like you said. It's temporary."

"Our marriage contract, maybe. But not your place in his life."

"Jay, eventually you're going to get married for real." Maybe to someone like Amy... "And then I'll have to step aside, to just be a fun auntie. And I will happily do that, for both of your sakes. Because your happiness means the world to me."

"Lee..."

My breath shakes as I exhale. I run my finger along the soft cotton of Jordan's shirt. "The fact is, Jay, that Ryder is probably the only kid I'll ever be a mom to. And I'm just determined to enjoy every moment that I get in that role."

There. I said it. Admitted the truth in a roundabout way. Though, if I know Jordan, he will dig deeper until he knows the whole truth.

I brace, waiting.

Finally, the questions come. "You're going to find someone else, Lee. Someone who you can love fully, who will love you the way that jerk never could. Just because one man disparaged his marriage vow to cherish you doesn't mean all men would do the same."

Is that what he thinks? My hand flattens against his chest, and I push up until I can look him in the eyes. "I know that, Jordan. You're proof that there are honorable men out there."

He blinks at me. "Then why do you say you'll never be a mom again?"

Here we go. "I...I don't know that I can actually have kids, Jay. I've already had three miscarriages." The words hurt leaving my mouth, just the way they did each time I had to speak them to Donny, then again to Lucy, the only other person who knows about my hidden horror.

"Lee." He breathes out the word like a prayer as his hand rises to cup my face, his thumb stroking along my cheekbone as his eyes melt into sympathy. No, it's more than that. It's empathy, like he's feeling the pain right along with me. "I'm so sorry."

"Me too." More words get stuck in my throat, but I don't need them. I think Jordan just knows. "Donny..." Tears come again, hot and fast. Ugh. I hate wasting even more tears on that jerk. "I'm sorry. I don't want to cry."

"Hey. It's okay, Lee." He holds me again. "You have a right

to cry. You lost something precious, and I'm sure Donny didn't make it easier on you."

"He said..." My heart wrenches with the memories. "That it wasn't a big deal. He didn't know why I couldn't just get back up and act like things were fine. Why I couldn't be fun anymore. Why I couldn't be intimate—" Oh sheesh, why did I say that?

I can feel Jordan's hand curl into a fist against my arm. "I never understood why..." He trails off, leaving me to wonder what he was going to say.

But honestly, I'm so tired of the wondering. I'm tired of everything right now except how it feels to be right here, in his arms. To feel understood and loved, whether as a friend or... maybe more. My brain decides now is the time to shut off. After the week I've had, I allow myself the luxury of sinking into Jordan, shutting my eyes, and falling into oblivion.

I wake up again—maybe it's been minutes, maybe hours— tucked against Jordan's chest as he carries me down the darkened hallway, nudging open the bedroom door with his foot and shutting it again behind us before depositing me gently on the soft mattress of his queen-sized bed. I can't see his face, but I feel the covers going over me, hear the warm intake of his breath as he smooths my hair out of my face and whispers, "You deserved better, Lee."

Then he places the gentlest of kisses against my forehead before starting to retreat.

And I'm not thinking fully—the edges of my mind still groggy with sleep—but I do know one thing.

I don't want to be alone right now.

So before he can leave, I catch him by the hand. "Stay."

He's quiet for a moment, and I wonder if I've drifted back to sleep. But then comes his soft reply: "I'll be right over there."

I assume he's pointing to the sorry excuse for a chair in the corner.

"No." My voice is thick with sleep, but I force determination into my tone and give his hand a tug. "Here. With me."

He squats beside me and a hint of moonlight through the window shows his eyes glittering back in the dark. "You sure?"

I answer him with a squeeze and another tug before rolling over to make space for him.

It takes a full minute, but then the mattress sinks behind me and it's warm and toasty under these covers, like bread out of the oven. Reaching behind me, I pull his arm around my waist. Then I finally drift off again, not knowing anything *for sure* except how Jordan Carmichael makes me feel.

Safe.

JORDAN

What did Marilee mean by reaching for me last night? Pulling me into the bed, against her, letting me hold her? And before that, opening up to me about her miscarriages, when it would have been easier to simply watch a movie together and slip back into the old patterns of our friendship.

The thought went round and round in my head all night, invading my dreams. In fact, I thought maybe I had dreamed the whole thing—until that moment when I woke up.

I was still tangled up with Marilee, my palm flat against her stomach. And my mouth... Shoot. My mouth somehow found its way to the bare skin where her shoulder meets her perfect neck. Those hazy first moments after waking tested the limits of my self-control. It took everything in me not to press a kiss there against the vein pulsing just within reach—especially when Marilee emitted the softest, sexiest little sigh and snuggled back against me.

Thanks only to my years of resistance to this woman and her charms, I was finally able to slip from that bed and into the shocking cold air of the room beyond the cave of warmth under the comforter, where I could have stayed forever.

Now, a half hour later, I'm beating my body into further submission by jogging down the boardwalk, trying to outrun all of the voices in my head.

Finally, I stop running.

Interlocking my fingers behind my head, I allow the deep breaths to come as my ribcage expands and contracts. A fierce wind blows up from the water, cooling my heated skin but making me shiver in my sweat-soaked, dry-fit tee. The waves are more tumultuous than usual this morning, a perfect reflection of the churning I feel inside.

I turn to head up the walkway between The Bluestocking Bookshop and Olive Paradise, neither of which will be open for a few more hours. I haven't passed many people on the boardwalk this morning, just the occasional jogger or walker out for an early morning stroll. But I know one person who will be awake. One person whose advice I trust.

Fifteen minutes later, I'm knocking gently on my parents' front door with a box of donuts from Al's Grocery in my hands. Mom opens up, smiling brightly at me, a book in her hand. She looks even better than she did a few days ago when I last visited. "Jordan! What a nice surprise. Come in."

"Morning, Mom." I lean down and kiss her cheek. This morning she smells like the cinnamon that's in her daily morning cup of chai tea. "Here. I brought breakfast."

"Your father will be happy."

I follow her into the kitchen, where she slips the box onto the round four-seater table along with her book and pads to the coffee maker, not even asking if I'll have a mug.

"Is he awake?" I kind of hope not. I don't want him involved in this conversation. Knowing him, he'll just tell me to man up—like that's the answer to every problem. *Man up. Stuff your feelings away. Better yet, don't feel at all.*

"Still asleep." Mom pours me a steaming cup of coffee,

which she keeps on constant refill for my dad—who likes to add a little Irish whiskey to his when she's not looking. She places it in front of me before sitting and folding her hands on the worn oak table. "Now. What's on your mind, sweetheart?"

"Can't a guy just bring his mother donuts?"

"Of course. But you've got that look about you."

"What look is that?"

"The same one you had when you were six and couldn't find the G.I. Joe I'd bought for your birthday."

"I don't remember that." I take a sip of the coffee, hot and black just like I prefer it. It burns going down.

"Mmm. Well, I do." Mom pulls her mug of tea closer. Her hands look a bit swollen this morning. "Poor thing. You had looked on your own for days and couldn't locate it. Finally decided to ask for help."

"And let me guess. You used your amazing mom instinct and found it in a few minutes."

She laughs. "Yes, but only because I'd moved it from the coffee table into a drawer when I was cleaning and then forgot to move it back to the toy bin. You couldn't have known."

"Guess I would have known if I'd asked."

"You were six."

"Sounds like I haven't changed much if I've got the same look about me now." I sit back in my chair and absently rub my left forearm.

"A boy always needs his mama, no matter how old he is. At least, I like to think so." She winks over the top of her drink as she takes a sip before lowering it. "Now, tell me what's going on. Is it the custody case?"

"No, that's all going well. As well as can be expected, anyway. We're on track for court, and my attorney is confident our angle will produce the desired result. He fully expects the judge to throw out Larry and Constance's petition."

"Good. The job, then?" Her lips quirk into the tiniest of smiles.

I think she very well knows I'm not here for something career-related, but I indulge her anyway. "No."

"Ah. A matter of the heart, then."

I sigh, not even bothering to answer.

"You still haven't told her how you feel, I take it?"

"Not in so many words." I stare at the lines of wooden grain in the table.

"Just in that kiss?"

My head jerks up. "You know about that?"

"Had to hear about it from the ladies at book club, thank you very much. My own son keeping me in the dark. Shameful." Another wink and smile. "It sounds like the two of you are moving toward something good."

"Maybe."

"You don't sound sure."

"I'm not." The refrigerator hums in the still morning air. "Things were really weird between us the last week. But last night, we finally seemed like ourselves again. She even opened up to me about something she never has before. Something that happened during her last marriage." When she told me about the miscarriages, my heart broke for her—for all the hurt she's experienced, even more than I ever knew. And when I heard Donny's reaction to their losses, well, I wanted to find the man and beat him to a pulp. A really, really bloody pulp.

So much for being a peacemaker.

"It feels like she's letting you in more?"

"I don't know. Maybe." I hesitate, and Mom's eyebrows go up as I continue. "She asked me to, um...to hold her while she slept last night."

"Oh my."

"Nothing happened, Mom."

"On the contrary." She gives me a knowing look. "I'd say something very significant happened."

"You think?" I scratch behind my ear. "I honestly can't figure it out. And I don't want to ask, to put another wedge between us. Because this week gave me a picture of what things would be like if I did lose her."

"And yet, didn't last night give you a picture of what you could gain?"

Yes. "Waking up with her in my arms was...indescribable, really. If I got to do that every day, I would consider myself the luckiest guy in the world."

"Jordan, I don't know exactly what Marilee told you about her past, but the fact she trusted you with that information speaks volumes. And then, right after that, to ask you to stay with her all night long? Sleeping is a very vulnerable position, but she still wanted you there."

"Yeah, but what does it *mean*?"

"I can't be sure, of course, but I believe that if she doesn't love you already, maybe she is at least open to the idea."

My heart leap frogs to my throat. "Really?"

"I'd say so." Mom leans forward and pats my hand. "And her reaching out last night... Perhaps that was her way of making a move toward you. But my guess is, she's not going to advance again. She's waiting for you."

"To do what?"

"To make the next move. The ball's in your court, son."

"All right." Mom knows I love a good sports analogy, so I indulge her. "But what if I overshoot?"

"Maybe don't go for the Hail Mary right away." She shrugs. "Take smaller shots. They'll add up."

When I just blink back at her, Mom cracks another smile, lines spiderwebbing out from her eyes. "Woo her, Jordan. Don't come right out and tell her you love her, but show her in several small ways. See if you can slowly start to get her to see you in a different light."

And suddenly, it's oh so clear.

It's like Kareem Abdul Jabbar's sky hook, during which he'd back his way down the court until he was close enough to shoot. With consistency and precision, he racked up the points for his team time and time again.

And it's time for me to create my signature move too.

"You're right."

"Of course I am. I'm your mother." She drains the rest of her chai. "Now, would you like some ideas?"

"Uh, *yeah*." I pull out my phone and open the Notes app, my thumbs hovering over the screen. "I'm all ears, Mom."

All ears—and all in.

The fear is still there, niggling at the back of my mind. The *what-if*s are strong, but I do my best to dull them. To ignore them. To remind myself that I can't live in the friend zone forever.

And that *this* just might be my ticket out.

MARILEE

It's official—I don't know what's gotten into Jordan.

But the past week, he's leaned hard into the fake husband role even more than the best friend role. Though come to think of it...

It doesn't feel *fake*.

The flowers he left on the kitchen counter Monday with a sweet note didn't feel fake.

The picnic he surprised me with at our special spot during lunch on Wednesday after cosigning loan documents at the bank didn't feel fake—especially when he casually took my hand as we ate and I told him about my fears and worries in taking over for Marla...and he reassured me that I had exactly what it took to do this and do it well.

As for the foot rub he's given me every night as we watch a different romantic comedy—many of them about friends who decide to date? Those haven't felt fake either.

And then there's the way we've slipped into a routine every evening of going to bed at the same time and talking until one of us (usually me) is yawning.

Every morning, somehow, I wake up in his arms.

It's driving me crazy. Because it can't all be in my head, right? Things have felt different between us since he came home from a run last weekend.

Sure, some things are the same as they've always been—like how he seeks me out just to tell me something funny that happened at work that day, or to ask my thoughts on the latest kids' TV show and whether it's age appropriate for Ryder.

But there are these little touches, little gazes he's given me, little ways our interactions strike a match inside me, leaving me warm and buzzing. It feels like things are shifting.

And I'm not going to lie—that still scares the sugar out of me.

But...I'm not running, either. I'm doing what April suggested, testing the waters, letting the possibilities sit and stay a while before automatically dismissing them. I told him one of my deepest secrets, and he's still here. In fact, ever since that conversation, he seems to be...pursuing me.

It's all a bit heady.

Which is why I'm, once again, baking—if one can call Saturday morning pancakes "baking."

"Lee-Lee, when will breakfast be ready?" Ryder's head pops up over the kitchen island, where I'm nearly done throwing the batter together and preheating the griddle. He's in his tight little Superman pajamas, complete with a Velcroed cape. "I'm starving."

"You are, huh?" I boop him on the head with the clean spatula, which makes him giggle. "Your dad should be home from his run any minute, and then we'll eat. You can keep watching *Paw Patrol* for now."

"'K." He runs back and tumble-flies over the back of the couch, unpausing the show, which plays at a medium volume.

I roll up the sleeves of my blue hoodie—well, Jordan's hoodie that I stole in addition to a pair of his flannel pants rolled ten times because I desperately need to do laundry—and stir the batter before opening the fridge for more ingredients, humming the *Paw Patrol* theme song to myself.

The front door squeaks open, and Ryder says, "Hi, Daddy!"

Jordan's baritone rumbles, "Morning, bud. Oh, I love this episode."

"Yup. Marshall's the bestest pup. Watch how he shoots that water!"

"Love how they're working together to save the day."

"Me too."

Smiling at their natural interaction, I reach for a container of blueberries, a bag of chocolate chips, a can of whipped cream, and a jar of chocolate sauce I made up last night from scratch. "Morning," I call as I close the fridge door—and nearly have a heart attack.

Because Jordan is standing beside the couch with no shirt on.

Biscuits and gravy. He's stretching his arm over his chest while watching colorfully clothed dogs on TV, and um, what is happening to my insides? I have seen Jordan in a bathing suit plenty of times. More than I can count. More than I remember.

But this? I'll never be able to get the image of his smooth, taut skin—just a smattering of dark hair surrounding his well-formed pectorals—out of my brain. His torso is streaked with sweat, joggers slung low on his hips, and his muscles are the perfect balance between ripped beefcake and barely there. Why are my eyes drawn to the veins in his tan forearms as points his elbow toward the sky and stretches his triceps?

The container of blueberries drops from my hands, and I yelp as the fruit scatters all over the floor.

"Whoa there." Jordan rushes to help as I set the other food on the counter and squat down to scoop berries into the flimsy plastic container.

"Sorry," I murmur.

"No big deal." He gently gathers fruit in his hands and helps me refill the container. Despite the sweat, he smells like ocean air and forest. His hand brushes mine as we close the container together. Then our eyes connect, and it's like he sees me for the first time as his gaze sweeps down over me. His irises seem to snap and darken. "What are you wearing?"

Is it just my imagination, or does his voice go all husky at the question?

I glance down at my sweatshirt. Well, *his* sweatshirt. "Um, I hope you don't mind, but almost all of my clothes are dirty, so I rummaged around in your dresser and borrowed these." And darn it, there's a splatter of flour on the front. I rub at it furiously. "Sorry, I'll make sure to clean this before I return it."

Then I'm breathless as he places his hand over mine, effectively stilling it.

"I don't mind." It's all he says, but the meaning pulses palpable between us.

Not just *I don't mind you borrowing my clothes*, but also...*I don't mind your mess.*

I glance away, swallow. "Thanks," I whisper. Then I stand, blueberries in hand, and set them on the island. The batter's ready so I ladle some onto the greased griddle. The sizzle pops and settles. I tuck an errant strand of hair behind my ear. "This will be ready in about ten minutes if you want to grab a shower before breakfast." And look at me, I manage to say it all without sounding like a nervous teenager.

"I'm okay." He hitches a hip against the island and reaches for a stack of mail.

"Oh." And I can't help but stare at the contours of his chest —a chest that has been hiding. Or rather, that I've never really noticed until now. "All right."

He peeks up at me, a tiny smile flicking over his mouth, and I avert my eyes back to my pancakes.

"Yikes," I say, pulling three nearly blackened pancakes off the griddle. Clearly, I wasn't paying enough attention. *Wonder why.* "Um, well, if you want to throw a shirt on, I'm sure you'd be more comfortable."

"I'm okay," he says again, the grin growing wider. "But if it's too distracting for *you*…"

"What?" I release a garbled laugh as I spray the griddle again and ladle out more batter. "Noooo. It's fine. I just want *you* to be comfortable."

"Great." Aaaaaand he proceeds to stand there some more, shirtless, his manly chest a glowing beacon for my eyes. This is getting ridiculous. "Well, um, would you mind washing the berries and putting both them and the chocolate chips into bowls? I thought we'd do a little pancake bar." And if he's at the sink, he's behind me. Out of sight, out of mind. Problem solved.

"Sure." He sets down the mail and rounds the counter, taking the bag of chocolate chips and the berries with him, his eyes glittering with amusement. I can feel the heat rising in my cheeks. Fine, maybe he's onto me, but so what? I can find him attractive. He's my husband. Fake husband, but husband all the same.

But for how long?

Exactly three hundred-forty-six more days. But who's counting?

I pull three golden pancakes from the griddle—much better—and add more to cook while cartoons drown out the doubting voice in my head. The sound of rushing water streams in and out of my consciousness as I give all of my focus to the pancakes. Finally, all of the batter is gone, and I've got a stack of perfect little pancakes, save the first three I ruined. Grabbing the dirty batter bowl, I turn toward the sink—and the edge of the bowl smacks right into Jordan's bare chest.

"Oof." One of his hands reaches out to steady my arm, and the other takes the bowl from me, depositing it into the sink. "You all right?" His thumb skates down my covered forearm to my hand.

Goosebumps are left in its wake.

"Yeah." I'm frozen at his touch. A shudder works its way up my entire body.

One eyebrow arches, and Jordan reaches for the zipper of the hoodie I'm wearing, which is hanging open, exposing a stained black tank underneath. He clasps the metal ends of the hoodie zipper together and slowly, achingly, runs it upward, all the while keeping his gaze steady on mine. When the zipper's to the top, he gives the hoodie strings a tiny tug. "There."

"What..." I swallow. "Jay, what are you doing?" Because suddenly, I have to know. Have to understand if I'm going crazy. If I'm imagining things.

But he just shrugs like it's nothing and says, "You seemed a little chilly." Then he steps around me, calls to Ryder, and turns to me with all the innocence in the world. "Ready to eat?"

And all I can do is nod dumbly, more confused than ever.

"Jay, what are you doing?"

Marilee's question echoes in my mind throughout breakfast, where Ryder enthusiastically devours three pancakes drenched in syrup and chocolate while passionately defending Captain America as the superior superhero. He talks for fifteen solid minutes, his eyes sparkling with excitement, and Marilee engages with him wholeheartedly, her laughter bubbling out like sweet sunshine.

But my focus drifts, lost in a web of emotions.

I catch glimpses of the confusion she wears like a lovely pendant—her little smile when I asked if she was ready felt muted, a flicker that didn't reach her eyes. The slight crease above her brow tells me something is off. She's wrestling with worries, perhaps even with the unspoken *something* that simmers between us.

I've been trying to heed Mom's advice: take it slow, don't scare her off with the force of my feelings. But every day spent as *just friends* gnaws at me. I can sense her shifting too. She might finally see me as more than the boy I used to be—after all, her reaction to me without a shirt was unmistakable.

Before breakfast, because I really *don't* want to make her uncomfortable, I hastily pulled on a shirt, and I noticed the flicker of relief that washed over her... And I'm not sure what that means. So maybe I'm just as confused as she is.

This is getting stupid, and maybe it's time to take a leap, to risk everything for a chance at something genuine between us. To make things ultra clear about how I feel about Marilee Moffitt.

After Ryder dashes off to play in his room, I seize my moment, speaking before Marilee can escape the lingering suspense between us. "Hey, about that glamping site I'm checking out next weekend..." I say, knowing that it also happens to be Valentine's Day, a detail that adds sweet, sticky weight to my invitation.

"Yeah?" She stacks Ryder's syrupy plate atop hers before reaching for mine.

Instead of handing it over, I get to my feet and grab all three plates. "I got to thinking." I walk the dishes to the sink, set them on the counter, and flick on the water to warm.

"And?" Marilee follows me into the kitchen.

"I was wondering if you wanted to come along." After a quick exhale, I continue, my heart galloping at the chance she'll say no. Reject me. Maybe I need to make it as non-threatening as possible. "I mean, this is a really lucrative opportunity for my business, and I'm hoping it'll work out, but I really value your opinion. So, if you're willing..."

At her silence, I turn to find her back to me, standing in front of the kitchen island, hands gripping the counter as if seeking balance. Shoot. Have I upset her somehow?

I turn off the water in the sink and approach her. "Lee?"

When she turns, her eyes glisten. "You care about *my* opinion?"

"Why does that surprise you?"

"Because you're the one with the business degree. You're organized, you make good decisions. Look at you—your life is always in order. And then, there's me, my life. My mess."

"Stop." I reach up to gently place a finger against her soft, smooth mouth—the mouth I dream of kissing again. It's been more than two weeks since Frederick and Chloe's engagement party, but my lips remember the taste of hers.

The memory sends sparks racing through me.

Her eyes widen, and the air shifts around us as it takes longer than it should for me to drop my hand.

"Lee, I need you to hear me," I say softly, my gaze locked onto hers. "Your opinion matters more to me than anyone else's. The way you see the world—it's a perspective I treasure. It's different from mine, and that makes it all the more valuable. So." I tilt my head. "Will you come?"

Her bottom lip begins to worry between her teeth, a gesture that tightens my chest with longing. This moment is too intense, and I suddenly realize how crucial it is for us to balance this heaviness with a splash of the fun that's always been part of our relationship. My eyes dart to the jar of chocolate sauce behind her. An idea strikes.

"Or do I need to threaten you?" I tease, reaching around her to drag the jar closer.

"Threaten me with what?"

"A good chocolate-ing, of course."

"What?" She bursts out laughing, and it's like music, a balm to the tension that envelops us.

Dipping my finger into the chocolate, I playfully lift it to her face, the air thick with laughter and potential. "Yep. Comply, or suffer the sweet consequences."

Her cute little hands fly to her hips, a defiant spark dancing in her eyes. "You wouldn't."

"Wouldn't I?" I wiggle the chocolate tantalizingly in front of her face.

"Jordan!" Quick as lightning, Marilee ducks from my reach, grabbing hold of the bowl of blueberries, one hand poised over the fruit as if preparing to defend herself with it.

I lick the chocolate off my finger, savoring its sweetness as it melts on my tongue. "What? At least it's tasty."

"Of course it is. I made it." She sets down the berries and tilts her chin, a playful challenge glinting in her eyes, before rolling them dramatically. "And I know you. You wouldn't waste a perfectly good sweet treat on a food fight."

Grabbing the chocolate once more, I advance toward her, heart racing as I set the jar down behind her. The space between us closes quickly as I pin Marilee against the counter, arms locked on either side of her. "Not sure you know me as well as you think, Lee."

"Fine, but I do know you wouldn't want to get your clean hoodie—well, clean-ish—dirty." She shimmies her shoulders airily, her taunt crackling in the air.

Oh, that hoodie—what a delightful distraction it's become. Because the sight of her wearing *my* clothes definitely does something to my insides.

"Easy fix." With another mischievous grin, I unzip the hoodie with a swift motion, letting it slide off her shoulders until it falls to the ground, exposing her smooth bare arms. "Not so tough now, are we?"

Her gaze locks onto mine, a mix of laughter and shock flitting across her face, and I can't resist. I dive into the chocolate once more, artistry taking over as I paint her face—a streak across her forehead, a swipe on both cheekbones, another playful smear along her chin.

"Jordan," she squeals, laughter bubbling from her as she pushes against my chest, but I can tell she's not truly trying to escape. A thrill runs through me, and I continue, letting my thumb glide down both sides of her neck, trailing along each earlobe, skating across her delicate collarbone. Goosebumps pop beneath my fingers as they explore the ridges of her shoulders and the skin of her upper arms.

Finally, I finish my masterpiece with a lively dusting of chocolate across her smiling lips.

"Done there, Picasso?"

I step back, feigning a critical examination of my work. "It needs whipped cream too, don't you think?"

"Don't you dare." She raises her hands in mock seriousness. "Now, how do I look?" Her gaze holds an impish challenge that ignites something deep within me.

"Delicious." My voice teases yet drips with sincerity.

She sputters another small laugh, that sound weaving its way into my heart. "Okay, playtime's over. You can get it off now."

And while I could easily reach for the rag that's neatly nestled beside the sink, my heart has other plans. I set the jar down. "All right." The moment stretches between us with palpable weight as I lean in closer and gently remove her glasses, placing them aside with care. Then my fingers move to cradle her face, taking in her delicate fragility, all the while knowing that beneath this surface lies the strength of the most courageous person I have ever encountered.

Perhaps one brave enough to step into the unknown with me.

And I know it's time...

Time for a *real* move. One that will leave her in no doubt of how I feel.

Slowly, I lower my lips to the hollow of her cheek, brushing them against her skin to kiss away the chocolate resting there. The sharp intake of breath that escapes tells me I've surprised her, but she doesn't back away. Instead, she remains, and her silence encourages me to follow the sugary path to her ear, my tongue darting out to taste her.

And whether it's the chocolate or Marilee's soft skin, I learn she's every bit as delicious as I hoped.

"Jay?" Her fingers rise to clutch the back of my neck, nails digging in, sending electric sparks through me. "What—"

"You said to get it off," I murmur as I trace kisses along the shell of her ear, feeling the warmth radiating between us.

"I did," she responds breathlessly. Her throat tightens against my mouth as I skim off the chocolate that's started to dry there, against the neck I've dreamed countless times of kissing.

The moment is so sweet, yet so complicated. And I want more. I want everything.

I just want Marilee. This. Us.

Forever.

"But..."

And that single word snaps me back to reality. I pull away slightly, resting my forehead against hers, our breath mingling in the charged space. My gaze slides down to the remnants of chocolate on her lips, a promise of what could be, but I won't risk nudging her too far, not when hesitation hangs in the air. "But what, Lee?"

Before she can answer, a blur of energy darts into my peripheral vision. "My turn, my turn!"

Ryder, ever the exuberant little whirlwind, hops into the space between us, unintentionally pushing me back from Marilee.

She blinks and shakes herself, producing a smile for my son as she crouches down in front of him. "Your turn for what, sweet boy?"

"For a kiss!" Then he smacks his lips against hers with an

innocent fervor that sends a shock of warmth through my chest. "There, Mommy!"

Oh, geez. I run my hands through my hair as he dashes away in a fit of little-boy giggles.

Marilee remains still for a brief moment, her eyes flicking up to mine, laughter vanishing like mist. "We're confusing him, Jay," she says, her voice quieter now, threaded with uncertainty. Then she sinks to the floor. "Maybe... Maybe we're confusing ourselves."

I kneel down in front of her, the gravity of the moment wrapping around us as I gently swipe the chocolate off her shoulders with my thumb. And then I speak the most honest words I've ever shared with her. "I'm not confused, Lee. I never have been."

Her trembling hand covers her mouth, and I can see the gears whirling in her brain. "I just...I need some time. To think."

"Take all the time you need. I'm not going anywhere."

And hopefully, even after a year's up, neither will she. But it's got to be her choice. So with a final squeeze, I stand and move back to the sink to grab her a clean rag for the chocolate still left behind, my insides jumbled from the intensity of what just happened, at finally making a move.

I pray that I haven't ruined one of the best things in my life by being too hasty. But I can still taste the lingering sweetness of her on my lips—and I can't find it in me to regret a thing.

There's nothing so funny—or so uncanny in its ability to distract me from my troubles—as seeing a gorgeous, legitimate princess shove her perfectly regal feet into hideous bowling shoes.

Chloe's blonde curls fall in curtains around her as she leans forward to tie the shoes. The red and black monstrosities clash horribly with her creamy white slacks and blue wraparound blouse, but she doesn't seem to care as she laughs while finishing up a story about the last event she coordinated through her business, Something Blue. "And then, the bride showed up with a replacement ring bearer—her pet piglet."

"No!" April cackles from her spot on the bench beside Chloe. She pours herself a glass of Dr. Pepper from the pitcher Lucy set down moments ago. "That's amazing."

"I can top that easy," says Elisse, who's sitting behind the computer inputting all of our names into the bowling lane we've rented for a Thursday girls' night out at the Bowl O'Rama one town over. Or rather, nicknames she's given us: Preggers (Lucy), Princess (Chloe), Sissy (Kelsey), Bestseller (April, who blushes and rolls her eyes at Elisse's belief in her author-ly future), Boss (herself), and Wifey (me...*yay, thanks for the reminder, Elisse*).

Elisse pivots to face the rest of us, save her twin, who is still at the rack of balls trying to use her big brain to select the one that will help her win (whereas most of us chose what was lightest or prettiest). "For the wedding at the vineyard last weekend, the bride told all of her bridesmaids to dye their hair green to go with the *Beetlejuice* theme. Which, ew, why?" As of last summer, Elisse works part-time for Chloe, coordinating events at her family vineyard and part-time for her parents doing marketing for wine tastings and purchases. "She changed the theme at the last minute, but one poor bridesmaid did not get the memo."

"Oh no!" We all laugh, and then Elisse launches into boss mode with a "Preggers, you're up."

Lucy stands and salutes, gathering a ball and tossing it granny style down the lane, where it gutters before even reaching the pins. She shrugs and sashays to the ball retrieval to wait. Several disco balls glitter overhead in the alley, which is hopping tonight, mostly with older ladies and church groups. Over the speakers, Kelly Clarkson's singing about being stronger even though she's gone through pain.

I'm not sure if that's true of me, but I want it to be.

Suddenly, there's a gentle hand on my upper arm. "Mare, you okay?" Kelsey's soft voice—the total opposite of her twin sister's—is low, but everyone seems to snap to attention around me.

Her brow furrowed, Lucy ignores the ball that spins up from the ball return and stalks over to sit on my other side. "I've been wondering the same thing. You've been so quiet."

Everyone else leans in.

Can they sense the internal battle I've been having for the last five days, ever since Jordan kissed chocolate off of me?

When my brain got so muddled that it couldn't catch up to what was happening, and I felt both relief and disappointment when Ryder interrupted us? When he called me Mommy and made every dream of mine come true—just before reality crushed my spirit?

"I..."

Just then, a waitress delivers two pizzas, three baskets of fries, and some buffalo wings. We all turn to Lucy with amused looks because she was only supposed to order us a few baskets of pretzel bites.

"What?" She snatches a fry. "I'm hungry."

It must beat being sick all the time. I bump her with my shoulder. "Glad to see you doing better."

"Same, girl, same." Lucy pulls a slice of pizza off the greasy aluminum platter and shoves it onto a paper plate, then glances around at all of us. "Well, come on. Don't let me be the only one eating."

That's all it takes for us to grab our own plates and dish up. "Chloe, how's wedding planning going?" The fries are a bit salty for my taste, but better if drowned in ketchup, so I dunk one and blow on it before bringing it to my mouth.

She fingers the tie of her shirt as she gently swirls a cup of ice water. "Flutterbum's at it again."

We all giggle behind our food because, thanks to Chloe, we are all quite familiar with the antics of Kentonia's official wedding planner, Felicia Butterflum, who is a force to be reckoned with. The thing is, so is Chloe, and as she launches into story after story of Felicia's attempts to overrun Chloe's big day with ridiculous royal demands, I find myself thankful that Jordan and I didn't have to go through all of that. The only regret I have is that all of our friends weren't there...

Then I catch myself.

Because what...?

I blink at my half-eaten pizza, which turns to cardboard in my mouth. When did I start thinking of our wedding day as *real?*

I push my plate aside and grip my stomach, which tightens.

"You look pale," Lucy whispers in my ear. "Like you're going to throw up. And believe me, I know what that feels like. You need help getting to the bathroom?"

"No. I'm okay. I think."

Lucy rubs my back, concern etched on her features. "What's going on, then? Is it work?"

"No, although..."

My friends are suddenly quiet again. Geez. I'm not used to being the center of attention. But each one of them—even the often-grumpy Elisse—is gazing at me with love in their eyes. Full acceptance. They want to know, truly know, what's going on in my life. And too often, I keep things inside or only share what I'm thinking with one or two people. Usually Jordan.

Lately, though...

Chloe wipes her mouth with a napkin. "Although what?" she prompts with her gentle accent. Despite the rocking music blaring through the space, we feel cocooned in this moment. "Last we heard, you agreed to take over for Marla. When's that go into effect?"

"Supposed to be the end of the month." So, like, two weeks. "We've spent the last week training on the budgeting and billing systems, the backend stuff. It's a lot more technical than I thought it'd be."

"I remember how overwhelming that was when I ran the Robin for a few months last year when Winona was out of town." Lucy pats my knee. "But you'll figure it out."

"Yeah, maybe."

"You don't seem all that excited about it, though." Kelsey shifts in the seat to face me better, smoothing her hand down the front of her denim bib pants she's paired effortlessly with a cute white tee. "Are you worried about financing? Or having second thoughts?"

Leave it to insightful, observant Kelsey to give words to what I've been feeling ever since I told Marla I'd take over.

A group of older ladies with bright pink jackets shuffle into the lane behind me, talking loudly. The shared bench creaks as a few of them take their seats.

I raise my voice so my friends can hear me. "I mean, I got the loan secured, thanks to Jordan. So that's not the issue." I press my lips together. "Something's been bothering me, but I'm not sure if it's just fear that I won't be able to do it, or something else."

"Maybe," Chloe says. "I was definitely fearful before I took over Something Blue, but there was also this excitement bubbling up inside of me at the thought. Do you feel any of that, or solely the fear?"

"Mostly the fear, honestly." I shake my head. "But I don't know why. It's the most practical option. When the custody battle's over, and Jordan and I get our marriage annulled, I'll need something solid to fall back on."

"You know, I haven't seen any of your cakes on display lately at the bakery." April refills her soda for the third time. Her hands shake a bit, and come to think of it, her eyes look slightly bloodshot, like she's fighting to stay awake. Maybe another one of her self-imposed deadlines is looming. "Are you still taking orders?"

I sigh. "I haven't had time."

"But you love that. Maybe once you take over for Marla, you'll be able to add more of that in?"

"I don't know. As she's telling me everything she does in a day, I can see why she doesn't do much of the baking anymore. I think I'll probably have to hire someone to do it once she's gone and I'm the one running the business end of things. Her granddaughter, Lexi, is willing to work more, but her college schedule keeps her pretty busy."

"Ugh, but Mare..." Lucy trails off, tugging on the end of her braid as she frowns. "Sweet macaroni. That's like *who* you are. You're a baker. A cake decorator."

I lift my chin. "And now, almost, a business owner."

"Of a business that's not your own," Elisse says.

She opens her mouth to say more, but at that moment, an employee with a mohawk saunters over, pointing at our lane. "Hey, if you guys aren't gonna bowl, we've got a line out the door waiting for a turn. Mind hurrying it along?"

In a flash, Chloe's bodyguard Tia emerges from the shadow and holds her hand to the guy's chest, her menacing dark eyes hovering over him. "Move along."

"Yeah, back off, dude." Elisse bares her teeth at him. "We paid for two hours on this thing, and we'll use it however we want."

The college-aged guy holds up his hands and backs away like she and Tia are both feral animals, muttering a few expletives under his breath.

Shaking out her short bob, Elisse returns her attention to me and waves her hand. "As I was saying, don't you want to make the bakery your own? Or better yet, go out on your own. I thought part of your agreement to marry Jordan in the first place was so he would invest in you."

"It was, but—"

"But what? So far it just seems to me like he's getting all of the benefits out of this arrangement. Free babysitting, a house-maid, a personal chef." She arches an eyebrow. "Unless there are *other* benefits we aren't aware of?" At that, her lips quirk into an evil smirk.

I press a fist against my stomach again, which roils some

more. Because all I can think about are his lips on my cheek. His tongue tracking down my neck. His warm breath gliding across my collarbone.

And how I wanted, how I *ached* for him to aim all of his attention at my mouth...

"Um."

That one word has my friends in hysterics. Lucy shakes my hand and practically screams, "What? Tell us everything."

I groan and bury my burning face in my hands. "I don't even know where to start."

"Let's start at the very beginning..." Chloe singsongs in a perfect Julie Andrews impression.

So I do. I let it all fall out—every word, every look, every shift in my feelings, my attraction, my fear.

My confusion over whether he actually sees me as more than a friend. (Every single one of my gal pals says, "Oh yes, absolutely, no freaking doubt.")

Ryder calling me "Mommy." (To which all of my friends say "Aw!!")

My fear of scarring him for life. (They reminded me that he's a kid, he's resilient, and to just think of what will happen if I *do* give this a chance and we *do* end up together and he's permanently *my* kid—something I cannot even allow myself to think about, because how can I ever come down from that hope?)

And, of course, they go absolutely bonkers—April even standing up and pumping her fists with a silly little dance— when I tell them about sleeping in the same bed, about the chocolate incident, and finally about how he invited me to preview the tent glamping site with him this weekend.

"You're going, of course?" Elisse says matter-of-factly.

"Well..."

"You're not going?" Lucy squeaks.

"I'm not *not* going..."

"Ah. You haven't answered him yet." That's Chloe, always the wise one.

"That's okay, Mare," Kelsey says, giving me a one-armed hug. "This is all a big decision. You don't have to do anything that makes you uncomfortable."

"Oh, I'm sure he didn't mean we had to stay in the same tent or anything."

"So, what's the holdup then?" Elisse crosses her legs and leans in tighter, ignoring the glares Mohawk Man keeps shooting her way.

"I just..." I blow out a breath, trying to quiet the noise in my brain, to tune out the noise in the room, the noise of everyone's expectations. "I just don't want to make another mistake, like I did with Donny."

Their eyes all shutter with sudden sympathy. "Aw, Mare." Lucy grabs my knee, giving it an affectionate shake. "This is completely different. Jordan is different."

"I know that. But I'm not different."

"Except you are. You're stronger with him by your side. An even better version of the incredible woman you already are. And that's because he loves you the way you deserve to be loved."

"I don't understand why he would." And that's the truth of it. "He should be with someone like Amy Montrose. Someone who's young and unencumbered. Someone who can give him..." I glance at Lucy, at her stomach. She licks her lips as her eyes fill with tears, and she grips my hand. "Who can give him what I can't."

The others squint at me, probably confused, but this isn't the moment when I want to go into all that I've lost.

April shakes her head. "Thing is, Mare, the heart wants what it wants. And I think that Jordan's telling you—that he's been telling you for a while—that he doesn't want Amy Montrose or any other woman you might deem perfect for him. He wants you. The question is simple: Do you want him?"

"Yes," I finally allow myself to admit.

The rush of joy that follows is drowned by the fear. But if I'm really stronger with Jordan, if he builds me up instead of tearing me down, then I can face the fear, right? "At least, I think so. But I don't know what to do about that."

"My dear, what you need is a proper date." Grinning, Chloe pulls a notebook and pen from her oversized Gucci purse. "And lucky for you, tomorrow is Valentine's Day—and I just so happen to excel at planning."

"We can all help," Kelsey says. "If you want our help."

"I do." I straighten, breathing in the stale bowling alley air. "Thank you, friends, for helping me to be brave."

"Thank you for letting us help you." April smiles through her clear exhaustion. "It's a privilege. You deserve happiness more than anyone else I know, Marilee."

"She's right." Elisse rubs her hands together. "And we're going to help plan the best Valentine's Day you and that fake husband of yours have ever seen."

"Maybe"—Chloe winks—"one so good that he won't be your *fake* husband for long."

The thought scares me to death, like the loop on a roller coaster I don't see coming. But I'm as ready as I'm going to be, and maybe it's time to just let go. To lift my arms into the air and enjoy the ride.

"Okay, then. Let's do it."

Come what may.

seventeen

JORDAN

Having dinner with another dude is not exactly how I imagined my Valentine's weekend starting.

I'd hoped to be driving up the mountain pass to Mitchell McGraff's glamping site tonight with Marilee, but she never responded to my invitation. And early this morning, I got a call from Mitchell asking for a deviation in our plans. Instead of our first meeting being at the camping site, he wanted to meet up in town at the base of the foothills tonight—Valentine's Day—and head up to the campsite tomorrow.

The guy must be just as single as I am.

And even though I'm married, I *am* single. The fact that Marilee's spent the week "thinking" in every place other than our home tells me that much.

But as I duck out of the rain with my small suitcase and under the awning of the boutique hotel where he requested we meet up, I realize Mitchell's plan is perfect. Like he said on the phone this morning, the views from the tents wouldn't be good due to the weather tonight anyway, but tomorrow's forecast is supposed to be clear. And meeting in town gives me a chance to see what makes this area special, as well as time tomorrow to explore other potential stops on my new adventure tour itinerary, should this partnership with McGraff Glamping work out.

Plus, apparently, this hotel makes a mean steak.

Raindrops splash in the large stone fountain in front of the hotel as I watch the valet take my truck from the circular driveway to an unseen lot, and the tinkling of classical music filters outside. I adjust my suit jacket—the same one I wore to my wedding with Marilee—and make sure my cuff links are still in place, all the while breathing through my nerves. This meeting could be a make or break for me. Not that Go Round Adventures isn't doing well. We are. But if I can secure this partnership, if it can truly attract a new clientele, it would allow me to step up my income. And that would mean I could hire more staff. Be there more for Ryder.

Because much as I love my job, I love my kid even more. And I want to do everything I can to be the best dad I can. To be present in a way my father wasn't for me, not because he was deployed, but because even when he was around...he wasn't.

A well-dressed couple steps out of another vehicle, and I turn to let them pass, taking in the outside of the hotel when I do. It's got a vintage Spanish architecture vibe, but with a modern twist because nothing looks old or crumbling. Staircases wind up the sides of the building. Colonnaded walkways lead to gardens and, in the distance, a rolling vineyard. The air smells crisp and cool, with a hint of earth that's sweet and stunning.

And when I step inside, it's more of the same. I remember going to some sort of military gala with my parents one time when I was young, and it was in a hotel like this. Massive chandeliers drip diamonds from the vaulted ceiling. Travertine marble glistens under my feet. Groups of dolled-up people gather on deep-blue, velvet couches drinking martinis and champagne. A split staircase with a decorative wrought-iron railing curls to a second floor, where I presume the guest rooms are located. Down on the far end of the lobby, I spy the restaurant where we're scheduled to eat in fifteen minutes.

I've got just enough time to get my room key and deposit my overnight bag upstairs. I don't see Mitchell anywhere, so I make my way to the reception desk, where an older gentleman with a bow tie nods solemnly at me and says it would be his pleasure to assist me. Mitchell said he'd be securing me a room, but now that I see the place, I feel bad that he dropped what was probably hundreds—maybe even a thousand—for me to stay overnight.

"Here you are, sir. Room Four-Fifty-Two." The gent takes a bit longer than I hope, and I keep an eye on the doorway until he hands me my key—a solid black card that's made of the same material as fancy, heavy credit cards. "Do you need bag assistance today?"

"No, thanks. I've got it." I wheel my suitcase to the stairs—the glass elevator looks crowded, and I'm only up four floors—and take them two at a time. Don't exactly want to show up to my meeting late, so when I reach my room, I shove my suitcase inside the door then hurry back to the lobby to wait for Mitchell. But as I descend the stairs toward the lobby, everything seizes up in my chest.

Because there, gliding in from the rain, is a vision in shimmering red.

Marilee stops in the middle of the lobby clutching a small purse. She glances this way and that—everywhere but at me—as if she is looking for someone or something. Her bottom lip is caught in her teeth, a sure sign of nerves, but I don't know how she could feel anything but amazing in the satin gown that hugs her curves all the way down to the tops of her white strappy heels. Her hair's pinned up, leaving just enough curls down to frame her face and sweep the tops of her shoulders. The dress isn't anything complicated, with its straight-across neckline and two thick off-the-shoulder straps that hug her upper arms.

But on Marilee, it might as well be a designer gown fit for the red carpet, because I've never seen a woman look as stunning as her.

I somehow reach the bottom step without stumbling and make my way toward her.

Just before I reach her side, she turns to find me there. "Oh. Hi."

"Hi, yourself." I stick my hands in my pockets, because otherwise I will reach for her and never let go. "What are you doing here?"

"Um, well." Her eyes dart to and fro before finding mine again. "I got hungry and heard this place had the best steaks." She shrugs her little shoulders.

But she isn't fooling me. "Is that right? Huh. I was told the same thing by Mitchell McGraff this morning."

She scrunches her nose. "Were you really? What a coincidence."

"Is it?"

Pressing her glossy lips together, Marilee pretends to think. "I'm going with a solid maybe." Then her eyes shutter again, and she waves her hand toward the restaurant. "But since we're both here, and dressed up so nice, and Blake and Lucy are watching Ryder...you wanna eat?"

"I could eat."

"Yeah?"

"Sure." I glance around casually, like I don't know what's

really going on here. Though to be honest, I am a little confused about what exactly has transpired. But hey, I'm not one to look a gift horse in the mouth. "I just need to find Mitchell and let him know someone better came along."

"About that."

"Mmm hmm?"

"Chloe-may-have-called-him-up-this-morning-and—"

I laugh. "Slow down, Lee." Then I extract my hand from my pocket, take a step closer to her, and take her fingers gently in mine. I rub my thumb over the back of her soft skin. "So, what you're saying is, I'm free as a bird?"

"No." She studies me from behind her glasses. "What I'm saying is, tonight you're all mine."

My lungs squeeze, and it takes a moment before I can talk after that kind of declaration. I lean down and press a soft kiss to her cheek. "Good," I whisper in her ear before pulling back. Then I give a gentle tug on her hand. "Then let's go find our table, shall we?"

She nods, color rising in her cheeks as she follows me through the crowded lobby to the restaurant. Here, it's dark, lit only by candles on each table and another chandelier hanging over a small dance floor. Harry Connick Jr. croons over hidden speakers that get quieter as our hostess leads us to a booth for two in the back corner, nestled away from prying eyes. The white linen-covered table is set with fine china, silver cutlery, and black cloth napkins. Water goblets have already been filled, and wine glasses await the possibility of a drink to go with dinner.

Marilee sits and adjusts her dress, and I scooch in on the other side. Our thighs settle against each other, but neither of us moves apart. A young waitress in a white shirt and black tie brings us our menus, asking if we'd like to start off with any of their finest wines.

"We won't be needing those glasses, thank you," Marilee says before I have a chance to decline for myself.

"You can have some if you'd like." I know she enjoys the occasional alcoholic beverage with her friends, and I don't want my decision not to drink to affect her enjoyment of the evening.

She pats my knee. "That's okay. I don't need it."

And that right there, folks, is why I love this woman. Because in that simple statement, she reveals her support. She doesn't even understand my reasons for not drinking—I've never fully revealed to her just why I avoid it, except for the obvious reason of my father's alcoholism—and yet still she supports me.

After perusing the menu, we both decide on steaks and a large side of mashed potatoes and asparagus to split.

Then the waitress leaves...and it's just us again.

My throat's suddenly parched and I take a drink of water. Then wait. Because this is her rodeo. Clearly, she arranged this dinner, going so far as to involve at least Chloe and Mitchell— and, knowing her, probably all of her friends.

But why?

Does she simply feel guilty about ignoring me this week? Surely she wouldn't dress up like this only to let me down easy? Then again, we've gone out to dinner together a thousand times. Maybe not on Valentine's Day, and maybe not in a different town where we dress up at a fancy hotel and—

Aaaaand yeah. I'm spiraling.

So finally, I shift a bit in my seat so I can look at her and ask the question: "Lee, what's going on?"

Just at the same time, she says, "Let's dance, yeah?"

Blinking at her, I nod and follow her from the booth onto the dance floor, where there are several couples swaying in each other's arms. I hold out my arms to welcome her into proper dance position, but she just shakes her head and places her hands on my chest, moving them up until they're looped around my neck. "Hold me for real, Jay."

"Yes, ma'am." My hands slide down and around that silky dress to press into her back, pulling her as close as possible. The heels help to iron out the height difference between us, allowing my lips to rest against her forehead. Michael Bublé serenades us as we fall headfirst into the moment, into each other. I have never wanted anything more in my life than this, with her, a woman who doesn't even know half of her value.

But I want to spend the rest of my life showing it to her, mining it from her depths and helping her to recognize the diamonds produced by all the pain she's gone through.

"Jay?" Her tenuous voice touches the deepest parts of me, and I move back slightly to take her in, allowing myself the pleasure of rubbing a silken strand of her hair between my thumb and forefinger. She sighs and leans her head against my hand. "I thought maybe...if the invitation is still open, I could go with you to Mitchell's site tomorrow."

"Really?"

She gives a slight nod.

"I'd love nothing more than that." I tilt her chin upward, bringing her lips oh so close to my own, which practically tremble with the need to kiss her. To make her mine for real. Our first and only kiss was done for Constance, for show.

But I want this one to be for us.

"Have I told you lately how utterly gorgeous you are, Marilee? How you wreck me completely in all the best ways?"

Her mouth opens slightly, like she can't believe what I'm saying, and I swipe her bottom lip with my thumb. Then I press closer, centimeters from taking—from giving—what I've always wanted—

"Well, look who it is."

The voice stabs me in the throat, and I freeze. Marilee's

sharp intake of air tells me she recognizes the blast from the terrible past as well.

My hands flex on her waist, I step back... And there he is, the smug idiot himself.

Donny Franklin.

The only man I've ever hated.

MARILEE

The edges of my vision go fuzzy as I take in the sight of my ex-husband, who I haven't seen since our divorce was finalized three years ago.

He's still effortlessly handsome with his broad football-player shoulders straining against a navy-blue suit, a cocky grin on face, his black eyes penetrating me with a stare that makes me feel like he's cut away my clothing to see the mess beneath the fancy dress.

Donny's arm is slung low around some blonde woman's hip. She's curvy and well-endowed in all the ways I'm not, just like most of the women he cheated on me with. "Good to see you, Marilee. You clean up nice," he murmurs in a low voice, his words a mix of condescension and charm as he leans in to whisper something into the blonde's ear. With a casual tap on her butt, he sends her drifting toward a distant table.

Over her shoulder, she shoots me a disdainful sneer—a silent girl-code proclamation that "he's mine."

Some part of me wants to warn her that he's not a prize. He's a hellion who will ruin her life, just like he ruined mine.

But no. My life *isn't* ruined. In fact, before he stepped onto this dance floor, I'm pretty sure I was about to kiss my best friend, a man who, even when we were just *friends,* treated me with more decency than the man in front of me ever did.

And if he can see beneath my mask, I can also see beneath his, to the black heart beating under his suit coat pocket. With Jordan's hand still looped around my back, I tilt my chin in defiance at this man who thought he could bring me down. Who *did* bring me down.

But because of good people in my life, I am back on my feet.

Jordan squeezes my hip, and I glance at him. Smile. "I think we were just about to go eat, weren't we?"

Donny hates nothing more than being ignored—something I learned the hard way. When I'd retreat into my baking to think, he'd take my supplies right off the counter in front of me and toss them against the wall like a toddler, demanding I give him the attention he "deserved."

The memory shakes me, just like all of them do, but then Jordan says, "We were," and we are walking off the dance floor, away from Donny Franklin, away from his hold on me.

Before I can fully exhale, Donny's hand seizes my arm with surprising force, nearly throwing me off balance with the abrupt stop it causes. "Are you two actually...together?" His sneer is laced with venom.

Jordan pivots sharply to confront him. "Let go of her. Now."

Donny's burly hand tightens on my upper arm. "Ooo, you're a real tough guy now, huh, Johnny?" he quips with a derisive lilt.

"Listen to him, Donny," I hiss. "Let go of me. You're making a scene."

"Whoa, whoa, whoa." With an almost casual chuckle, Donny releases his hold and raises both hands in a theatrical, playful surrender as if we were old acquaintances sharing a private joke. "No need to get all defensive, sweetheart. I was just surprised to see you here is all."

He runs a palm through his slicked back hair, and a designer watch glints in the light. Something rumbles in my gut... Did he buy that with *my* money? Or is he honey trapping that blonde woman? Maybe she's a rich heiress. He's clearly set his sights higher than me. I never quite knew why he chose me in the first place. Probably he sees me as his greatest mistake.

Ironic then, that I feel the same way about him.

Judging by the fumes coming off of Jordan, staying in Donny's vicinity for any longer is probably unwise. But I have to know what he means. "Why would you be surprised to see *me* here?"

"Oh, it's just that Johnny boy doesn't exactly have the capital to afford a place like this, what with his crappy job, stuck in that useless town. Not unless he struck it rich or inherited something from dead parents like you did." Donny tilts his head to look at me with something like pretend pity. "And we all know *you're* worth nothing now, so..."

Growling, Jordan lunges. "How dare you—"

I pull him back. "Stop it. He's not worth it, Jay." Because the last thing Jordan needs is for anyone to see him attack Donny. Not when he's got an ongoing custody battle over being a negligent father. I glance around and see more than one person subtly videotaping our interaction. We've definitely attracted an audience. "Let's go sit down."

"Good, yes, rein in your attack dog, Marilee." Donny laughs, his tone mocking as he addresses me. "He always *was* making puppy dog eyes at you back in school. Made it all the more delicious that he couldn't have you." His words slice through the air as he steps closer, towering over me. His finger glides down my arm—exactly where he had clutched it moments before—as he lowers his voice to a conspiratorial hum. "It's the only reason I kept you as long as I did...so he couldn't have you. What other reason would I possibly have had to want such a mess for a wife?"

I shudder at his touch, but I don't have to for long, because Jordan's there, shoving him back, his voice steeled with raw protection. "That's my *wife* you're talking to, so you'd better watch your stupid mouth."

I can't even speak. My whole body strums with his words—with the delight in them, with the horror in what I see shifting in Donny's eyes. Oh no. If possible, they've gone blacker, deeper and darker, the way they always would before he flipped the switch from charming guy next door to calculating villain.

"Oh ho, now, really? Your *wife*? Bravo, Johnny." Donny slaps Jordan on the back, and I want to slap *him*. "You finally got the girl." His wilting gaze rakes down every inch of me, and I feel naked and exposed under the chandelier light that's suddenly blinding and intense. I want nothing more than to crawl into a hole. Then, he pivots back to Jordan. "I shouldn't be surprised. You always *did* want my sloppy seconds."

And Jordan—my peace-loving, tender-hearted best friend—hauls off and punches Donny Franklin in the nose.

Howling, Donny grabs his face and screams. Blood falls between his fingers. "I think you broke it, you complete lunatic!"

"And I'll break more if you come near her ever again." Jordan reaches for my hand. "And for the record, it's *Jordan*, not Johnny, you total waste of space."

Then he pulls me to the hotel lobby, not stopping to look backward, not stopping to grab my clutch. We just keep barreling toward the elevators. I don't know where, but it's with Jordan, and I don't care.

Before we step through the open elevator door, I glance over my shoulder at my ex, who is ordering someone to call a doctor, and the blonde who has leapt to his defense, and the waiters all crowded around him. I'm shaking from the inside out—with relief, with terror, with his words still bouncing around in my head.

Sloppy seconds.

Worth nothing.

A mess.

And when the doors finally close and we are alone in the small space, the noise of the lobby cuts out, and Jordan turns to me. "Are you okay?"

It's then that every bit of emotion seeps from me. All I can do is slump against him and sob.

He tucks me against his side and murmurs soothing words of comfort, his lips pressing a gentle kiss to my temple. His protective grip is fierce, a reassurance I've never known before —not from my dad, not from Blake. For the first time, someone has physically defended me like this, punching away my past and guarding my future.

Nobody has been a truer friend than Jordan Carmichael.

And I...I absolutely love him for it.

nineteen

JORDAN

I can't believe that just happened.

As I pace the hotel room—a surprisingly expansive suite with a separate living area, bedroom, and bathroom—I loosen my tie and toss it over the back of the ruby-colored couch next to my suit jacket. My shoes trample the delicate trail of red rose petals strewn from the front door to the closed bedroom door, a barrier that feels all too solid right now. The sound of running water filters through the air, and I can't tell if Marilee is washing away the lingering touch of that demon, or simply changing into something more comfortable. I'd understand either way.

I'm just sorry I didn't hit him harder.

Donny ruined what could have been one of the sweetest nights of my life, intruding upon our moment like a shadow that wouldn't dissipate. This place—this beautiful, romantic haven clearly orchestrated by someone with a penchant for love—deserves better than the chaos he introduced. Candles cast muted light against the elegantly papered walls, while a gentle fire dances in the hearth, its warmth a stark contrast to the chill in my heart. Raindrops patter rhythmically against the patio, where the French doors stand invitingly open, gauzy curtains swaying with the breath of the night.

We should be sharing laughter after indulging in a feast of steak and potatoes, curled up on this couch, lost in a show, the world melting away. Maybe we'd explore the thrill of a kiss, wrapped in the warmth of each other's arms.

Instead, Marilee is spent from crying, and my insides still roil with the desire to march back down those stairs and take another swing at Donny.

After what feels like an eternity of pacing, I sink onto the couch, resting my hands on my knees, staring into the fire's flickering embrace as I wait for her to emerge. I just wish I knew what she needs from me, because I've never felt more helpless.

Finally, the bedroom door creaks open, and she steps out. My breath catches. Her face is cleansed of makeup, her hair cascading in soft, loose waves, pins discarded. She's wearing my flannel pants and a T-shirt that swallows her smaller frame whole, a sight that twists my heart and elicits a primal, possessive urge to claim her as mine.

"Hey," I manage to choke out, my voice rough. "I ordered room service. They'll bring it up with your purse. Are you sure you don't want me to grab your suitcase from your car?"

"No, thanks." Her voice is flat, a stark contrast to the vibrant woman I know. She crosses the room and pushes the gauzy curtain aside, gazing out at the fog creeping in with the rain. It settles over the foothills, softening the vineyard's familiar outlines, wrapping everything in a shroud of secrecy and romance. It feels like a poignant embrace, a lullaby inviting us into a quieter, more contemplative space.

And yet, I don't know if we'll get there. I don't know if we can. The shadows feel close by, waiting to snatch away the light.

I watch Marilee, admiring the elegant curve of her silhouette and the tendrils of hair dancing around her waist, and an ache of longing cracks deep within me. When she turns back, her expression is a mixture of sorrow and vulnerability. It's heartbreaking, and all I want is to pull her close and shield her from pain.

"What is it, Lee?"

"I'm just..." Her voice quivers, and my heart sinks. "I'm so sorry. About Donny."

"You never have to apologize for that creep. Ever."

She exhales slowly, glancing upward as if seeking solace from the ceiling. "But I do, because *I* picked him. Chose to marry him."

"That may be true, but tonight, you stood up to him. I was so proud of you."

"Really?" Her hands clasp at the hem of her shirt.

"Of course. And I'm not gonna lie...I've wanted to knock him down since the first time I met him." I pat the couch beside me. After a moment of hesitation, she plops down facing me, one leg folded on the couch. Our knees touch.

"The day he hit you with a football?"

"Yep."

"I saw it happen. The way he treated you, like you were beneath him—like everyone was beneath him, unless they were useful to him. But I chose to ignore it. Made excuses for him."

I take a breath, my heart pounding as I finally ask the question that's haunted me for years. "I'm not blaming you one bit when I say this, but what *did* you see in him, Lee?"

"Ah, the million-dollar question." She tilts her mouth up on one side. "At first, he was...sweet. We had yearbook together my freshman year. He took it his senior year as an easy A, and he needed as many as he could get since he played football and had to keep up his GPA." Somewhere outside, there's a ringing like wind chimes sighing. "Back then, I was super insecure. I always knew I was flighty, kind of a mess. Someone who didn't use her brain enough."

The pain in her voice stabs me. "Why did you think that? Because for the record, I think you're amazing—smart, talented, and much more than you give yourself credit for."

A faint smile flickers on her lips, like a sunrise breaking through the clouds. "You always know how to boost my ego."

"That's my specialty." I wink, trying to lighten the moment, but the heaviness still lingers between us.

Marilee chuckles softly, then her fingers drift to the fabric of her pants, tracing a zigzag pattern as if trying to ground herself. "I remember when I was in junior high, helping my dad wash his sports car. I was so excited, because he never trusted anyone with his baby. But then I sprayed the hose all over the car with the top down."

"Uh oh."

"Yeah. My dad rushed out, bucket in hand, and yelled at me. He said I had no sense in my brain and that he couldn't trust me with anything important again."

"Geez, Lee. That's terrible." Mr. Moffitt was a tough man—someone who loved his work and loved his wife but was really hard on his kids—but I had no idea his words had left such scars on Marilee. "Surely he apologized later."

"Did you ever know my dad to apologize for anything?"

"Good point."

She shifts, her tone growing contemplative again. "There was that, not to mention the fact that Blake's brilliant and always got high marks in school when I was a solid C student. So I went into high school with my self-esteem already crumpled. The only thing I was ever good at was baking, but I wanted to show my dad there was more to me than that. Unfortunately, he just never really seemed to see it." Marilee shrugs.

"Then I met Donny, and he was this big football star—like a knight in shining armor. I was in awe, and my dad... It was like he finally approved of me."

Ugh, I hate that for her. "Donny definitely put on a good act." For others, anyway. I always saw him for exactly who he was, but I think that's because he wanted me to. He didn't care about hiding from me, because he never really saw me as a threat to what he wanted. "Most narcissists do."

"But you'd think after a while, I'd see through the facade. I saw cracks occasionally, but I wrote them off. He was the great Donny Franklin, and I was just...me. Out of all the girls, he wanted *me*."

"Like that's so hard to believe?"

I want to blurt out that *I* wanted her the moment I first saw her. But tonight isn't about my confessions. It's about her, and I have this feeling she needs to get it all out. She needs to come full circle with her emotions and realize that this was not her fault.

A sigh slips from her lips, heavy with regret. "I ignored the signs. I got so tangled up that I didn't know who I'd be without him. And I was scared to find out."

My heart clenches at her tone, so vulnerable and defeated. "Lee, I know I've asked this before, but...he never hit you, did he?"

"No. And that's the thing. He wasn't outright abusive. He just made me feel...less than." She pinches the bridge of her nose, fighting back tears. "When I miscarried over and over again, he joked that I was defective. Said nobody else would put up with my mess, with my broken pieces, the way he did."

"That absolute piece of—" I trail off, biting the inside of my cheek until I taste blood. I shift closer, unable to restrain my desire to comfort her. "You know it's not true, right, Lee? He said that to feel powerful because *he* was weak."

She wipes away a tear, shaking her head, and the sight shatters me. "I believed him, though. I still kind of do sometimes. I thought I deserved the pain, like I was being punished for not leaving him sooner. No children should grow up in a household like that. So it felt like...feels like...my fault—every bit of it."

A fresh wave of tears spills down her face, and I'll be darned if I let her suffer alone. I surge forward, pulling her into my lap, wrapping my arms around her like a fortress. "No, Marilee. You did NOT deserve any of that. Not one bit. And if you believe anything he said, you're just allowing him to win."

She clings to me, soaking my shirt with tears. After a moment, her breathing slows and she shudders. "You're right." Pulling back, she looks me in the eyes, her arms still draped around my neck. With trembling fingers, she runs her palm down my cheek, a touch that sends shivers coursing through me. "You've always been right, Jordan. I should have left him when you begged me to, but I was too scared."

"We don't have to talk about that now."

She shakes her head, something fierce and determined in her expression. "But it matters. I pushed you away that night, told you that if you were a friend, you'd support me. I threatened to cut off all communication if you said anything bad about Donny. Who does that?"

"Lee, it's okay."

"But it's not okay," she insists, her voice rising slightly, filling with emotion. "You were there for me, and I just...I never appreciated it. Never appreciated you." Her gaze locks onto mine, and there's an intensity in the moment, something raw and honest that sends my heart racing. "I should have seen you."

Then, as if time suspended, she leans in, and I can feel the electric tension crackling in the air. Her lips hover tantalizingly close to mine, and I can't help but want to bridge the gap. I'm on fire. Every part of me screams to kiss her, to drown in this moment, but my instincts hold me back.

Honorable is the last thing I want to be right now, but it's what's right for her. For us. I have to be sure that she's sure. I don't want any regrets between us. So I gently place my hands on her arms, slowly pushing her back. "Lee," I murmur, my voice barely above a whisper, heavy with the weight of desire and restraint.

She blinks, a blush creeping up her cheeks, and I see the realization dawn in her eyes. "Sorry, I just..."

"No, don't be sorry," I say quickly, searching for the right words. "It's just that..." How to find the words? "I don't want you to kiss me just because I'm not Donny, or because I've said something that's always been true."

Her brow furrows in confusion. "You don't want to kiss me?"

"Not tonight." I squeeze her arms, grounding us both. "Tonight's been a whirlwind, and you look exhausted."

And as if punctuating my point, she yawns adorably, small and vulnerable, and I can't help but chuckle as I pull her back into my chest, cradling her against me.

"Tomorrow, though," I murmur. "If you feel the same way, then..." I trail off, feeling the promise hanging in the air, fragile and intoxicating.

"Tomorrow?" she asks, her voice laced with sleepiness.

"Tomorrow. Or whenever. If you still want to."

"Promise?" Her eyes flutter closed, bewitching in their innocence.

"I do."

The words hang between us, a sacred vow. With her nestled against me, the world outside fades, leaving only the soothing sound of rain and the steady beat of our hearts. Tomorrow holds the unknown, but tonight, we exist in this cocoon of warmth and unspoken possibilities, the embers of something real flickering ever so gently, waiting to ignite fully under the right kind of spark.

For the first time in a long time, I have hope.

And that's a beautiful thing.

MARILEE

I truly couldn't imagine a more perfect day. So far, it's been one for the books.

After our tumultuous evening—during which I cried more tears than I have in a good, long while—I woke up in the California king-sized bed under the softest duvet. Jordan was nowhere to be seen, though sunlight streamed in through the window and my suitcase sat on the footboard bench. Not only that, but a lidded cup of coffee rested on my side table, still warm to the touch.

I was up and showered before Jordan returned in his running clothes, pulling AirPods from his ears. *"There's a cute breakfast cafe in the hotel. Hungry?"*

"Starving." Especially considering I fell asleep before the room service came last night.

Breakfast wasn't the only thing I was hungry for, but first thing in the morning didn't feel like the right time to continue our conversation from last night.

It also didn't feel like time when we explored the town together after breakfast or met with a few local vendors Jordan might consider partnering with if he secures this contract with

197

Mitchell McGraff. And it wasn't the time as his truck chugged up the mountain pass to Mitchell's land, which is gorgeous in its own right. We're so far up that our cell phone reception is spotty, surrounded by trees and wild flowers.

It's been good to have the time to reflect though. Because it was a hit to my pride when he stopped my kiss last night. It took a lot for me to reach out—and then he stopped me.

I understand why, but it's taken me a while to know what I want to say to him. To be sure.

Unfortunately, we haven't had two minutes to ourselves since arriving early this afternoon. After checking in, Mitchell took us around his property, telling us all about how he'd inherited the land from his grandfather and cut down just enough trees to create a clearing for twelve tents. They're smaller than I imagined, but cozy, each with a queen-sized bed with a rustic luxury frame, a small bathroom with a rainfall shower, and a completely clear dome overhead. The front of our tent is also see-through, but a curtain can be tugged closed for privacy. A series of paved walkways connects the tents, and the resort features a hot tub, pool, kids' playground, and dining dome where Mitchell brings in a five-star chef to create truly gourmet meals.

Throughout the tour, Jordan asked insightful questions, his voice calm and steady, but I could see the thrill building in his eyes. He wants this to work—and I don't see why it shouldn't. Obviously we haven't tried the tents overnight, but Mitchell has graciously provided us with one to test out tonight.

Now, as the tour finally ends, perhaps we'll have our chance to have that conversation after all...

But then Mitchell invites us to his home, a beautiful two-story log cabin that sits on the edge of a nearby lake. Mitchell and Jordan hash out some details as we roast hot dogs and marshmallows over the fire pit.

My impatience grows, but I keep a smile pasted on.

Finally, as the sky starts to darken, Mitchell claps his hands together. "Well, it's getting late, and I shouldn't keep you newlyweds any longer."

"Oh, we're—" Jordan looks over at me for a split second, then back at Mitchell. "Thanks, man." He reaches out, shakes the guy's hand. "This place is great."

"Hopefully great enough for us to work together?" Mitchell smiles, Jordan laughs, and we all stand.

"It's a definite possibility," Jordan says.

"Fantastic." Mitchell stretches his lower back. "Have a good night, you two. If you need anything at all, just shoot me a text. I want your stay to be as comfortable as possible."

Jordan glances at me again. "I think we've got everything we need." He takes my hand.

I shiver at his words. At the implication there. And once again, something in my soul whispers…*"you're enough."*

Mitchell douses the fire and waves as he heads inside.

We make the quiet trek back to our assigned tent. Jordan quietly offered to ask for a second tent if I wanted my own—the resort is only half-booked, probably due to the chilly weather— but I said that would look funny for his wife to stay in her own tent.

I mean, that's not the only reason I want to stay with him, but again… It wasn't time for that conversation.

Now, though?

The rain from last night is nowhere to be found, and stars pepper the sky like a spicy soup. Streaky cloud wisps resemble spun cotton candy stretched out beneath the crescent moon. It's the perfect night for stargazing.

The perfect night for love.

If we have the courage to speak our truth.

We don't spy a soul as we walk the path. Thanks to the

higher elevation, I'm bundled in my red winter coat and Jordan's in a black hoodie—not the one I stole from him. That one's mine forever, stuffed away in my suitcase to prove it.

My teeth start to chatter, but finally, we reach our tent. Dropping my hand, Jordan kicks at a clod of dirt. "Do you want to sit out here and look at stars for a bit?"

I exhale, and my breath's visible on the air. "It's a little cold for me. Plus, we can see stars from inside the tent." I tilt my head, shooting a reassuring smile his way. "Kind of the point of this place, right?"

"Right." Humorless, he's rigid as he opens the tent flap.

Ducking inside, I am instantly grateful for the installed heater that allows me to strip off my jacket. "Be right back, okay?"

He nods absently as he stands at the open front of the tent, looking up at the sky.

Grabbing my pajamas, I step into the bathroom and change. Not sure what I was thinking, only bringing shorts and a spaghetti strap shirt, but the big fluffy orange duvet should keep me warm tonight.

That...and hopefully, Jordan.

My bare feet pad quickly back into the main tent area. Jordan glances back at me and coughs, laughing as I jump into the bed and pull the duvet up to my neck while I sink back against the headboard. "Cold?"

"I'll be fine." I pause. "You gonna jammy up?"

"Jammy up? Who am I, Ryder?"

"Ha ha. Fine. Are you going to change into your pajamas?" Jordan's normal bed wear is actually just boxers and no shirt (Ryder is a fount of information you never asked for), but since I've lived at his house, he wears a white undershirt and basketball shorts to bed.

Jordan hesitates, then nods, disappearing and reappearing

in his usual fare before he exhales and climbs into the other side of the bed. He leaves an entire foot of space between us.

I arch an eyebrow. "You think I have cooties or something, Jay?"

"What? No." Another exhalation. "I know we haven't talked yet, and I didn't want to...presume."

This sweet man. I scoot over to him and lift his arm around my shoulders, snuggling up against him. "No matter what we say tonight, the basics will not—cannot—change."

He relaxes against me. "And what are the basics?"

"You and me have each other's backs. Forever."

His breath warms my ear as he sets his mouth against the side of my head. "Yeah?"

"Yeah. Whatever happens, we will always be in each other's lives." I place a hand flat on his chest under the comforter. "Deal?"

"Deal." His free hand covers mine. "Do we need to add it to the contract?"

I love this guy's ability to tease me, to make me laugh, even when we are navigating something new between us. "Could be we need to renegotiate some of the terms of said contract."

His finger traces the top of my hand. "You think so, huh?"

"I do." Pushing myself back up, I turn to face him, my hand still lying against his heart as I peer through the starlight into his eyes. He's the most handsome man I've ever seen, and I don't know why it took me so long to realize it, so long to face the fact that I've probably been in love with him for a good while now.

"Jay, I didn't want to kiss you last night simply because you're the opposite of Donny. It's because you're *you*."

His eyes flicker. "So, it wasn't just because I punched that scumbag and stood up for you?" The fingers that were around me fall to my right shoulder, and Jordan's thumb draws a line down the delicate strap of my shirt, leaving fire in its wake.

"Well, that definitely helped." I laugh and push against his chest. He holds tight to my hand, and I grow serious again. "Nobody has ever treated me with the tender care that you have. I convinced myself for so long that it was just as a friend, because I couldn't accept the idea that you'd think of me as anything more."

"Why, Lee?"

"You know why. I didn't think I was worthy of the kind of love you showed me day in and day out. As a friend, I could accept it, but as more than that, I just couldn't." My lips press together. "Speaking of presumptions, I know I'm presuming a lot here..."

His hand slides up the side of my neck, fingers teasing into the roots of my hair, which is up in its usual bun. "I think you can safely presume away." Jordan straightens and draws closer to me. "Marilee Moffitt, everyone is worthy of love, but most especially you. You are an angel to everyone around you, leaving sprinkles of sunshine wherever you go. You've brightened my life from the moment I first laid eyes on you baking in our home economics class."

I laugh at the memory. "Talk about a mess."

"A beautiful mess." Reaching up, he gives the rubber band in my hair a gentle tug and tosses it aside. As my hair falls around my shoulders, I feel the softness of it against my skin. Jordan presses closer, and his hand plunges deeper, nudging me forward until we are nose to nose, breath mingling. "That day changed my life forever. It was the day I first saw you. The day I first fell for you."

"What?" I can't help but laugh out the question, awe filling my chest at the pure devotion in his tone, at the crazy words he's speaking. "What do you mean?"

"I mean that I've loved you half of my life, Lee... And I don't think I'll ever stop."

Oh, this man. This wonderful, beautiful man. "I love you too, Jay. And I—"

But I don't get to say any more, because he hauls me up and over his lap, where he holds me close and kisses me like there's no yesterday or tomorrow.

Just today.

Just us.

Just this tent, and this bed, and this moment.

Just his hands skating up the sides of my thighs until our breaths are one and the same as we give and take years of love and wanting. Secret longing, now exposed.

His lips move to my neck, the movement curling my toes with delicious pleasure that expands when his attention moves to the hollow of skin above my collarbone, nerves popping one by one. Then he captures my lips again and the kiss deepens quickly, a small sound escaping my throat as his tongue traces my bottom lip.

And I can't help but melt into Jordan.

The world outside is lost to us, and each brush of his lips against mine sends tingles down my spine, igniting every part of me that has been waiting for this moment. His mouth is warm and soft, molding against mine as if it's been waiting too. The taste of him—the sweetness of marshmallows from earlier— lingers on my tongue, making me crave more.

I never knew a kiss could feel like this, like falling and flying at the same time.

Like coming home.

I clutch at his shoulders as if he is my lifeline, and in that second, I realize he truly is. Perhaps he always *has* been, but I've been too scared to see it. With every soft caress, every gentle push of his mouth against mine, he ushers me into a world where we exist solely for each other. I can feel his heart pulsing against my chest, and it matches the rhythm of my own, a drumbeat only we can hear.

His hands travel up and down my back, exploring the curve of my waist before he grasps my hips with a firm tenderness. I lift my chin and wrap my arms around his neck tight, needing to bridge the small space that still feels too wide, but the boundary only fuels the yearning inside me.

Jordan pauses for a moment, his forehead resting against mine. "I can't believe this is real," he murmurs, his voice low and thick like honey.

"It's real." And because I don't want this moment to end, I kiss him again, more fervently this time, pouring every ounce of my love and longing into it. Our mouths move together, perfectly synchronized as if they were always meant to meld this way, like chocolate and peanut butter over a gentle flame.

I have never felt so utterly seen, so cherished as Jordan's fingers tangle in my hair, pulling me closer, as if he is afraid I might drift away.

As we pull apart briefly, he cups my cheek with his palm, his eyes locking onto mine with an intensity that makes my breath catch. "Marilee," he whispers, "you have to know that this doesn't change anything... Except maybe everything."

I nod, heart racing at his words. I don't know what the future holds, what will happen after tonight, but I know that I want to be with him, whatever that means. "I know."

He leans in again, and I can feel the heat radiating between us, the space that we've once kept so carefully defined now feeling impossibly small. The midwinter chill outside contrasts sharply with the warmth enveloping this tent—and I am here for it one thousand percent.

Jordan's heated palms drift from my hips to press against the small of my back, guiding me gently off his lap as he lowers me delicately onto the mattress, his body hovering over mine but not pressing down. Every brush of his skin against me sends shivers through my body. I run my fingers down his arms, feeling the muscles ripple beneath his shirt, marveling at how right this feels. At how well we fit.

The stars outside highlight the scruff on his jaw that only adds to his rugged charm. I can't help but touch his cheek, feeling the faint stubble beneath my fingertips—a reminder that this moment is real and tangible. That it exists. That we exist. That we are alive.

That we are in love.

And yet...

His head dips to kiss behind my ear. My eyes flutter shut, because it feels amazing. But I finally force them open and whisper, "Jay."

He sits up on an elbow, his breathing labored. "Yeah?"

"Can we..." My eyes blink into the dim light. It's like coming back to myself. "It's just...I know we're technically married, and with that might come certain...um, expectations. But this is still new."

His look softens, and there's a flicker of understanding in his eyes. "You want to take it slow."

"Yes," I breathe, relief flooding through me. "I'm not saying never. Just..."

"Not right now. I understand completely."

"Are you sure?"

"Of course, I'm sure." With that, he leans in for another kiss. It's feather-light but filled with warmth—and over far too soon when he lies back down beside me and tucks me into his side. "I want to savor every moment with you, Lee. We don't have to rush a thing. Just kissing you is more than I ever dreamed possible."

"Thank you." I should have known this would be his reaction, because whether he's my friend Jordan or my husband Jordan...he's still just Jordan. A good man. The best man. My protector. My champion. "So, what now?"

"Now, we look at the stars."

"And maybe kiss a little more?" I say playfully, pinching his side.

Groaning, he slicks a hand down his face. "Woman, you're killing me, you know that?"

"You love it."

"I love *you*," he says, and the conviction in his tone is like a tuning fork to my heart, making it sing. "And as for *now*...now I get to date my wife."

His wife. Wow. How strange...and yet, wonderful. I think. It's been an unconventional path, but that doesn't mean it's wrong. Right?

Okay, yeah. I'm tired. So much has happened in the last twenty-four hours. But we have time to figure it all out, to process and see what works best for us. For right now, I'm just going to enjoy this moment.

"Well, Mr. Carmichael." I cuddle up against him, pressing the bottom of my foot against the top of his, deep under the blankets. "I really *do* like the sound of that."

twenty-one

I'm standing on top of a jagged rock, overlooking one of California's most beautiful waterfalls, my very kissable wife tucked under my arm...and wow. This is my life.

"It's so gorgeous," Marilee whispers. "So quiet too."

"That's the thing I love most about getting lost in nature." After waking up to the sun streaming all around us from outside the tent, we snuggled for a bit before getting dressed and eating stuffed French toast at the dining dome. We have to head home in a few hours, but I wanted to check out a hike in the area, another activity to add to my tour itinerary if I take Mitchell up on the offer he presented to me at breakfast—a very lucrative offer that has my insides twirling with possibilities.

Somehow, things are all coming together with my career... and the rest of my life too.

I continue. "The peace I can find here. The way it silences my mind."

"That's how I feel when I'm baking."

I squeeze her shoulders. "I know."

She smiles. "You think you know everything about me, huh?"

"No way." Leaning down, I give her a gentle kiss. "But I'll always want to know more."

Lee grows quiet, contemplative again, as we take in the view, breathe in the clean air. The water below us cascades from two main points, converging into a pond eighty feet below that Mitchell says is swimmable in the summer. An entire forest of sycamores and oaks grows up around the falls. Squirrels scurry up their trunks, birds twitter in their branches, and moss grows on the rocks at their bases. The ground is soft from the rain, but yesterday's sun dried it enough so it's not muddy.

I'm honestly surprised we're the only ones up here, but you won't find me complaining. This is our own little retreat, our haven from the world. Last night was incredible, but I'm not dumb enough to think that everything's solved between us. Not only that, but court's just two days away.

And Marilee is still quiet.

Removing my backpack, I set it on a rock and lower myself to the hard ground, tugging on her hand. "Whatcha thinking about now?"

"Hmm?" She joins me, bringing her knees into her chest. "Oh. Nothing." A shiver racks her body despite the rays of the mid-morning sun.

I reach into my backpack and remove an extra hoodie—the one she stole from me that I found hanging out of her suitcase this morning. It made me smile to see it there, mingled with all of her other clothes. Like it belonged. "Unacceptable answer." I set the jacket over her shoulders.

"That's rather bossy of you." But she smiles, and I know she doesn't mind. "And thank you. For keeping me warm."

"I can keep you warm other ways too, you know."

She laughs and bumps me with her shoulder. "Yeah, I *know*." And yet, she doesn't move any closer.

"Okay, spill. Unless you really aren't ready to talk. But I can tell something's bugging you."

The gentle rush of the water fills in the cracks of her hesitation. "I'm worried about court. Aren't you?"

"Of course. But we have to trust our attorney, right? And he thinks we've got a solid defense. I cannot fathom a world in which a judge would take Ryder away from us." And yes, I said us, because I'm hoping...praying...she decides to stay. "Is that really what you're thinking about? Or is there more?"

She sighs and closes the jacket tight around her, over her whole body, her knees, as she huddles. "You really do know me, huh?"

A bird of some sort swoops into a nearby tree. I freeze, thinking it might be a bald eagle, but I can't be sure. Either way, the possibility is there, hanging out, so close we could snap a photo.

But Marilee's my focus right now, and I have a feeling I know why she's feeling unsettled. I place my hand on her back and make soothing circles there. "Yes, but I'd like to hear it from you."

"It's just everything, I guess. The custody battle, taking over the bakery. Not even sure I really want that. And then... Last night was amazing, but it's a lot, you know?"

"I know. But we can figure it out. Like we said, we're not in a rush. We love each other. That's enough for now."

"But what if it's not enough forever?"

"That's the thing, Lee. It's not."

Her head swivels, eyes wide. "What do you mean?"

"Love itself isn't enough."

"What else is there, then?"

"Choice. Love is an emotion, sure, but it's also a choice. And when the hard times come, sometimes we might not feel in love. But the couples who survive those times survive because they choose to stay together. Choose to work it out." The bird flies away, toward a rocky outcropping that's higher than we are. "Take my parents. My dad is a hard man to live with. Once, I asked Mom why she's stayed with him. She told me just what I'm telling you. Love is a choice, and if the person you're with is good-willed and not abusive in any way—even if they're not perfect—you can get through anything."

She lays her cheek on her knees and looks over at me. Her glasses are slightly crooked, and it's adorable, but it's her eyes that grab me. So big, so full of vulnerability. "A choice. I like that. And it's something I never had with Donny. Something I never *thought* I had, anyway."

I nod. "But I want you to know something, okay? You will always have that with me."

She bites her lip. Waits while I continue. "Just because we are technically married right now doesn't mean we have to stay married if you decide this isn't what you want." It hurts to look at her while I say this, so my gaze wanders, finding peace in the beauty surrounding us, the proof that there's a bigger something out there holding it all together when my shoulders feel too heavy. "Obviously, things have changed since our original agreement, but I won't trap you, Lee. It has to be your choice. As for me and what I want..."

Well, I don't think I need to say it out loud. She has to know.

"Jordan?" Her hand finally reaches out for mine. "Why did it take you so long to finally tell me you loved me?"

"Guess I didn't want to rock the boat and lose you. Life had already taught me that speaking up about something I wanted might cause irreparable rifts between me and the people I love."

"What happened to make you think that?"

"Well, there was the time my dad told me to go to college

away from here, so he didn't have to hear me 'harp at him' over his drinking anymore."

"That was totally out of line." She squeezes my hand. "Any other instances?"

"I don't know." I squint, think. "I remember when I was maybe eleven, and we had to move yet again for Dad's job. I pleaded with him to change his mind—I knew it wasn't totally his decision, but thought maybe..." The water falls into the pond below, and even if I can't hear it, I'm hyperaware of the thrashing it makes at the bottom. "Anyway, I didn't want to leave another school, to leave the friends I'd just made. Dad said it was selfish of me to speak up when this job was what kept a roof over all of our heads. Told me that throwing a tantrum wasn't going to change anything, so I might as well be quiet and have a good attitude about it."

"Aw, Jay. I'm sorry." She sighs. "I wish your dad had been more understanding. You were just a kid."

"At least he bothered to say something at all." I huff out a sardonic laugh. "It was almost nice to get his attention for once."

Marilee hmms. "I remember you told me he never came to any of your school programs or track meets, right?" Her long, lithe fingers—capable of creating and giving so much love—stroke the veins at the top of my hand. At my nod, she contin-ues. "I'm so sorry he wasn't there for you."

"I got used to it." But did I, really? Or did his absence, in mind and body, become like a splinter in my nail bed that got infected and festered until the nail stopped growing...and I stopped remembering it was supposed to?

"Was he always an alcoholic, or just after his injury?" she asks.

"I have a few memories of him laughing, going with us to the park, that kind of thing, when I was super young. He was a good dad back then. But after his deployments, that dad disappeared. I don't remember him drinking until the injury that ended his career, but he found other ways to escape before that."

"What do you mean?"

"He worked all the time. And even when he was home every night, he wasn't really there, you know? He ate dinner most nights in relative silence. Even when Mom would try to engage him in conversation about what she'd done that day, or what me or Claire had learned at school, he just sat there shoveling food into his mouth and staring at us, grunting. Or he'd watch TV. Or just...disappear into his office and work some more." I scrub a hand down my face. "It's why I hate working so much now, why I've been trying to find a way to be home more with Ryder. Love means showing up, and even though my dad didn't show up for me, I'll be darned if I do the same thing to Ryder. I want him to tell me every single thing he does, to know that I'm going to be there whether he messes up or is victorious. It's why it kills me that Constance and Larry think..."

"I know. But I meant it when I told Sam you're the best dad in the world. I wish my own dad had been half as encouraging as you are to Ryder." She tries for a smile. "I loved him, but he wasn't perfect. No father is, and I'm sure yours loves you even if he doesn't know how to show it."

"If my dad did love me once upon a time, it's hard to see it now—not when he's never there for anything important in my life."

"Maybe he'll surprise you one day."

"Yeah, maybe." I say it with zero conviction in my voice. "But I've learned to stop expecting it. And stop asking for it. Makes it easier than being constantly disappointed. Or worse, him pulling even deeper into his abyss." A small lizard darts across the rocks near the waterfall's edge, bringing me back to the present. Back to why we're even talking about this in the first place. "So—in an extremely large nutshell—I guess that's why I put off telling you how I felt for so long, even after you and Donny ended."

"I understand." She takes her time, blinking at the ground. "With that fear weighing on your mind, it's a wonder you ever got the courage to beg me to leave Donny that night almost six years ago."

Oh, that night. The night that changed everything for me. The night we've never spoken of until two evenings ago in our hotel room.

The night of my biggest regret. But also, one of my biggest joys. It all mingles together.

And I can't avoid talking about it anymore.

"Ironically, that was my pathetic attempt to tell you how I felt. I just wanted you to know that there were people out there who loved you. That you didn't have to put up with someone who made you cry."

I can still picture it. I'd just moved back to Hallmark Beach not long before that. We hadn't kept in super close touch while I'd been away—probably because of Donny—but when I found out Marilee's parents had died, I realized everything that was important to me existed in that tiny town and made plans to return after business school.

So I graduated, moved back, started up Go Round Adventures, and hung around with Marilee as much as I could without disrespecting her marriage and causing a wedge between her and Donny. But the jerk did that all on his own.

"When I started to see how he treated you—the little things he'd say, the way you'd hide yourself away, the fact he was spending all of your money on gambling and other women—I got really concerned. And then, that night, I found you curled on your couch, a shell of the vibrant woman I knew, crying, and I couldn't stand it anymore. I had to speak up."

"And I rejected you." Her eyes go misty. "That night...I'd just miscarried for the first time the week before, Jay. And when I finally told Donny, he laughed it off. Said it would be fine, that we could just have another go round in the sack, make another baby—" Her words cut off and she shudders out a breath.

I want to hold her, but I give her space to speak. To remember. To process.

Her voice is small but strong when she continues. "And when I told him I wasn't able to...that it might be a while before I could...he got angry. He didn't touch me, didn't throw anything, but his eyes went all cold, and he grabbed his keys and said not to wait up for him. Then he went out the front door all calm. And I just knew that he was going somewhere to find someone who could give him what he wanted."

"That's so messed up, Lee. He should have held you, should have cried with you, should have reassured you it wasn't your fault."

"I know." She sniffs. "That was the first time I realized he was probably cheating on me. I mean, there were signs before that, but I always thought—no. Not Donny. We're high school sweethearts. Meant to be. He wouldn't do that to me. Pretty stupid, huh?"

"It's not stupid to believe in love. He just wasn't worthy of your love. That's all on him, not you."

"I know that now—in my head, at least. But back then, I just couldn't see it. So when you showed up and were against him, I defended him because, well, I couldn't face the truth that I'd chosen so poorly. Couldn't face the idea of another loss. Of another failure. But you didn't deserve that, and I'm sorry. I'd go back and change it if I could."

"I've already told you it's okay, Lee. Do I wish you would have gotten out of that situation sooner? Yes, but for your sake, not mine. Besides, I'm not sorry, because everything that happened led us here. It led to Ryder, to me becoming a dad, however different a path than I saw it happening. It led to us, being a family. So in the end, all things worked together for good."

Her mouth hangs open.

And it takes me a moment to figure out why. At the same time, she asks, "What do you mean, it led to Ryder?"

And I know it's time to tell her the truth—the whole truth about what happened that night. All my cards on the table. All *my* mess spilled out.

I can only pray it doesn't change how she feels about me. Though I wouldn't blame her if it did.

twenty-two

MARILEE

"Jordan?"

He's gone still beside me.

"Hey." I wait until he's looking at me. "Whatever it is, it's okay."

He gives me a small smile—one that doesn't reach his eyes—and then stands, holding out his hand to help me up. "We should get going back to our tent. Pack up. Get back to town."

Back to reality.

"Yeah, okay."

We both gather our packs and silently pick our way down the rock to the path. It winds to the bottom of the waterfall and another few miles through the trees, and we follow the loamy forest floor as it weaves. The sun's hidden here, the branches overhead choking out its rays, and I find myself shivering again—though not just because of the breeze that's kicked up.

It takes him a while, but finally, Jordan speaks. "After I left you that night, I did something I swore I'd never do."

I stop and squint at him. He's so solemn, and if I know Jordan, he needs me to remind him to laugh, even when things are hard. "Please don't tell me you murdered someone."

"I wanted to."

Oh. Donny. Right. I start walking again. "Did you deface a building?"

"No."

"Kick a puppy?"

"What? No, of course not!"

"I get that reaction over kicking a puppy but not murdering someone?" I tease, gripping the straps of my backpack and looking over at him. "Where are your priorities, Jay?"

"Hey, when we're watching thriller movies, *you're* the one who's always way more concerned about one of the animals dying than the people. Remember when we watched that opening scene of the original *Twister* movie, and you said 'at least the dog didn't die' when the girl's dad gets sucked up by the tornado?"

"What? I was glad the dog didn't die." I stop at the sight of a huge stick on the path, pick it up because it reminds me of something Ryder would snatch. "Besides, this is why I watch romcoms. People don't die in romcoms."

"Except that creepy zombie movie you insist is a romcom but is literally filled with dead people."

"Are zombies really dead, though? And *Warm Bodies* is totally a romcom!" I jab the air with the stick, and Jordan snatches it from my hands.

"Whoa there, Braveheart. Settle down." Laughing, he tosses the stick aside, much to my protest. "Thanks, Lee. I needed that."

"Feel better?"

"I do, actually."

"Ready to tell me what terrible, terrible thing you did?"

Stopping along the side of the trail, he sticks his hands into his pockets and leans against a massive tree. "I went to a bar one town over and got completely wasted."

Oh, Jay. To him, with a father like his, that *would* be worse than almost anything. Copying his position, I face him. "Okay." I hate that my actions turned him to drink. But this isn't about me. It's about him, and I want to hear him out, however painful it is.

His chest rises and falls more rapidly than before. "That bar...that night." Jordan glances up into the treetops as if trying to find the light. Then his eyes settle back on me. "That's where, and when, I met Georgia."

Oh, peanut brittle.

But the timing tracks. I don't know why I didn't think of it before. Probably I was just so lost in my own grief...

He continues. "We were both sitting at the bar, both drinking to drown our sorrows—hers over a recent breakup. I felt like I'd lost you too, like all hope of ever seeing you happy again was gone. Like I'd endangered our friendship. And I just wanted it all to go away, you know? The pain. And here was someone who seemed to understand. Who wanted to help me escape. Who wanted to escape herself."

I swallow, throat thick with emotion. "So, you...?"

"I'm not proud of it, but yeah. It was mutual and all that, but I still can't help but feel like I used her. I was drunk, but I was still aware enough to know I was acting like the kind of guy I never wanted to be." He swipes a hand along his forehead, under the brim of his hat. "The next morning, she was gone from our hotel room, and I thought I'd never see her again. Then six weeks later, she showed up in town and told me about Ryder."

"And you stepped up."

"I did what any decent guy would do."

"That's not true, though. A lot of guys would have let her do things on her own, but you changed your whole life to accommodate that little boy."

"And that little boy has been the biggest blessing in my life. I can't imagine not having him. Which is why it scares me, this thought that I might lose him."

"You won't." I step forward, grab his hand. "We did everything we could to make sure that won't happen, remember?"

"Thanks to you." His fingers trail up my arm and find a home against my cheek as he searches my eyes for something. "Lee, if this changes how you feel about me—"

"What? Of course it doesn't." Lifting up on my tiptoes, I give him a kiss. One filled with promise. "It honestly makes me love you more."

He steps into the gap between us and crushes my mouth with his before hauling me into his arms. I wrap my legs around him as he backs me up against the tree, kissing me until a gentle rain starts falling. Raindrops dance on my cheeks and weave into our hair, mingling with our laughter as it escapes between kisses. Each soft patter on the ground is drowned out by the sound of our hearts, and the air is invigorating, cleansing us of our doubts and fears. I am alive, vulnerable, and utterly cherished in Jordan's arms.

"Ready to go home?" he finally says.

It's not the first time he's asked me that question. The last time was after our wedding, when things between us were so fragile and new.

They're still new now, but there have been so many confessions between us since then. Instead of our past mistakes coming between us, revealing them has only strengthened our bond. "So ready," I say.

An hour later, we're in his truck, headed back down the mountain to fetch my car from the hotel, when Jordan's phone starts going crazy with texts and voicemails finally coming through. He laughs. "Think I should advertise the lack of reception for potential tour takers?"

"I'm not sure. It'll be a turnoff for certain clients and a bonus for others."

"True." His phone is nestled in a car mount attached to his truck's air vent, and Jordan frowns as his eyes flick back and forth between the phone and the road. "Sorry, can you check these for me? My mom texted me a whole bunch."

"Oh no. Yeah, sure." I grab his phone and input his pin, something Donny never gave me for his own devices. A flood of texts from various sources swoop in my vision.

LANDON

Bro, way to go! That guy deserved what he had coming to him.

LUCY

Are you guys okay? Is Mare? She's not answering her phone either, but I saw the video. I hate Donny. CALL ME.

CLAIRE

Um, did you know you've gone viral? Check out this link.

MOM

Honey, there's news with the custody case. Please call when you can.

SAMUEL GRANGER

We need to talk. Now.

"Oh no," I breathe, my chest tightening with each text I read.

"What?" Jordan's hands tighten on the steering wheel. "What's going on, Lee?"

I click the link in Jordan's sister's message, and it pulls up a video someone posted to social media. It already has 1 million views and climbing. It's labeled *The Hottest That's My Wife*

Moment Ever, and it's footage of the restaurant on Friday night. I can't hear what Donny's saying, but I can see the contorted rage on Jordan's face as he shoves Donny back, can hear "that's my *wife*" spoken in a raw, menacing tone that is so opposite of Normal Jordan that I almost wouldn't believe it had happened if I hadn't been there.

This is bad. This is so, so bad.

"Is that...?" Jordan's skin goes pale.

"The good news is...you're famous!" I try for a chuckle as I wiggle the phone at him. "The bad news is...well, I'm not sure. Your mom said to call because there's something new about the case. And your attorney left a very terse text. Oh, and look, a voicemail too."

"Play it, Lee. Please."

I press the speaker button and play Sam's message. "Hi, Jordan, this is Sam Granger." His voice, so genial the few times we met, is now clearly filled with annoyance. "It's Saturday evening, and I don't know where you are or what you're doing, but your custody case just got a lot more difficult to win." The man huffs out a loud sigh. "There's the little matter of this video that I'm sure you've seen. It doesn't look good, but we can probably explain it away. But then... Look, I understand that you felt desperate, but I didn't mean for you to get married under false pretenses."

My eyes widen, and Jordan curses under his breath.

"And I'm your attorney. I would have advised against it, but once it was done...I just would have rather had the information ahead of time and not been blindsided. But I got a notice today from the Comers' attorney that they'll now be seeking full custody—"

"WHAT?" Jordan roars.

"—because they claim to have proof, both in writing and

because of some overheard conversation in a bowling alley, that your marriage is fake."

Bowling alley? Oh no. I shrink in my seat.

"Give me a call and we'll figure this out. Our biggest hurdle is Judge Terpstra, who was new to the area when we first spoke but has had a chance to try a few cases since then. Turns out he's a stickler for two things: honesty and non-violence. So, we've got our work cut out for us. And before you ask, no, we can't delay the case. I know his clerk personally, and she said he won't reschedule cases because he wants kids to be in limbo for as short a time as possible. Okay, I think that's everything for now. Call me and we'll meet up to discuss the best course of action."

The message shuts off, and I just stare at Jordan. I can't speak, can't swallow. I'm drowning with a lack of breath to my lungs.

Because Jordan might legitimately lose Ryder, and it's all my fault.

twenty-three

JORDAN

It's been the longest day of my life.

I pull into my driveway beside Marilee's car, cut the truck's ignition, and just sit there slumped at the wheel, staring at the front of my house. The dull front sconces need a bulb change. The grass is overgrown, weeds and leaves overtake the yard, and the storm from Friday night broke a few large branches off the tree.

My property here is in a similar state as my work email, which has piled up over my long weekend away. Since it's President's Day and Ryder had the day off preschool, I was already planning to be home from work, simply looking over emails while he played and Marilee took a shift at the bakery. Instead, Mare had to call off work to stay home with Ryder, and I had to spend the day at Sam's office, trying to figure a way out of this mess I made of the custody battle.

I still don't have an answer. But I know one thing—telling Marilee about it will at least soothe the ache. She's always been good at calming me down, helping me breathe easier. Climbing from the truck, I head through the unlocked front door, and my heart squeezes at the sight in front of me.

The kitchen's seen a hurricane—a Cat 4, at least—with flour, sugar, and butter sprinkled all over the counters and dirty bowls and other dishes in and beside the sink. But in the middle of the counter is the world's coolest two-tiered cake resembling the outside of the Avengers Compound, with various Avengers action figures placed strategically along the top, and the words *Daddy, you're my hero* written in Marilee's perfect print along the bottom.

But that's not the part that has my heart in a vice. No, it's seeing my son curled up on Marilee's lap asleep, a book lying beside them on the couch. He's tucked against her, and she's got her head down too, clinging to him like she's never letting go.

I set my wallet and keys on the counter. Her head pops up, and I can see she's been crying—her mascara smudged, her eyes red. I don't wait another moment before moving the book and joining them on the couch. Then I hold them both while she holds Ryder, my fingers smoothing through his thick red hair that's sprinkled with flour.

"He wanted to help make your cake."

"It's amazing." I lean in, kiss the side of her head, breathe in the sweetness of her. "You're amazing."

"Jay." She sighs. "We need to talk."

"Yeah, I'll tell you all about the attorney's office. Just let me get this guy to bed."

Her face is stone, unreadable and strange, but she nods. I lift Ryder from her lap and walk him back to his bedroom, tucking him under his Captain America sheets and giving him one last glance before I turn out his light and close the door. Then I follow the hallway back to the living room, where Marilee is no longer sitting on the couch, but standing by the Christmas tree.

She's taking down ornaments one by one, rewrapping them

in tissue paper and placing them in the tub I keep in the garage with holiday decorations. And she's crying, again.

"Hey, hey, hey." I gently take her shoulders, turn her to me. "What's going on?"

"I'm sorry. I'm just a waterworks festival lately." She gives me a brave smile and pivots back to the tree, continuing to remove hooks off the artificial branches. "What did Mr. Granger say?"

"He confirmed what we suspected. Some old biddy that's a friend of Constance's heard you talking with your friends at Bowl O'Rama—"

"I'm so, so sorry." Her hands go faster, removing the ornaments at lightning speed. "I should have kept my stupid mouth shut, especially knowing we were in her town."

"Lee—"

"Don't try to tell me it's not my fault. It is." She stops for a moment, glances over at me. "And what about the supposed written evidence?"

"Apparently Constance found a copy of our contract. The rules we wrote up."

She gasps. "What? How?"

"That one's on me, I'm afraid. Ryder asked me a week or so ago for some paper to color on, and I told him there was some in the printer in my bedroom…"

"Let me guess. You had just printed the rules out?" Ornaments fly again, one at a time, from her hand into the box.

I cringe watching them go, but nothing breaks. "Yep, it was an earlier version of the contract I printed here—the final one that we signed was printed at my office. But after printing that earlier version, I got distracted and forgot to grab it off the printer. When I finally remembered, it wasn't there, but I just figured my computer had malfunctioned or I hadn't hit the Print button like I thought."

"So Ryder used the contract as a coloring sheet…"

"And it was in his backpack when he was playing at their house last week. Yes."

"Ugh."

"Ugh is right." I unhook the lights from the tree and start winding them up. I still don't understand why she's choosing to tackle this tonight, but I'm going to help so she knows she isn't alone in it. "Anyway, Sam basically spent hours grilling me about every aspect of our relationship, and he still wasn't satisfied that our position is strong enough to win. I told him I'd like to speak, to tell our side of the story, and he said no way."

"Really? Why?"

"Said there are too many holes in our story, that the judge might not believe us. And it opens me up to their shark of an attorney's cross examination. Who knows what else they could bring up."

Marilee's fingers tremble as she reaches for another hook— and she yelps, yanking it back.

"You okay?" I reach for her hand and pull it close to find her fingertip bleeding from a prick. "Hang on."

In the bathroom, I find a Band-Aid and some first aid cream and rush back to her. She's sitting on the couch, tears streaming down her face yet again.

I slide onto the coffee table in front of her. "Does it hurt really bad?"

"No."

"You sure? It seems like it does." I reach for her hand again.

"I'll do it," she says softly.

"I don't mind."

"Just…please hand me the bandage, Jay."

My forehead furrows as I place the Neosporin and Band-Aid beside her. "What's wrong?"

She uses her teeth to unscrew the lid of the cream. "Other than the fact you might lose your son because of me? Oh, nothing much." A large blob of the Neosporin shoots from the tube onto her finger.

"Because of you? The bowling alley was a simple mistake, just like leaking the contract."

Marilee rips open the Band-Aid next, and the disposable flaps and wrapper float down to the ground at her feet. "This whole marriage of convenience was my idea. Another stupid idea from my stupid brain—not thinking things through, just like always. I've brought my chaos into your life, into Ryder's life, and I will never forgive myself if you lose him because of me."

She flicks the bandage around her finger, and tears dot the lenses of her glasses.

What is she saying? "Geez, Lee, come on. It doesn't matter how this marriage started. We'll just tell the judge how it is now—"

"Like Sam said, he'll never believe us."

"He might."

She stands again abruptly, and I do too, reaching for her— but she's back at that darn tree.

And I see what she's doing now, why she's yanking those ornaments off with fervor. "I'm not letting you do this." I reach into the box and rehang ornaments at the same speed she's pulling them down.

"Jordan." She stomps her little foot, and it would be adorable if it didn't terrify me. If this—her attempt to put away the thing in this house that I left up for her and her alone— didn't mean...

"You can't leave, Lee. I know what you're thinking here. That you have somehow ruined my chance to keep Ryder. But I don't think that's true. I think if we tell the judge that you're here and this is real and you're what is best for Ryder because he loves you like a mom—"

"But I'm not, am I? His mom. However much I want to be. And I'm not your wife, not really."

She might as well have taken a whisk to my insides, scrambling them up like eggs. "Look, I know what I said yesterday, about not trapping you in this marriage." And I meant it. But I didn't tell her what I really want. I should have and I didn't. But I'm going to now. "But—"

"And you were right. I have a choice here."

My heart pounds in my throat because, yes, she does. "So you're just going to, what? Walk away?"

Stepping forward, she grabs my hands, and I can feel the rough bandage covering her soft touch, a barrier between us. "I will always be here for you. For Ryder. But right now, I think it's better if we get a little space to think about what's best for all of us. So I'm going to go stay with Blake and Lucy for... Well, I don't know how long. Okay?"

I want to pull her in, hold her there forever, remind her of the love we just spoke about on Saturday, yesterday, this morning when I kissed her forehead as I slid out of bed and headed for the attorney's office.

But it's not enough. It's never been enough.

Because Mom is right—love requires a choice.

And Marilee is not choosing me. Again.

And I could sit here and beg and cajole and try to get her to stay, but whether it's my pride or my battered heart or the pure exhaustion of this fight I've been fighting for fifteen years— trying, desperately, to make her mine, to love her like she needs me to—I just can't.

"Okay." I slump onto the couch, leaning forward, elbows on my knees. Then I spy something I didn't before—her suitcase, right beside the door.

She was planning this all day. From the moment I walked in, she knew she was going to leave.

She'd already made her choice. Nothing I said was ever going to stop her.

"Are you still going to come to court tomorrow?"

Marilee grips the edge of the mantel. "Of course I am. But I think it's best if I drive myself there."

I exhale. "Fine."

But I don't feel fine. Nothing's fine. I'm pretty sure I just lost the love of my life. Maybe my best friend too. And if I also lose my son?

Yeah. I'm the exact opposite of fine.

twenty-four

I am a sobby, sodden mess.

So, naturally, I find myself in the kitchen of The Blackberry Muffin on my day off, my hands flecked with pink and purple frosting as I attempt to make a unicorn cake for Scarlett's upcoming eighth birthday.

But right now, I'm failing even at that, because it more closely resembles a scary clown blob.

Staring at the mess on the yellow granite island, I wipe my trickling nose with the back of my hand, and instantly I know I've smeared frosting there.

At that moment, my boss Marla swoops into the kitchen via the swinging door connected to the lobby and freezes upon seeing me. Her eyes flit between me and the cake, and her lips purse.

"Go ahead. You can laugh." I push the cake away and slump onto one of the three black stools pushed under the edge of the island. "It's awful."

"It is." Marla, while sweet, is also no nonsense. She'll tell it to you straight, but always with a silver lining. "May I?" Her finger hovers over the cake.

"Why not?"

She dips it in and takes a lick of frosting from her finger. "At least it tastes good, honey." Then she winks, and the woman's rosy cheeks are almost enough to cheer me up for the moment.

But then the moment is over, and I remember that the court case is in two hours—and after that, I don't know what's going to happen to me and Jordan.

Marla must sense my distress because she wipes her finger off on a towel and comes around to give me a solid pat on the shoulder. "There, there, dear. It's just a cake. And I know you're sad about not having much time in the kitchen once you take over for me—"

"You do?"

"Of course. I felt that way too, at first. But then I got invigorated by the prospect of growing something beyond myself, beyond my skills." She studies me. "You don't feel that way, though, do you?"

I blow out a breath. "I confess, I don't. But maybe I will." I try to infuse hope into my tone. "That's not why I'm upset, though."

"Hmm." She gathers the supplies I've left dirty on her counter and carries them to the sink. "It's about Mr. Carmichael and your fake marriage then?"

I choke on a sputter. "How did you—"

"Small-town living, dear. You cannot escape the gossip." Almost instantly, a bottle of cold water appears before me. "But based on your reaction, I'm guessing there's an element of truth to it?"

I nod, unable to keep what I'm sure is a miserable expression off my face. "It was my idea, a way to show the judge in Ryder's custody case that Jordan had a stable home. Only now..."

"Oh my. Well, that is a conundrum, isn't it?" Marla slowly lowers herself onto the stool beside me, and her knees and joints pop loudly.

Sighing, I fiddle with the cap of the water bottle, flicking it open and then closed again. "I'm just so tired of making the wrong choice, Marla. Of screwing up my life and others' lives in the process. That's not what I want to happen, but inevitably...it does."

"And what's the alternative to making the wrong choice?"

"Making the right one, of course."

"And how are you supposed to know what that is?"

I frown. "If I knew, then I wouldn't be in this mess."

"Maybe, maybe not." Marla's frail shoulders lift and lower. "My dear, life is full of choices—some big, some small—and you can't very well not make them. Just by not making a choice, you're making a choice."

My head spins and I place it in my hands.

The weight of her comforting touch lands on my back. "You simply have to do the best you can with the information you have. Use the things God has given you—like a sound mind, and friends who love you, whose advice you trust. Not to mention that precious heart that's beating in your chest."

I glance up at her, and she's gazing at me with so much grandmotherly affection I want to cry.

She reaches a veined and wrinkled hand toward me, tapping my chest right below the clavicle. "Honestly, Marilee, the fact that your heart is not hardened after your first marriage, but still soft and open, is a testament to the strong person you are."

"Thank you, Marla. But this heart has led me astray more times than I can count."

"It does that sometimes. But usually it's because we've allowed other voices to invade our minds."

"What voices?" I ask softly.

"Well, the voices of those who want us to fail. Or the busy-bodies, who don't have any stake or say in your life." She looks at me pointedly. "The biggest voice keeping us from making the right choices, though, is usually the voice of fear. But baby, fear is a liar. It will twist up the truth and turn you upside down with it."

My heart swells and contracts. "Oh, Marla. I've just been such a mess."

"I know, honey, I know." Like a mother would, she sweeps her thumb under my glasses and gathers my tears, carrying them away. "But here's the truth—we are *all* a mess. We all need a little saving. We all make bad choices sometimes. But leaning into love instead of fear? That's never a mistake."

"Even if you choose the wrong man like I did?"

"Tell me this. Have you learned from your experiences? Have you grown? Because that's what life is—a series of experiences that we can either use to make us better or bitter. And from where I'm sitting, you, Marilee Moffitt, are far better now than where you began. You've taken what could have been bitterness and invested it in those you love."

"But I've also hurt the people I love." Oh, Jordan. And Ryder—what must *he* have thought when I wasn't at the house this morning to see him off to school?

"We all do that sometimes too. It's called being human." Marla's eyes spark. "The question is, what are you going to do about it now that you recognize the hold fear's had on you?"

Oh, Fear...my old friend. But it's not, is it? It's been my frenemy, keeping me close, pretending it cared about me, only wanting to protect me from danger. But all the while, it's been holding me back from really, truly living. From making choices, because making a choice could lead to mistakes. But like Marla said, making the choice to stay in my comfort zone is still a choice.

I push to a stand, the legs of the stool scraping the tile floor. "Marla, I have to go."

"I know you do, baby."

I lean down to kiss her weathered cheek. "Thank you," I whisper. "And maybe, later this week...we can talk about the bakery." Because fear's been keeping me rooted in that decision too. And maybe it's time to face what I really want...and be okay with failure if it comes to it. At least I'd have tried.

"That'd be fine."

With another goodbye, I'm out the front door of the bakery and in my car, racing up Hillside Drive to Jordan's house, praying I'm not too late.

And when I arrive and don't see his truck in the driveway, my heart seizes.

Still, maybe there's a slight chance...

I run inside. "Jay? Ryder?"

But the hallway is dark, and the air feels sad. I peek out back, just in case. But reality settles in.

Nobody's home.

I'll have to meet them at the courthouse after all.

And by not being here for him, I've fed into Jordan's biggest fear—that the people he loves won't show up for him.

But there's no time to dwell on my mistakes. Only time to fix them. And I suddenly know what I can do to show him I will always have his back. That we all do.

Turning toward the front door, something on the refrigerator catches my eye. A drawing in color—a new one, with a big *Ryder* scrawled in the corner in red crayon. As I study it, my jaw drops at the picture's simplicity. At its profoundness. Oh, this sweet, sweet boy...

My sweet, sweet boy.

I pull the drawing off the fridge, tuck it into my bag, and make a mad dash for my car. I know exactly where I need to be and what I need to do.

I just hope I'm not too late.

The hearing starts in ten minutes, and my tie is choking me.

Reaching up, I give it a tug while I walk up and down the courthouse steps. It's a relatively small building as far as courthouses go, an attractive white with a red-tiled roof. A round planter with flowers between the steps and the front doors. Some pleasant grassy areas where court employees eat their lunch on this blustery, beautiful day.

But all of that means nothing.

Because inside, the fate of my family will be determined.

And my wife—the woman who said she'd always have my back, no matter what—isn't here yet.

"She'll be here." Mom sits on the edge of the stone planter. She drove down with me and Ryder, who is currently in the care of my older sister Claire. Dad couldn't be bothered to show up, but at least my sister—who I'm not even as close to as I'd like to be—took the day off work from her fancy banker job in San Francisco to help look after my son during the hearing. They're sequestered away in a room next to the courtroom where Judge Eli Terpstra will preside over our hearing. "Traffic's really bad, what with that construction on the highway. It's a good thing we left extra early, or we'd have been slowed down too."

"Maybe." I check my watch again before running my hands down the sides of my face, smooth from my morning visit to the Golden Highlight for a haircut and shave. "I already don't know how I'm possibly going to win this hearing, but it's going to look especially bad if my wife doesn't even show."

"Oh, Jordan." Mom looks extra tired, and I feel terrible that she's here in the middle of a flare-up. But when I saw her condition and mentioned she should stay home with Dad, she lifted her chin and said nothing was keeping her from being here to support me today. And I'll admit, I was so grateful I didn't have the energy to try to stop her. "Your attorney still doesn't have much confidence?"

We didn't have a chance to talk in the car since Ryder was right there and I've tried to keep him in the dark about why we're here today. He just knows he's hanging with Auntie Claire and might have to talk to a judge in a really cool courtroom like the one in *Bee Movie*.

"Sam wants me to let him do all the talking, for me not to testify."

"That's silly. How are you supposed to show the judge you're a stand-up guy, that you don't have anything to hide?"

"But I lied, Mom."

"What lie did you tell? You've loved that girl forever."

"But she didn't love me." And I'm still not sure she really does—not if it was so easy for her to leave last night.

I guess that's not fair. She did look wrecked. And yet, when I watched the taillights of her car driving down the road, the gut punch felt the same either way.

"The judge will think I lied or tricked Marilee. Either way, it's not a good look." I sit beside Mom. "And Sam just doesn't want to give Constance and Larry's lawyer a chance to pounce on me. She's pretty tough, I guess."

She pats my knee. "You're tough too, you know. And while I don't think you should discount all of your attorney's advice, in the end, it's your life, your son, Jordan. If you feel like you need to speak, do it."

Her inner strength and confidence flow toward me, holding me up. "Even if it rocks the boat?"

"Especially then. Take a risk for love, son, and speak from your heart. If the judge has any sense, he will see the love you have for your son and know exactly where he belongs, whether Marilee shows up or not." She stands. "Though for the record, I still think she will."

Exhaling, I rise too. "I hope so."

Then, together, we walk into the courthouse and toward Courtroom 2, where Sam meets us down the hall. He's wearing a brown suit with a briefcase tucked under one arm and reassures me that everything's in order. Larry and Constance stand on the other side of the doors with a middle-aged woman in a striking blue pantsuit, her brown bob cut at a sharp angle. Constance glances my way, purses her lips, and turns away. At least Larry, for his part, gives me a small wave before frowning and scratching the back of his bald head that shines under the harsh fluorescent lighting of the courthouse.

My chest tightens at the sight of our friends—Landon, Lucy, Blake, Chloe, Freddy, even April and the twins— huddled in a quiet group, all dressed nicely in skirts or slacks. Sam said he might call Landon, Lucy, and Blake to the stand as character witnesses depending on how the trial is going, but I didn't expect the rest of them to be here.

I guess I should have, but I didn't.

There are a few glaring absences, though. My dad, no surprise. And—

"Where's Mare?" Lucy's hand finds my elbow, her voice wrapped in concern.

Shoving my hands into my pockets, I shrug. "We didn't drive together."

"What? Why? And why is she back sleeping at our house?" she hisses, glancing over her shoulder toward Constance and Larry, who don't appear to be paying us any mind. "She wouldn't talk to me about it last night, and she was gone before I got up, but something has to be very wrong for her not to be here."

"That's a question for her, I guess. If she shows up." I have the sudden urge to rip this tie from my neck and toss it away, because breathing has once again become a chore.

"Jordan! Of course she's going to show up. She loves you and Ryder."

Does she, though? The question burrows deep in my subconscious. I hate doubting her. And the thing is, I'm not mad. Just sad. And oh so tired.

Exhausted, in fact. But that will mean nothing to the judge, and Ryder needs me to be strong. And despite the crowd here today, nobody else can fight this battle for me.

Lucy frowns, Blake at her back, and she looks like she's going to say more, but then the bailiff calls us in. We shuffle through the thick beige double doors. The room's smaller than courtrooms I've seen in movies, with only a few rows of chairs set up on either side of the short aisle. A waist-height paneled wall divides the gallery from the two basic wooden tables equipped with three chairs and a pair of microphones each. The courtroom echoes with the sound of everyone getting settled. A court reporter and clerk take their seats at a desk that stands between our tables and the elevated judge's bench, to the right of which is the witness stand.

"All rise," the bailiff announces.

I draw in a sharp breath. It's here.

We all stand, and the back door opens. A man in a black robe and graying hair walks through and takes a seat as the bailiff continues. "This court with the Honorable Judge Eli Terpstra presiding is now in session. Please be seated and come to order."

Here we go.

My palms sweat as the Comers' attorney—a Sheila Devoney—launches into the reason we are all here: sweet Ryder. She's very dramatic as she paints a picture of what a great mom Georgia was (a picture I agree with) and how she was taken too soon. How the Comers had concerns over my parenting, but when they raised them with their daughter, she said she wasn't worried because she was in his life to balance things out. (Not sure how true that was, because Georgia never expressed concerns to me.)

I have to sit there while Sheila disparages my character, parading witnesses in front of the judge, whose expression is solemn. He's clearly invested, nodding along. Then Ms. Devoney calls a waitress from the hotel restaurant to the stand and enters the social media video into evidence. The moment I punch Donny is displayed on the television for all to see, and I catch a hint of disapproval cross Judge Terpstra's face.

Great.

Sam cross-examines the woman, but she wasn't close enough to overhear our conversation, only enough to know I was angry and upset and Donny seemed to be laughing and "not causing any problems."

When he sits down, I lean toward him and whisper, "If I don't say something, the judge is going to think I'm violent for no reason." How else is he supposed to know that the man I hit was my wife's abusive ex, saying very derogatory things? Sure, maybe violence was not the best course of action, but I definitely didn't hit an innocent man out of nowhere.

"If you get on the stand, you'll open yourself up to a lot more criticism than that, because you'll be obligated to tell the truth about your marriage." Sam's eyebrows give a knowing jaunt. "Don't worry. We'll have a chance to tell our side through our witnesses."

But that's the thing. *I* won't have a chance to tell my side. Not if I sit here and stay silent.

My eyebrows narrow as I listen to Constance's friend on the stand talking about the bowling alley incident, then Constance as she tells about her discovery of our marriage contract. She does seem genuinely distraught over the whole thing, but I can't tell if it's just a ploy to get sympathy, or if she really, truly believes that I'm the scum of the earth.

Who knows. Maybe I am.

But I love my son, and I'm not done fighting for him.

Sheila pats Constance on the shoulder as Constance returns to her seat. "We rest our case, Your Honor."

He nods, then turns to Sam. "Are you ready to call your first witness, Counselor?"

"Actually—"

"Yes." Pushing back my chair, I stand.

Murmurs from the audience create a kind of white noise behind me. I can't hear what they're saying, but the noise feels frenzied.

And yet, everything in me has stilled. I am calm. I know what I need to do.

Take a risk for love, son...

"What are you doing?" Sam hisses at me.

"I'm sorry, Sam. I have to do this."

"Even if it costs you everything?"

I glance back at my mom, and she pats her chest—right over her heart—as she nods.

"I'll always wonder if I should have testified."

"Counselor, is there a problem?" the judge asks.

"No problem, Your Honor." Sam looks at me and rubs the corner of his eyes, sighing. "We call Jordan Carmichael to the stand."

I make my way to the witness stand, shaking out my hands before the bailiff brings a Bible over and swears me in. When I'm done saying the words, the door to the courtroom opens.

And sunshine plows right in.

Marilee steps through the door, her hair windswept and her skirt crooked. She's got something—maybe a paper?—clutched in her hand and looks right at me, wide-eyed, mouthing "Sorry" before stepping aside.

Revealing my father behind her.

Dressed in a suit that barely buttons, his thin wisps of hair combed over his otherwise bald head, he shuffles inside, toward my mother, whose hands are over her mouth.

Marilee scoots past Lucy and Blake, who squeezes her arm, to join my parents. She grips the low wall in front of her, where she's set the piece of paper that was in her hand upon entry. Her earnest look is a balm. No matter what's between us, she's here—and she brought the one person I never thought would show up for me. If that's not having my back, I don't know what is.

And it gives me the extra bolstering I need.

Sam approaches the stand. "Jordan, please tell the court in your own words why you believe the Comers' petition—and their classification of you as violent and a liar—to be false."

Instead of looking at Marilee, I turn my attention to the judge, the one who will decide our fate. And I do what Mom suggested and speak from my heart. I explain the video. I know sharing the details of her ex with the court will be painful for Marilee, but I also know she won't mind, not if it helps us keep Ryder.

"And what about the marriage, Jordan? Was it indeed fake, as Ms. Devoney so disparagingly put it?"

Now for *this*, I look at Marilee. But she's not looking at me. Her gaze is on her shoes until I speak my next words.

"Not for me, it wasn't."

At that, her head snaps up, eyebrows knit together.

"Can you expand on that, please?" Sam asks. I'm sure on the inside, he's annoyed with me—I'm definitely going off script here—but he's maintaining a patient facade at least.

"I've always loved Marilee. Since the first moment I saw her, I knew I'd always love her."

Her chin trembles, and her friends issue a low murmuring chorus of "Awww!"

I take a breath. "I love her when she's covered in flour from head to toe. I love her when she's crying over a romcom. I love her when she's wearing that smile she gets when she's creating something delicious and beautiful. I love her when she's teasing me, and I love her when she's indignant for her friends. But most of all"—I lean into the microphone, my voice strong and crisp and clear, leaving no doubt of the truth of what I'm saying —"I love her when she's a mom to our son."

My voice cracks at the last words, and I quickly swipe at a tear that finds its way down my cheek. "I love Ryder fiercely, but that woman right there... She loves him tenderly, the way a mother should. And if you truly want what's best for him, you wouldn't dream of taking him away from her."

And I didn't think Marilee had any more tears left, but I should have known better, because my sweet, sensitive best friend—my wife for who knows how much longer—is crying again.

"But she's *not* his mother!"

This from Constance, who has shot to her feet.

The judge seems taken aback. "Madam, it is not your turn to speak."

Constance shakes her head vehemently. "I'm just making a statement. He's calling that woman Ryder's mother, but his *real* mother—my daughter—wanted us to have custody of him. You saw the will."

"Again, Madam, it is not your turn to speak. I realize that family court is a bit less formal than other proceedings, but we will still have decorum and order." The judge turns to Sam. "Counselor, you may proceed."

"No further questions."

"Ms. Devoney, would you like to cross-examine the witness?"

Sheila glances at me, then at Constance, who has slumped down in her chair. She must decide that my testimony was either damning enough, or that asking me further questions will not be good for their case, because she mumbles, "No, Your Honor."

The judge tells me I can step down.

I slide back into my chair and feel a strong hand on my shoulder. Surprised, I glance back to find my dad blinking at me. He gives my shoulder a squeeze and releases me, sitting back.

It's brief. To anyone else, it would seem like nothing more than a passing affection.

But to me, it's everything.

And it's all because of Marilee.

The rest of the trial feels like a whirlwind as Sam calls Landon and Blake both to the stand, and both confirm my story. After brief cross-examinations, in which Sheila tries to catch them in lies—and make me look like an irresponsible liar—my attorney says we rest our case. He wanted to get Marilee on the stand, but I said no. She's already done enough by being here, and I'm not going to put her through that.

Sam gives me a firm nod that tells me we've got a good shot at winning this thing.

At the other table, Constance and Sheila are whispering loudly. I can't hear what they're saying, but the tension snaps in the air like a whip.

I have no clue what Judge Terpstra is thinking. I can't decipher the expression behind his glasses, and he merely sits there, head tilted as he appears to study us. Finally, he sits back in his seat. "I know this is most unusual, but I feel I need more information before I can make a decision. Young lady." His eyes find Marilee—and she freezes. "Would you mind joining me at the bench, please?"

"Um. Yes. I mean, no, Your Honor." Marilee stands, at first leaving the paper behind on the wall. Then, with a glance back at it, she hurries to snatch it up before approaching the judge.

What does he want to ask her? I glance at Sam, but he just shrugs and redirects his attention to the front.

"Please state your name for the court."

"Marilee Moffitt. I, um, haven't had a chance to change it to Carmichael."

Aw, Lee.

"That's all right." Waving her off, the judge leans forward and studies her. "I cannot force you to take the stand, but I do have some questions for you if you wouldn't mind answering them."

"Oh, um. Of course." She's standing at a slight angle below the judge, so I can see her profile. Her fingers crinkle the paper.

The judge seems to notice too. "Is that paper relevant to today's proceedings? You seem particularly attached to it." And that's when I notice it—a shift in his demeanor. His voice is soft and pliable, almost fatherly.

I want to laugh. Without meaning to, Marilee's cast her spell over him, the same way she does most everyone she meets.

"Yes, well." Her eyes flit down to the paper, then over to Constance of all people. "Sorry, it's just... Do you mind if I..." She indicates holding it out to Constance.

"Please let me see it first."

"Of course." She does, and one of his eyebrows quirks.

The judge points to the clerk. "Hand it to her, please. Clerk, please show this over the projector and enter it into evidence."

Marilee glances back at me before shuffling toward the clerk, who fires up the projector and sticks the paper there. It appears on the screen—and I huff out a laugh.

Brilliant woman.

Because projected for the courtroom is a drawing Ryder presented me with this morning. It cut me to the core, but he said he'd made it with Miss Lucy over the weekend and wanted to display it for Marilee to see "when she gets home."

I didn't have the heart to tell him that might be never.

But my wife has clearly been home—and she's brought with her the key to winning this battle if ever there was one.

"Please explain what we're seeing, Ms. Moffitt."

"It's a drawing Ryder did. As you can see, it's labeled 'my family.'" Marilee walks to the screen and puts the full force of her attention on Constance—and then she speaks directly to her. "There's him in the very middle, and Jordan, and me." Under the stick figure with big glasses, it says *Mommy*. "And over here, to the side, you can see four people with canes. I think that's supposed to be all of his grandparents."

Mom and Dad chuckle behind me, as do all of our friends (and some of the women are definitely awww-ing again). Even Larry has to fight a grin. But Constance is still staring at the photo, squinting. "And what about there? What's that in the upper right-hand corner?"

Marilee taps the part of the picture in question. "That is an angel with long red hair and a halo." Her eyes shimmer. "And it says Mama."

"What? Oh..." Constance's voice breaks as she starts to cry.

Marilee hurries toward her—probably breaking all sorts of court rules, but the judge is allowing it—and drops into a squat beside Constance, grabbing her hands. "Constance, Ryder hasn't forgotten Georgia, and we won't let him forget her. I know you miss your daughter, but don't rip this little boy from a home that's good and right, where he feels safe and loved. There's not a competition for his love. As you can see, he's got enough to go around."

Constance's sobbing now, and she grips Marilee's hands right back. "I'm s-s-sorry. I just...I miss my girl so much."

"I know the pain of loss. I know."

Gah, how I love this woman. Her ability to love even those who have wounded her astounds me daily.

The judge seems thoroughly captivated by the display in front of us but still asks for order in the courtroom—though honestly, it seems more of a formality for the records than a request. Marilee goes back to her seat, and the judge asks for Ryder to be brought in, just to confirm nobody coerced him into drawing the picture.

When he sees Constance crying, he runs to her and gives her a hug. "Don't cry, Grammy. It's okay." Then from her lap, he sees the drawing on the screen and exclaims, "Hey! I drew that."

The judge says, "Hi, Ryder. I'm Judge Terpstra."

My kid wrinkles his nose and says, "You don't look like the lady judge in *Bee Movie*."

That gets everyone laughing. Even the judge, who says, "No, I don't guess I do." And when he asks Ryder if anyone made him draw the picture, Ryder holds up his fingers and wiggles them, shrugging and saying, "Just my hands. And my brain."

Constance laughs, hugging Ryder to herself and catching my eye over her attorney's head. With eyes full of unshed tears, she says something to Sheila, who hisses back at her.

Finally, the attorney stands. "Your Honor, in light of...well, everything we just heard, we'd like to withdraw our petition for custody."

My heart stutters.

What?

The air buzzes as the judge declares this hearing officially over, as he sees no reason why the custody of Ryder Carmichael should change, so long as I agree to continue granting the Comers visitation rights.

And then I'm leaping from my chair, hugging my son—who has no idea why we're having a party in the courtroom—and shaking hands with Constance and Larry to show no hard feelings, and thanking my parents and sister and friends for coming. Everyone starts talking about grabbing dinner at a local restaurant together and Ryder asks my parents if we can go to the park and it's a ruckus as the judge slips away and we celebrate this happy ending.

But I have an even happier end in mind.

Finally, I turn toward Marilee. She must sense my gaze because she glances over from her conversation with Chloe and

Lucy and immediately walks toward me. We step slightly away from the group.

"We did it," she says. Her soft smile is everything I want to wake up to every morning, everything I need day in and day out.

"*You* did it." And I want to reach for her, want to fight for this, for us. I don't want her to feel pressured, but I also have to show her what she means to me. So I gently take her hands in mine.

And she doesn't pull away. In fact, she steps closer.

"Jay." There's chaos swirling around us, but Marilee's zeroed in on me. "I'm so sorry I left like that."

"I understand why you did."

"And I'm sorry I was late."

"You had a good reason." I glance over at my dad, who's got his arm around Mom, Ryder tucked against his leg as they chat with my sister. His eyes look clearer than they have in a long time. "How did you get him to come?"

"Let's just say I summoned every bit of bossy I had in me—and also plied him with close to a gallon of coffee." A pause as her face softens. "But for real, I just reminded him that it was literally his job to show up for you today, and that if he loved you at all, he'd be here. Because love is showing up, right?"

"Right." I give her hands a squeeze. "I'm honestly surprised that convinced him, though."

"Jordan, he was horrified. He said, 'Of course I love him. But he's better off without me there.'"

I frown. "How could he actually think that?"

"You two have a lot of talking to do, but I think..." She bites her lip, smiling. "Maybe something I said shook loose his own demons. I'm not sure, but I think he's open to the idea of doing better now. He's here, anyway, and that's the first step."

"You're amazing, you know that?" Because if anyone could

change a hard-hearted man, it would be her—pure sunlight cracking its way through dried-out concrete.

"Not really. I just thought you could use all the support you could get," she says. "Though if I'd known traffic would take forever..."

"I love that you did that for me." I close the final bit of a gap between us. "Thank you. And that picture—wow. You saved the day with that. Guess you found it at the house?"

She nods. "Marla helped me to realize a few things this morning. Once I did, I raced to your house to see if I could still ride with you. You were gone, but I found that instead. It was a beautiful reminder from that little boy, that love surrounds us... if only we hold it close. If only we choose it. And I've made a choice."

Her voice is shaking, and I can tell the words are hard for her.

Oh man. This could be bad.

I brace for the truth.

Her chest expands with a deep breath. "If I thought I wouldn't be kicked out of this courtroom, I'd march over to the clerk, grab the so-called evidence of our contract—and rip it to shreds."

"Wait...what?" Laughing, I cup her face gently between my hands. "What does that mean, exactly?"

"It means that I choose you. I choose Ryder. I choose us." Her smile lights up all my dark places and doubts. "No more fear. I choose love. Because I love you, Jordan, and not just as a friend. As a woman loves a man who is everything to her. And you're everything to me. You and Ryder—you're my family."

"Marilee Holly Moffitt, you are unreal." Smiling, I shake my head. I can't even believe this woman's sweetness and goodness. The fact she's picking me, a guy who has screwed up more times than I can count, who will inevitably screw up again. "I love you *so* much."

Eyes shining, she taps her chin playfully. My little minx, always bringing a spark of fun to my life. "Since we're in a court of law, it feels appropriate to ask you to present evidence of that love."

"Hmm. All right." I gather her into my arms and tug her right up against me. "Allow me to present Exhibit A."

And I don't care that everyone is probably watching us. I kiss that woman like it's the first time, pouring every memory into it—the beautiful, the painful, the hilarious, the everyday, the special, the angry, the quiet, and the unforgettable.

I want to kiss her like that for the rest of our lives...if she'll have me.

But I can be patient. I can savor and enjoy. I can date my wife, give her time to make sure this is the life she wants to choose. And once she's sure, I'll ask her to marry me again...

This time, for real.

Eventually, she pulls back, laughing. "Hmm, that's certainly a start, but I think I'm going to need more convincing. What other evidence do you have?"

My hands flex against her waist. "This may take a while."

"I'll allow it."

And I don't wait for her to change her mind. I dive in for another kiss and another and another.

Because when something matters as much as this, I'm nothing if not persuasive.

APRIL

Five months later

I'm a romance writer who hates weddings. Go figure.

Some might infer it's because I never had one of my own, despite being a mom. And fine, *some* might be a little right. A teensy, teensy amount of right. A minuscule amount.

Really, the biggest reason I hate weddings is because they require me to get dressed up. And for someone who is the poster child for women who wear yoga pants but don't do yoga, dresses are a veritable form of torture.

But for one of my besties, I will make an exception. I'm sacrificial like that.

The timer on my phone goes off, and I swipe the reminder upward. Sighing, I close my computer and lean back against the headboard of Elisse's queen-sized bed. No inspiration's coming anyway, not today, not surrounded by the chaos brewing outside on the Loveland family's vineyard grounds. After a long day of mimosas, nails, hair, makeup, photos, and more tulle than a person should have to endure in a single lifetime, the sun's finally setting.

I can hear the strings of the quartet Chloe and Elisse arranged to play at Marilee and Jordan's second—but first and only *real*—wedding, and I know the little bit of writing time I had available to me today is over and done. At least until the ceremony is finished and my services as bridesmaid are no longer required.

So much for my looming deadline. So much for the writer's block keeping the story just on the other side of the clouds. I can see it like a hazy silhouette, and I think it's laughing at me.

But between parenting, working at the bookstore, and spending the last several Saturdays I've had off at bridal showers, baby showers, and dress fittings, the only time available has been the quiet of the evenings. After Dad's shut off his baseball games, and Mom's turned in for the night after an evening of quilting, and Scar's well into dreamland...

And it seems to be at night when my brain likes to retreat to the past. To the *what-ifs*.

Also, it's hard to write romance when you haven't been so much as kissed in nine years. So, you know. I feel a bit justified at the paltry word count on my computer.

Not that Cynthia will care...

My phone buzzes again, and this time, I shut off the alarm and stand from the bed, smoothing the front of my strapless, tea-length gown. Moving to Elisse's floor-length mirror, I examine myself from side to side, making sure my dress isn't tucked up into my underwear or some other such romcom *faux pas*. I give the top of my dress a tug, and it goes...exactly nowhere. With no real boobs or curves or height to speak of, the thing kind of just hangs on me like a drape, but at least Marilee put me in one of the green dresses (along with Kelsey and Jordan's sister Claire). With my auburn hair and pale skin, the red dresses worn by Chloe, Elisse, and a very pregnant Lucy as part of the bride's Christmas in July-themed wedding would totally wash me out.

Elisse flounces into her bedroom. Her short hair parted on the side and done in waves would soften her were it not for the look of pure exasperation on her face. "What are you doing back here, April? We needed you five minutes ago for some last-minute photos on the deck."

"Sheesh, sorry. I was trying to get some writing in."

"Write on your own time, girl." Elisse snatches a little box off her white dresser and shoves it at me.

Opening it, I find a pair of Christmas tree earrings inside. I smile. So very Marilee.

"Let's go, let's go." Hands clapping, Elisse leaves just the way she came.

I salute her back with a "Sir, yes, Sir," then stick the earrings in before snatching up my computer and whisking outside to the home's back deck overlooking the hills and valleys in the distance. The chatter of guests drifts over from the ceremony site, where white chairs sit on the cleared lawn beside the vines.

All of my friends, including the groomsmen, are clustered around a grinning Jordan and a gorgeous Marilee. Her long brown hair is gathered over one shoulder in curls. A simple tiara adorns her head, simple heels on her feet. The real star of the day is her mother's wedding dress, altered to fit her to perfection.

She really is the most beautiful bride I've ever seen, and after all she's been through, the most deserving of happiness too.

"Sorry, guys," I say as I ferret my computer away on an out-of-the-way side table. "Got distracted by the electric glow of my computer screen and the fictional world found within."

"Hey, no worries." Marilee smiles softly from where she stands tucked against Jordan, the photographer pushing wisps of hair from her face as she positions the rest of the wedding party around where the happy couple stands on the steps. "Chloe just wanted one more shot of us all on the deck right before sunset."

Jordan whispers something in her ear, and her cheeks go red as she scrunches her nose and only half suppresses a goofy grin.

Watching the two of them earlier across the vineyard as they did a private reveal ahead of group photos—and watching them, anytime, really—is proof that true love does exist.

Even if it doesn't exist for *me*.

I don't know how they still manage to look that giddy, that in love, after being technically married for six months and living together again for the last few months after "dating" and then getting "engaged for real" in May. It's all very confusing, but it works for them, and I couldn't be happier for my friends.

I feel a squeeze on my hand and glance up at Kelsey, my closest friend. "You get any words written?" she whispers. She's the only one who knows my secret. My current stress.

Claire peeks her blonde head out the door, her perfectly plucked eyebrows raised. "You guys ready for the kiddos?"

"Yes, bring them out," Chloe says, a clipboard in hand. The woman looks like a freaking model with her long hair in curls down her shoulders and back, heels the length of a football field on her feet, and curves that wind up and down her whole body. We each chose our own style of dress—Mare only cared about the colors—so Chloe's picked a sleek halter gown with a slit that reaches mid-thigh.

Next to her, I look like a child playing dress-up.

Maybe I can finagle it so I'm standing on the exact opposite end of the bridesmaids' line from her... Though, honestly, all of these women are beautiful in their own right, even my poor cousin, who needs both Frederick and Blake to help her off the couch where she's been lounging, a mostly empty bag of potato chips on her round stomach. But even with swollen ankles and more filled-in cheeks, Lucy's got the pregnancy glow working for her.

"April." Kelsey squeezes again.

I shake myself from the distractions of my mind—the hazards of being a writer. "Not many words written at all. Like two."

"Two thousand?" Her face brightens as she fiddles with the straps of her corset-tiered, ruffled gown, which I happen to know she designed and put together herself.

"Nope. Literally two."

"Oh. Well—"

"Kels!" her sister barks at her from a spot at the steps next to Landon. She points and widens her eyes in a look that communicates something to her twin I'm not privy to.

"Sorry," Kelsey mutters. She gives my hand a final squeeze before letting go. "You'll get there. I believe in you."

"Thanks." I sigh and wait my turn to be positioned.

Claire brings Scarlett to my side, and she spins her little white flower girl dress with a hearty laugh. I have to stop her from throwing flowers in the air right here and from chasing a tuxedo-wearing Ryder (the cutest ring bearer ever) around the little yard as we wait for the photographer to make up her mind about how best to place our huge wedding party.

Watching my daughter, with flowers in her hair and a gap-toothed grin that sparks joy in anyone she meets, is both a blessing and a curse. She looks so much like her father some-times, especially when she's wearing a mischievous grin or when she states something so matter-of-factly, with otherworldly confidence. Then there are her eyes. When she looks at me, it's like looking back at him.

And I remember.

Those eyes, his eyes, used to drink me in, make me feel like the most beautiful girl in the room. From the moment we first connected to the last moment we breathed the same air, Ethan was my whole world.

And even though he didn't want to be part of our lives anymore, at least he gave me a new world—the one that starts and ends with Scarlett. Unfortunately, even when I want to, I can't escape him. Can't go to a bar during hockey season without seeing his jaw-droppingly handsome face splashed on the screen, making heart-shaped gestures over his chest and grinning like a man without a care in the world. Without a regret.

And maybe he truly doesn't have any.

I both want to smack him and kiss him—and that's just not okay. I wish my stupid heart would just forget.

But then, there's Scarlett, and I know I never will.

Finally, the photos are done and the music lilts through the air, and we walk down the simple grassy aisle toward the holly-wrapped arch flanked by classically lit Christmas trees. And Jordan and Marilee promise each other forever—this time, for real—and their kiss sets the tone for romance as couples in the audience give each other pecks as well, and the couples among our ranks make eyes at each other across the aisle.

When the ceremony's done and we make our way to the reception area—expertly bedecked by Chloe's team at Something Blue, with lights weaving overhead, silver-draped round tables covered in glittering snowflakes, and a cake table featuring a three-tiered Christmas-themed delight that Marilee made and decorated herself as part of Holly Cakes, the new cake decorating business she started while staying on part time at the bakery instead of buying it—we all find seats at the head table facing the rest of the crowd, which is made up of most of the town regulars.

We laugh at best man Blake's stories of a threatening game of pool he and Jordan played months ago, and at matron of honor Lucy's tales of how she knew before anyone that Jordan and Marilee would be a forever kind of couple.

Scarlett sits between me and Claire, but she keeps darting off to sit with my parents. I watch her dance with Papa Burt, and there's a tiny ache inside me knowing she will never have a daddy-daughter dance with her own father. Never have anyone but me to walk her down the aisle. Then again, Marilee's father is gone, but she still asked Jordan's dad to give her away, and the man—who you'd hardly recognize since he started attending AA meetings and getting sober—said he'd be honored. Marilee seemed content with that, so maybe there's hope for Scarlett.

Amid the scrape of forks against porcelain, the raucous laughter of the "Cupid Shuffle," and the sparkling cider toasts (because ironically enough, Jordan and Marilee chose a dry wedding at the vineyard), I eat and laugh and raise my glass with everyone else.

But my mind is a million miles away.

It's back with my characters, Emmett and Ava, with the fundamental problems between them. It's wondering how there can ever be a happy ending with the disastrous past creating a chasm in the middle of their love story.

And I just can't see it.

But when dinner's finally over and all of my friends are up dancing, I sneak away to the deck, pop open my laptop, and settle in on the couch with a piece of cake to do my darnedest to figure this story out.

Because whether I know where it's going or not, whether I feel inspired or not, this deadline is rapidly approaching.

And the next Abigail Fox novel isn't going to write itself.

Ahhhhh. Jordan and Marilee. Alllll the heart eyes.

Can you tell I've loved this couple since the first time they stepped onto the page? (And sweet little Ryder too!) I know many of you have felt the same way and have been so patiently waiting for this story. I'm sorry it took so long to get here, but I hope you feel I've done it justice.

And now, it's time for April's story. Oh, April, our spunky single mom with a loaded past...and some very juicy secrets! Want to read a second-chance romance sure to make you swoon?

Order *Beachside Kisses With My Famous Ex* now.

If you do want a bit more of Jordan and Marilee's story, I've written a bonus scene where you can read how he proposes to her...for real, this time. ;)

Grab that one at kristincanary.com/BeachsideBF.

Finally, read on to snag a free prequel novella that kicks off my California Dreamin' series...

This series is all about a San Diego friend group that, much like our Hallmark Beach crew, is total #friendshipgoals. This series also includes some of the best tropes and swoony book boyfriends you could ask for!

a free story for you

Enjoyed *Beachside Kisses With My Best Friend*? Not ready to quit reading yet? If you sign up for my newsletter at kristinca nary.com/freebook, you will automatically receive *Enamoring Her Amnesic Ex*, the love story of Connor's brother Kevin and his wife Lola (who you briefly met if you've read Book 1 in my California Dreamin' series, *Loving the Ladies' Man!*). This is just a gift from me to you as a thank you for choosing to hang out with me.

Enamoring Her Amnesic Ex:

Two years ago, he broke my heart—and now he's forgotten all about it.

When my sister goes into labor, what are the chances that the nearest hospital would be the one where my ex, Kevin Bryant, is a surgical resident?

You know—the man who decided being a doctor was more important than love and left me reeling. Hard.

But when we run into each other—quite literally—he falls, hits his head, and wakes up with amnesia.

And he still thinks we're together.

His brother Connor asks me to pretend we're dating, just for a little while, so we can ease Kevin into the truth.

But the real truth is that being around this strong, capable man again is making me remember things *I* would rather forget.

Yeah, hi, my name is Lola, and I'm clearly a glutton for punishment. Because here I am. Pretending with him. Taking care of him.

Kissing him.

Just waiting for the bubble to burst.

Because as soon as Kevin snaps out of this and remembers the past, there WILL be another heartbreak.

And all I'll have is the memories of what was.

Read on for a sneak peek of the California Dreamin' prequel novella, Enamoring Her Amnesic Ex...

Of all the hospitals in San Diego, my sister had to pick the one where *he* works.

Fine—if we're being technical, she didn't really have a choice. Her water breaking in the frozen foods aisle of her grocery store wasn't exactly Theresa's plan.

But come on, universe. Did the closest hospital have to be *his*? I feel I have a right to be upset by this, but since I can't be mad at Theresa, here I am with the biggest bouquet of flowers I can afford (hint: it's not THAT big) obscuring my face as I slink down the brightly lit hallways. And you'd better believe that anytime I see a tall doctor with brown hair, I hug the wall like it's wool and I'm static, baby.

But I'm not letting a potential encounter with my ex stop me from meeting my newest niece. Because family trumps everything—even if being in the place where Dr. Kevin Bryant is a surgical resident is giving me sweaty pits and an itchy nose. Or hey, maybe that's the flowers shoved in my face.

Wiggling my nose like that girl from *Bewitched*, I book it in my jeweled wedges down the hall, almost to the magical door where Theresa and Jake await with their new bundle of joy.

And then, I hear it—that voice I'd know anywhere, even though it was only part of my life for five months.

And yeah, they might have been the most intense and wonderful five months of my life, but phantom whiplash still hits me when I think about them. Because all the intensity, all the wonder, came to an abrupt halt when Kevin figured out I didn't fit into the picture he had for his life.

Now, I can't help the yelp that comes from my mouth as I stop and peek through the flowers. My traitorous heart—which shouldn't care one fig about the man standing at the nurses' station after he broke my heart into a million pieces nearly two years ago—thumps a happy jig against my chest.

Down, girl.

Because he may have the same high brow, the same tousled dark hair, the same strong arms and lean body that suggest he still runs and lifts weights every morning like clockwork, but the harshness in his tone, the rigidness of his stance as he yells directives at the nurses and disappears behind a set of doors are proof that he's not the man I thought I knew.

My Kevin was sweet. A little uptight, yes, but considerate and generous. My Kevin would never treat people like that.

But maybe I just saw what I wanted to see back then.

"Lola?"

I turn to find my brother-in-law standing in the hall outside my destination door, his brown-gray eyebrows raised. Jake's eyes are a bit red, probably from crying—he's a freaking waterspout, I tell ya—and his clothing is rumpled, I assume from the long night at the hospital.

Striding forward, I raise on my tiptoes and brush a kiss against his cheek. "Congrats, Daddy."

"Thanks. How's Sami?"

After Theresa went into labor and Jake joined her at the hospital yesterday, they asked me to pick up my five-year-old niece Sami from kindergarten and keep her at my apartment overnight.

"Wonderful and precocious as always." In fact, the girl asked me a million questions about birth and babies that started making me sweat. Thankfully, I was able to distract her with a Disney movie and pizza night. This morning before grabbing the flower bouquet I'm now holding, I dropped Sami back at school, where Jake will pick her up this afternoon so she can officially meet her baby sister.

"That's my girl." A grin sweeps his face and he pushes glasses up the bridge of his nose. Then he scans the hallway. "By the way, why were you standing there like Harriet the Spy just a minute ago?"

Note: Sami is obsessed with Harriet the Spy, so it's completely adorable that Jake uses it as a reference point in conversation. Not so adorable is the fact he caught my strange behavior upon seeing Kevin.

"No reason." I straighten and tug at the hem of my aqua-colored blouse. "How are Theresa and Baby Girl? Did you guys come up with a name?"

"Not yet."

"All right, all right. You twisted my arm. I guess I don't mind."

"Mind what?"

"Sharing my name with her. Lola Warren's got a great ring to it, don't you think?" I wink and breeze past him. As I step inside the room, my sister's tired voice wades out from the other side of the privacy curtain—and an older voice responds.

Mom.

Ugh. Is it too late to escape? I turn on my heel, but Jake shakes his head. He juts his chin toward my sister's bed. "I need you to stay with her. Theresa's craving a breakfast burrito from Dos Brasas."

"Fine," I hiss out. "But I expect one too. As payment."

"Payment for spending time with your sister and adorable niece?"

I stick my tongue out—not so mature for a twenty-four-year-old, but when did I ever claim to be mature? "For forcing me to talk with my parents."

"She's already been on the phone for fifteen minutes." There's a bit of sympathy in Jake's voice now. He knows why this is hard for me. "I'm sure you won't have to talk long."

"Still, you'd better throw in a Diet Coke to revive my energy when you return."

He chuckles, pats my shoulder, and leaves.

Groaning inwardly, I brace myself for the inevitable. Then I throw on a happy face and walk around the curtain, ginormous bouquet in tow.

Theresa's blonde hair is a bit grungy, tossed up in a messy bun on the top of her head—stay-at-home mom style, as she'd say—and her face is devoid of makeup like always, but the tiny smile lines around her lips are on full display as she snuggles her infant daughter against her chest with one arm and holds up her phone with the opposite hand.

When she sees me, Theresa turns the screen my way. "Look who's here."

I wave at the grainy image of my parents, who are squeezed in front of their computer in Zambia, where they teach English to underserved communities. Apparently they do a lot of good in the village where they've lived for more than a decade.

I hope so, considering what it's cost them—what it's cost all of us.

Stuffing down the bitterness, I set the flowers on the windowsill of the small room. "Hi, Mom. Hi, Dad."

"Lola! So good to see you." My mom looks older every time I see her on-screen—her hair a little grayer, the wrinkles around her eyes a little more prominent—but maybe it's just the terrible Internet connection. I wouldn't know, since they haven't been back to visit since Sami was about six months old and I've never been to Africa.

"You too, Mom." I move to the head of the bed, and Theresa flips the phone back around so it's fixed on her youngest daughter, who is sleeping and breathing in and out with an adorable little mew. At 8 pounds, 6 ounces, she's bigger than Sami was, though her legs are scrunched up like a little frog. Theresa has dressed her in pink footy pajamas that are just about the cutest thing I've ever seen.

Bending down, I kiss her sweet downy cheek, then the top of Theresa's head. "Good job, Sis."

"She's pretty great, isn't she?" My sister yawns and nearly drops the phone. "Sorry. Long night."

"We won't keep you, dear." Mom clicks her tongue. "Oh, I just wish I was there to hold my grandbaby."

"You could come home, you know." The words are out before I can call them back. I know better. Nothing is going to change. At this point, why would it?

"Lo ..." Theresa warns.

Dad sighs deeply, taking his glasses off and rubbing his chin with a big meaty fist. "You know we would, Lola, but the people here need us."

We *need you*.

They're the words I've longed to say for eleven years since they left a thirteen-year-old me in the guardianship of my twenty-three-year-old barely married sister because their new life was "too unstable for children." But I don't say those words, because they're not true anymore. Nope. Theresa and I have learned to rely upon each other. We are all the family we need.

I force another smile. "I know."

After a few more pleasantries, my sister says goodbye and hangs up the phone. "That wasn't so bad, was it?"

"Torture." I tilt my head. "But worth it to meet this sweet girl."

Black-as-night curls stick out the bottom of Baby Girl's white cotton beanie with a pink satin bow. Apparently all Flanagan girls are born with dark hair that eventually falls out and comes back in nearly white blonde. At least, that's what happened with me, Theresa, and Sami. "Can I?"

"Of course."

My long hair falls forward over my shoulder as I gather the tiny bundle in my arms and get her situated. Her button nose and rosy lips remind me so much of her older sister, it's uncanny. "The Flanagan genes are strong with this one."

"Right?" Theresa pours a glass of water for herself from a pale pink jug. There's only enough to fill half her cup, and she downs it quickly. Then she relaxes against the bed. The room is small but thankfully private, and it smells like a mixture of baby formula and lemongrass. A large window lets in the morning light of another gorgeous mid-September day in San Diego.

As Baby Girl coos and inhales, I sigh in contentment. This is where I belong. With my family, who need me. I'll never regret choosing this life.

"So." Theresa studies me then tugs at the thin sheet covering her. "Did you see that job opportunity I sent you yesterday? You know, before I made a complete mess in Aisle 3." She hangs her head. "I'll never be able to show my face in my favorite grocery store again. Can you imagine the person who had to clean that up?"

"Oh, stop it. The staff will take one look at this sweetness and forget all about how she came hard and fast into the world." I run a fingertip along her forehead, tracing her cheeks, her nose. "Although maybe it wouldn't hurt to get them all gift cards as a thank-you. I'm definitely glad the manager acted quickly when she realized your contractions were coming so close together."

"Me too. And so grateful Jake made it just in time." Theresa, who is not the crier in the family, sniffles despite herself. "Find yourself a nice guy like him, Lo. It may have taken me a few years to see him as more than my nerdy lab partner, but now I find him the most handsome man alive. There's nothing sexier than watching him hold our daughters. Daughters. As in, more than one." Tears start streaming down her cheeks at an alarming rate. "Oh my gosh, I'm sorry. These postpartum hormones are something else."

I reach across to the counter and snag a few tissues, shoving them into her hand. "You definitely scored one of the good ones."

And once upon a time, I thought I'd done the same. From the moment I met Kevin at the diner where I still work—and accidentally served him a hamburger instead of his requested pastrami sandwich—things were like lightning between us. Hot and charged, yes, but deep too, leaving a lasting trench, a mark, on my heart.

Theresa blows her nose and then fixes her eyes on me again. "You didn't answer my question."

My nose scrunches. "What question?"

"The job opportunity. Did you look at it?"

"Oh." I kind of want to ask her which one she means, since she sends me several each week. But I'm not sure if she's in a teasing mood, given the sheen of tears still coating her eyeballs. "Um, no, haven't had a chance yet."

"Well, I think it's perfect for you. Assistant costume designer at a theater in Los Angeles." She straightens and I can tell she's about to go into teacher mode—I guess she can't help it after teaching science to middle schoolers for so many years.

"Now, I know it doesn't pay all that well, so you might have to have a second job, but you're basically working two jobs now anyway. And this way, you'd get paid for the theater work. No more of this volunteer stuff. Which would be fine, but you have a bachelor's degree in costume design, for goodness' sake. You should be paid for your genius."

Baby Girl rustles and makes a sound like a grunt. *I agree, girl. I agree.* "It does sound like a great opportunity." I let my words trail off.

"But?"

"But you know how I feel about moving. I'm not going to be some distant aunt who never sees her nieces."

"Lo, Los Angeles is only a few hours away."

"I know, but—"

"And"—I hate how big-sister bossiness pervades her tone— "if you're ever going to go to New York and design on Broadway, then this might be a good step in the right direction."

"New York isn't happening, Reese." I try to infuse a lightness to my tone, as if my statement doesn't prick my insides.

"But it's your dream."

"Was my dream. In middle school. But now that I know what it would require ... well, I'm just not willing to make that sacrifice."

I refuse to abandon the people I love like my parents did.

Like Kevin did.

Not for a million dollars—and not even for the chance to design costumes on the Great White Way.

As if I've somehow summoned her help, Baby Girl opens her big beautiful blue eyes—and starts to wail. It happens so suddenly that I jump, but Theresa just laughs and holds out her arms. "Saved by the cry of hunger."

Standing, I hand over the hangry monster who has replaced my sweet little niece. But as soon as Theresa has her suckling—

like a freaking boss, I might add—she turns her pointed gaze to me again. "Now, where were we? Oh, yeah. About to dissect the trauma our parents unwittingly unleashed on you by sticking you with me as a pseudo mom. Is that about right?"

"I mean, when you put it like that ..." I tease.

Thankfully, I'm saved by yet another interruption when Jake waltzes through the door, a brown paper bag in hand and a soda. He wiggles them in the air and Theresa nearly leaps from the bed—but doesn't, of course, because I'm guessing Baby Girl would deafen us all if she unlatched. But when Jake places a foil-wrapped burrito the size of my forearm on the table in front of Theresa, she gives him the most solemn expression before saying, "I don't think I have ever loved you more than in this moment."

He turns amused eyes to me before handing me a burrito and the soda. "Do you feel the same?"

"Would it be weird if I said yes?" I grin. Living with him and Theresa for five years before living on campus at the University of San Diego for my undergrad gave Jake and me lots of time to perfect the brother-sister relationship. Even though I have my own apartment now, I still spend lots of my free time at their house, watching Sami and doing movie nights with my sis.

Theresa rips into her burrito, taking a bite and sighing with pleasure. The scent of sausage and cooked eggs makes my own stomach rumble, and I start to unwrap my burrito, which is warm in my hands.

"Do you have to work today?" Jake asks.

I freeze. Shoot, what time is it? My eyes land on the ancient clock above Theresa's head and the tension leaves my body. "Not for another hour." Which is good, because the lunch rush at Dom's waits for no one. Of course, I've told my boss that I might be switching shifts a lot in the next few weeks as Theresa might need me. And thankfully, the first costume fittings for *The Music Man* aren't until this weekend, so I don't have any set times I need to be at the theater until then.

Before I can even take a bite of my burrito, Theresa has inhaled hers, all while Baby Girl happily nurses. Jake is watching in awe of them both, and suddenly I feel like the thirdiest third wheel ever. I should be used to it by now—it's basically been happening since my parents foisted me on the newlyweds—but I still can't seem to escape the ick swirling in my stomach at the thought that I'm more an invasion than a help.

I stand, set the burrito on my chair, and grab the now-empty water jug from Theresa's side table. "I'll get you a refill."

"Oh, thank you. That would be great." My sister strokes Baby Girl's back. Both of them look like they're in a food coma.

Hustling from the room, I quickly find the kitchen area where the nurses stash little packets of crackers, containers of applesauce, and sandwiches for hungry mamas. There's an ice and water machine and I use both to refill the container to the brim. Once I set the lid on top, I take my time moseying back to the room. I stop to study a wall papered with children's artwork from the pediatric wing, smiling at the crooked lines and creative shapes.

"Lola?"

For the second time in an hour, someone is calling my name. But this time, it isn't my brother-in-law.

It's *him*.

And his voice in my ear is so unexpected that I shriek and jump, forgetting that there's a full container of water in my hands.

Liquid careens out of the top—guess I didn't secure that lid as well as I thought—and all over Kevin. As if that wasn't bad enough, I drop the jug, allowing what's left inside to spill out onto the floor beneath him.

Eyes wide, he's staring back at me with a look that likely mirrors my own. Along his strong jawline is a dusting of stubble, which is kind of a surprise given his propensity to shave every day. He always said doctors should present themselves as professionally as possible.

I lift a hand and give him the tiniest wave known to mankind. "Hi, Kevin."

"What ..." He looks down at his green scrubs, which are drenched. Then his gaze moves back to me. "What are you doing here?"

The once-bustling hallway is now strangely devoid of people, as if the universe knows this moment is embarrassing enough. "I didn't come here to see you, that's for sure." I cross my arms over my chest.

"That's not what ..." Kevin tugs at the badge on the pocket of his scrub pants. "Sorry. It's, um, good to see you."

"Sure it is."

Kevin shifts from one foot to the other. I'm shocked he's still standing here, to be honest. Maybe he's expecting me to go quietly like I did the last time we spoke. But I've got two years' worth of pent-up anger and hurt just begging to be unleashed on him. The only reason I'm keeping them in check? I don't want my sister's care to suffer. Not that a surgical resident would have anything to do with Theresa. But still.

Oh, yeah. And I guess I also maybe feel like he wouldn't care one way or the other. He was so clinical when he dumped me.

No feeling. No heartache.

It was so ... *easy* ... for him to let me go.

So sue me if I'm relishing his discomfort in this moment just a tad.

A pager on his belt goes off and visible relief finds the cracks in his face. "Well, I'd better go. I hope ..." He swallows. "I hope everything is okay."

Dang it. There's a sliver of the Kevin I knew—the one who understands what it is to lose someone and works desperately hard so others don't have to. I can't leave him thinking that there's something wrong with my family. Or me. "Theresa had a baby."

"Right. Of course. That's why you're in this wing."

"Yep." My smile hitches one corner of my mouth at his logical brain at work. "Why are you here though? Doing a rotation in OB?" While dating him, I acquired quite the medical vocabulary.

"Just covering a shift for a colleague." He checks his watch. "Speaking of."

"Right." I bite the inside of my cheek, because the idea of saying goodbye ... "Well."

"Well." His eyes connect with mine and spear me right there on site. I can't move, can't breathe. Their deep chocolate tones wash me in their sweetness, in the depths of what was. What could have been. If only ...

Then the connection is severed when he pivots quickly.

But instead of moving away, he slips in the puddle of water that—until this moment—I'd forgotten completely about.

Apparently he did too.

His head bangs against a medical cart behind him. Before I know what's happening, his eyes loll back into his head and close.

"Kevin?" I drop to my knees, and my jeans are soaked in an instant—not that I care. He looks really pale, though I don't see any blood and his breathing seems okay. I pat his cheek but he doesn't wake up. Turning my head toward the nurses' station down the hall, I cry out. "Help!"

A few people come running and they push me aside while I watch them take stock of the situation. They call for a bed and a woman in a white coat hurries over and examines him. It's all happening so quickly and my own breath is coming in short bursts. I clench my fists at my sides.

Finally, as they lift him onto a bed, his eyes flutter open.

"Thank you," I whisper as I step forward.

But the doctor gives me a side-eye. "Sorry, miss, you need to step back."

"Don't talk to my girlfriend like that," Kevin says before his eyes roll back into his head and he passes out again.

Did I miss the "ex" in ex-girlfriend? Maybe I'm the one who hit my head. And no, it's NOT wishful thinking, thank you very much.

The doctor and team start wheeling him away and I realize I'm biting my lip so hard that I taste blood. One of the nurses—a sweet older woman with a white poof of hair—puts her hand on my lower back. "We're taking him to the emergency department to get a full workup. Don't worry, we'll take good care of him."

And I do the only thing I can do. Because this is Kevin, and even though he is the absolute last person I wanted to see today, this is kind of all my fault and I owe it to him to make sure he's all right.

After shooting Jake a quick text, I follow the nurse down the hall.

Enamoring Her Amnesic Ex is ONLY available by signing up for my newsletter. Grab it here: kristincanary.com/freebook

Kristin is a wife and boy mom who functions best on peach tea and cookie dough ice cream. A desert dweller, she always has her eye on the next trip to a beach somewhere—and if she can't travel there in person, then you'd better believe she's going to write about it. Kristin is never fully satisfied with a movie, TV show, or book without a hefty dose of romance in it, and she's grateful to be living a true-life love story with her own crazy little family. Connect with her at KristinCanary.com.

facebook.com/kristincanary

instagram.com/kristincanaryauthor

www.ingramcontent.com/pod-product-compliance
Lightning Source LLC
Chambersburg PA
CBHW021042310726
48969CB00006B/1765